LETHAL PERIL

Rinaldi Romances

Gianni & Leah:

Leah's Seduction – Book 1
Leah's Seduction – Book 2
Leah's Seduction – Book 3
Leah's Seduction – Book 4
Leah's Seduction – Book 5
Leah's Seduction – Book 6
Leah's Seduction – Book 7
Leah's Seduction – Book 8
Leah's Seduction – Book 9
Leah's Seduction – Book 10

Kyra's Story

Stay With Me – Book 1: Lust
Stay With Me – Book 2: Secrets
Stay With Me – Book 3: Betrayal
Stay With Me – Book 4: Confessions

Cooper & Daniela

Daniela's Crazy Love: The Prequel
Daniela's Crazy Love: The Novel

Bend To My Will:

Forbidden Passion
Seductive Affair
Intimate Kiss
Deep Longing
Illicit Craving
Wicked Obsession
Luscious Sins
Sexy Addiction
Secret Torment
Daring Confessions
Eternal Love
Sweet Promise

Fighting For Gisele

UNLEASHED
UNTAMED
UNBROKEN
UNDEFEATED

Military Romantic Suspense

Cold Peril
Lethal Peril

LETHAL PERIL

Stealth Security

Emily Jane Trent

Lethal Peril Copyright © 2017
by Emily Jane Trent

Printed in the United States of America
First Printing, 2017

ISBN-13: 978-1545510483
ISBN-10: 1545510482

Camden Lee Press, LLC
12112 N Rancho Vistoso Plaza
Suite 150-101
Oro Valley, AZ 85755

www.EmilyJaneTrent.com

Acknowledgements

No book is published in isolation. So many helped me, some in ways they never imagined. From my friends and family, my mentor, and a long list of indie authors, all have contributed to my success. Without my editor, cover artist, formatting expert, and others who played a part in making this book, I'd never be able to create these books for you like I do. I want to thank each of them for their good work.

A special thank you to all my readers: I hope you enjoy this romantic tale. It's been very rewarding to write. It's my pleasure to continue to create stories for you. I look forward to meeting you at my fan page, Emily Jane Trent Books, or at my website. My success is only because you read and enjoy these stories. I appreciate each of you.

CHAPTER ONE

Elizabeth Marie Foster had been born into wealth with the apparent enviable advantages. It wasn't that she lacked gratitude for her fortune, but more that she'd witnessed the darker side of money and control.

Her father insisted on calling her Elizabeth, but she preferred Beth. She wasn't some snooty heiress who commanded awe from the masses—quite the opposite. She was a rebel and had been from the time she was a young girl.

Behaving properly and dressing to impress were trappings that boxed her in. At the age of twenty-eight, Beth already had a long list of offenses. Not one of them was noteworthy, taken on its own. But viewed as a whole, the acts had given her a reputation for causing trouble.

Not that Beth cared. She preferred to live on the fringes, to ignore demands, and to be her own woman. Although she hadn't quite figured out what that was, it definitely *was not* being the woman that she was expected to be—but one of her own design.

Elizabeth, the only daughter of shipping magnate Stephen Charles Foster, breathed in the brisk Manhattan air. The walk through Central Park had been invigorating. She glanced back at the fall colors of the leaves, dangling from the trees and scattered across the lawn. As a young girl, she'd spent time at the park, frequently in the company of her mother.

But her mother had passed away, a victim of cancer, long before Elizabeth graduated from grade school. To this day she missed her, and the loveliness of the park was a stark reminder of the motherly love that had been taken away much too soon.

Turning toward the street, she focused on her plans for Saturday. She cherished her liberty from the confines of an office, and embraced the relief of being away from her stifling life. In his generosity, her father had given her a job, doing accounting for Foster International. Despite her assumed untrustworthiness, he had faith in her.

Thus Stephen Foster had entrusted his billion-dollar baby to her, allowing her to work in bookkeeping, as part of his accounting team. Not her preference at all. But she hadn't had the heart to reject his loving gesture. Of any family member, apart from her dearly departed mother, Elizabeth loved her father most. More accurately, she adored him.

Reflection on her employment at Foster tightened her chest and brought tears to her eyes. She brushed them away with the back of her hand. This was no time for sentimentality. What she'd been accused of was beyond the realm of possibility. Yet it was so damn easy for others to believe it of her.

Elizabeth stuffed her hands in her pockets and strode toward Fifth Avenue to catch the subway. She'd remembered to wear a jacket, but not her gloves. Her hand closed around a tiny sketchbook that she carried with her. Drawing caricatures was her hobby, so in the park she'd sketched a couple of the tourists. Such were simple to spot, since they gawked at the scenery—something a New Yorker was not prone to do.

The walk from Central Park to the metro station

was short, so didn't require taking a cab. Elizabeth far preferred walking, in any case. She rarely opted to ride in the family limo, as it was pretentious and claustrophobic. Pedestrians filled the sidewalk, confirmation that she wasn't alone in her choice to walk instead of ride.

Up ahead, her friend waved both hands in a joyful frenzy, most likely pleased to be out of the office also. Amanda Moreau waited by the subway station, waving her arm for Elizabeth to hurry up. Shopping held an allure for her friend, not that Elizabeth objected. She found plenty to add to her wardrobe during their outings.

While hanging around the newsroom at one of the small daily papers, Elizabeth had recently met Amanda. The friendship had begun with little effort, since they had much in common—especially a sharply condescending attitude toward politics and the crimes of the wealthy.

Elizabeth drew cartoons derived from her observations, satires on political absurdities, while Amanda wrote scathing editorials on similar topics. But their friendship wasn't limited to the newsroom. In the months since Elizabeth had found her new friend, she'd agreed to various lunches and shopping sprees.

"Hey, Amanda, sorry I'm a little late. I should have picked up my pace in the park."

"Let me guess. You were sketching and lost track of time?"

Elizabeth raised her hands. "Guilty as charged."

Amanda looked her over, then grinned. "You wore that great jacket. I'm jealous. Turn around."

Elizabeth spun in a half-turn, and Amanda pulled on the hem of the bomber jacket. It was pink with black cuffs and hem. On the back was a striking logo, a symbol that had become a trademark of sorts.

"I love this thing," Amanda said. "The eagle on the back is just so...spectacular. He's magnificent outlined in rhinestones."

Slipping off her black leather jacket, Amanda grinned. She dropped her purse to the sidewalk between her feet and reached out her arms. "Okay...trade. I want to trade...just for today."

Elizabeth laughed. "Sure, why not?" The jacket was silk, a designer fashion personalized with the unique logo. The stylized eagle represented individual freedom, and served as a symbol of Elizabeth's art. She slipped her sketchbook, phone, and wallet from the pockets, then handed over the treasured garment.

Amanda put on the shiny jacket and Elizabeth donned the leather one, slipping her items into the pockets. Interests weren't all she had in common with her friend. Amanda was barely five feet two, the same as she, with a similarly small build. And the petite journalist's hairstyle was a copycat of Elizabeth's punk look—buzzed around the left ear, long on the right side, with some stray tendrils at the neckline. And her friend had a row of piercings along the curve of one ear, matching hers. Elizabeth couldn't claim credit for that, since Amanda had worn tiny hoops on that ear when she'd met her.

The identical black hair finished the look. Amanda hefted the strap of her purse over one shoulder, then motioned toward the entrance. "Shall we?"

The subway gave Elizabeth the creeps. It wasn't the safest way to travel, but she refused to wimp out. After all, thousands of commuters rode the trains each day, so she could too. The stench of the underground and the graffiti magnified the unsettling atmosphere of public transportation.

Crowds parted and moved toward their individual destinations. "We can get off at Madison Avenue," Amanda said, "exit near Calvin Klein."

"I need some new jeans," Elizabeth said. "What you looking for?"

"Hermès has a special on shoes. Maybe I can find a pair to match the bag I snagged last time."

A group of guys bumped into Amanda, knocking her into Elizabeth, but didn't acknowledge the collision. Dressed in low-hanging baggy jeans and sloppy shirts, not one of them could have been over the age of sixteen—some high school kids, hanging out.

A tall, bulky dude leered at Elizabeth, and she gave him the stink-eye. *Asshole*. Sticking close to Amanda, parting the sea of people with an outstretched hand, Elizabeth threaded her way toward the waiting area. The station was busy, and throngs of people pushed them off course.

"Sheesh, we should have taken a taxi," Amanda said.

Elizabeth caught sight of a man she had noticed earlier, near the entrance. Unlike the other commuters, he focused on Amanda and pushed people aside, coming toward her. The fleeting thought that maybe he admired the jacket vanished when he made a beeline in her direction.

"Amanda, that guy is following us."

"Who?"

"Don't look, just keep moving." Elizabeth grabbed her arm and dragged her forward through a break in the crowd. "He's some weirdo."

But it seemed there was more to it. The man wore sunglasses and a ball cap. He was broad-shouldered and appeared intent on something. Elizabeth feared it was Amanda, or maybe both of them. But what idiot would kidnap two women in the middle of a subway station? Then again, this was New York.

Elizabeth moved faster. The waiting area was near; she could see it. Glancing back was a mistake. The pursuer was just a few people behind. Her heart pounded. It made no sense. Some strange guy wouldn't grab them in broad daylight, or in this dark subway tunnel filled with witnesses.

"We're late," Amanda said.

As if to confirm that fact, a mass of people pushed toward the edge, leaning to see if the train was coming. The noise of the subway train drowned out conversation, yet the roar of voices of the waiting passengers blended with its reverberating sound.

"We better get up there," Elizabeth said, nearly shouting. In the same instant, a frantic crowd swept her friend away, like driftwood at sea. One minute they were together inching ahead, and the next, Amanda was carried forward into the crowd.

Giddy with the fight for the subway train, Elizabeth clung to the assurance that if Amanda got in first that she'd save her a seat. Then the man in the ball cap broke free of the mass of people, like some bizarre superhero, who was stronger than anyone near him.

Elizabeth couldn't breathe. The air was stifling and the crowd suffocated her. Then the scary man was only inches from her friend. "Amanda," she screamed, but it was futile. Her friend didn't look back.

The ground rumbled as the heavy train approached. Elizabeth stood tall to look over the crowd; Amanda was at the edge, close to the rails. The

6

strange man was next to her, as if he might say something. Then he lurched against Amanda, knocking her into open space and onto the tracks.

Elizabeth screamed and thrust her hands into her hair. It was a nightmare. It had to be. Soon she'd wake up to find that she was still in her bed, away from the horror she'd witnessed. Her heart sank to her feet, and on trembling legs she staggered forward.

The crowd had backed away, leaving an open path. Frantically, Elizabeth made her way to the scene and looked down at the tracks, before she thought better of it. Tears streamed down her cheeks, and she hugged her arms around her waist, rocking back and forth as she wailed with distress.

Amanda was dead.

Elizabeth turned and moved away from the disaster, hardly able to see through her burning tears. She bumped into a row of wooden seating. Instead of sitting down, she slumped against the wall and slid to the floor, shivering uncontrollably. Images of the incident flashed through her mind. The man had pushed Amanda. She'd witnessed it; seen it with her own eyes.

Looking up through blurry vision, Elizabeth couldn't pick the man out of the crowd. *Gone. He's gone.* Shock engulfed her, rendering her speechless and preventing her from moving. She reeled with confusion. *Why?* It was so senseless.

Elizabeth put her hands over her eyes and sobbed. Amanda was gone. It was a tragedy, one that couldn't be undone. Confusion addled her brain. She scanned her memory, trying to get a grip on what had transpired, but was unable to sift out the truth.

Why would anyone want to kill Amanda?

*****

7

A cacophony of voices and people moving about drew her attention. Elizabeth had to do something, tell someone. Numbed by the loss of her friend, she stood on shaky legs and returned to the rails, having no concept of how long it had been since the accident.

The police were there, questioning a few people. The crowd had noticeably thinned. She put her hand on the arm of a cop holding a walkie-talkie. He looked down at her and frowned. "Did you see what happened? Did you know the deceased?"

Tears rolled down Elizabeth's cheeks. "She was my friend. We were together. Her name is Amanda Moreau. She's...*was* a journalist."

The cop lowered his radio and gave her his attention. "Did she jump?"

Elizabeth shook her head. "No. No."

"Was she drunk or high?"

"She was...*murdered.*"

The cop didn't seem alarmed. "Do you realize what you're saying?

His disbelief cut through the haze, stirring anger. "Yes. I do. I saw it happen. A man pushed her."

"And what's your name?"

"Elizabeth Foster."

"Lady, I don't mean to be disrespectful, but do you know there have been over eighty deaths this year alone, from people falling on the metro tracks? Most are suicides, the rest are accidents, as a result of intoxication with alcohol or cocaine."

Elizabeth glared at him, irritated by his reciting of statistics. "I don't care. I'm telling you that my friend was pushed."

"We've spoken to the motorman. He didn't see anyone else. What he did see was a woman's body plummet to the tracks in front of the train, so he hit the emergency brake and laid on the horn."

The denial of her allegation infuriated her.

The cop's gaze hardened. "So where have you been, then...if you saw it happen?"

"I was...over there." Elizabeth waved her hand toward the wall. "I couldn't get to her. I couldn't...do anything."

After a moment, the cop huffed. "I need you to give a statement, then. Let's go down to the station."

He proceeded to escort her to his vehicle, and, considering his attitude, it was surprising that he didn't cuff her. The cop talked on his radio, letting the station know he was coming in. Elizabeth rested her head against the seat and stared up at nothing.

This was all a horrible mistake. It had to be. She'd known Amanda. The woman didn't have enemies. She'd worked an entry-level position at a daily paper. Not the stuff notoriety was made from. She hadn't developed the kind of career that could get her killed.

Elizabeth struggled to recall if Amanda had mentioned anyone in her private life who posed a threat, but came up blank. Amanda dated but wasn't hooked up with anyone. There was no man who'd abused her or wished her harm. Not that she'd spoken of.

When Elizabeth closed her eyes, the image of her silk bomber jacket filled her mind. Her gut twisted as she recalled the pink, sparkly garment that Amanda had worn to her death. Elizabeth's eyes flew open. *Oh my God. Could that be?*

Spotting Elizabeth would have been an easy task, even for a man who hadn't seen her before. The logo on the jacket was a giveaway. Even those who hadn't seen Elizabeth's cartoon drawings recognized the logo. That vector image of an eagle was plastered in news media, on publications that printed her art, and, most prominently, on her jacket.

Amanda had looked enough like Elizabeth to be her twin. From the back: same height, hair color, and style. Both had on jeans and boots. Yet there was one significant difference, the one thing that set them apart—the logo jacket.

Her friend may not have had enemies, but Elizabeth sure did. Playing the role of the rebel hadn't endeared others to her, even her own family. And recently, she'd been on the outs with them. Yet she couldn't envision it was sufficient motive to kill.

But the alternative, that the killer had been after Amanda, didn't ring true. It was more likely, as absurd as it seemed, that the killer had been sent to take out Elizabeth. She shuddered. Her family was wealthy, rich from billions handed down for many generations. Old money garnered from the lucrative shipping industry.

There was no doubt that her family had the resources to remove any person that got in the way of finance. But murder? That was beyond any improprieties she had knowledge of. Yet could she really put it past them?

And who would commit murder...who was that desperate? Certainly not her father. But other than him, Elizabeth considered any family member capable of such a deed. Not personally, of course. But for the right price, a killer could have been hired. A tingle of fear ran up her spine. However incredible, she was unable to brush aside her suspicions.

Elizabeth sat up. The cop glanced over at her, then turned into the parking lot. She needed her lawyer; things were out of hand. Pulling her phone from the pocket of the leather jacket, she dialed the family attorney.

"Who are you calling?"

"My attorney," Elizabeth said. "I'll have him meet me at the station. You'll just have to wait until he arrives."

The cop clenched his jaw.

"I'm not under arrest, am I?"

"It's just an interview." The cop pulled into an open parking space. "You're the one that's so anxious to turn this into a murder investigation."

"Hardly." Elizabeth glared at him. "But a friend of mine died. I'm not about to keep quiet."

*****

The police station was no more welcoming than the subway had been. Thomas Stapleton, attorney-at-law, had represented the family for as long as Elizabeth could recall. He was a welcome sight, striding toward her, sporting an expensive leather briefcase. Even on such short notice, he'd managed to arrive in a tailored suit.

"What can I do for you, Elizabeth?"

Thomas didn't seem all that surprised to find her at the police station. He had been around so long he was like part of the family, thus he knew of her escapades. Yet this went far beyond her mischievous games. This was for real.

Elizabeth gave him the punch line first, letting him know that she'd witnessed a murder. He raised his brows. "We need to speak alone before you agree to an interview."

The cop reluctantly agreed to let them have an empty office, and Elizabeth proceeded to relay her version of the event. She clarified that the cop asserted the death had been an accident, and was skeptical of her claim that it had been murder.

Having heard the blow-by-blow of what had happened that morning, Thomas expressed concern over her emotional state. After her assurance that she was all right for now, he leaned back in his chair. "I can't advise you to give a statement at this time. The situation is quite volatile. If you are to be interviewed, it should be in a formal setting where I am present. I'd like to look over all the facts, and the police investigation, before such an interview takes place."

It wasn't lost on Elizabeth that her attorney's first priority was the family's reputation. Any story that involved Foster International, or any member of the Foster family, spread like wildfire. Mere rumors turned into headlines overnight. An incident involving alleged murder would spiral out of control.

Elizabeth studied her attorney. "So I can count on you to keep this quiet?"

"What do you mean by quiet?"

"I'd rather you not tell anyone just yet."

"I'm not sure that's a good idea. Your uncle should be told. He will be furious if something like this is withheld from him."

Elizabeth shrugged. Martin Foster, her father's younger brother, would hit the roof when he heard about this. But she needed time. "Yes, but my uncle knows me." She gave Thomas an impish grin. "He won't blame you. I promise not to tell him that I called you to the station. I'll take the fallout for any upset."

"Elizabeth..."

"Really, I promise. So please, just for a day or two, until I can figure things out. And it's a given that you won't relay any of this to my father either." That last stipulation likely wasn't necessary, but she had to make sure.

Thomas shook his head. "Against my better judgment. But I need your agreement not to speak to the authorities unless I'm present."

"Deal."

"You realize that your uncle will find out anyway, as well as your father?"

"But not immediately. And when it does come up—because I'm sure the police won't keep a lid on a story like this—you can use your standard line that the family wishes to maintain their privacy."

Thomas stood and lifted his briefcase from the table. "Okay, but I insist on driving you home."

*****

Home was a three-story mansion in Manhattan, where Elizabeth had lived with her father for many years. It had five fireplaces, a basement swimming pool, and two gardens. She found no joy in the fact that she had it all to herself.

Other than the maids who came in to clean, or the maintenance man who tended to the upkeep, Elizabeth rambled through the spacious quarters quite alone. The reason saddened her, yet she was at a loss on how to make her life any different than it was.

After Thomas dropped her off, she went up to the rooftop patio to gaze at the scene below. It was one feature of the house that pleased her. Up so high, with a view of the city, Elizabeth was above it all. She often gained perspective on things while lounging on the terrace, alone with her thoughts.

She would have much preferred for her father to join her, but that was no longer possible. Only months before, the sudden onset of Alzheimer's had taken him away. For his own safety, her loving father

Stephen Foster had been placed in a nursing facility with twenty-four-hour care.

Plopping into a cushy patio chair, Elizabeth looked up at the sky. It was a gorgeous shade of eggshell blue with a few wispy clouds slowly drifting, languidly progressing over the city without a care in the world. If only she could claim the same.

Until a week ago, Elizabeth had spent much of her week as an accounting department employee at Foster International, doing her part to keep the books straight. She wasn't destined to be an accountant, but her father had employed her in that department due to her talent with software and computers.

She'd grown up using computers, so it was no special talent. Or so she claimed. Yet she understood such things better than some, and she tinkered incessantly, playing around with software as a hobby. It was interesting, which was something she needed.

Yet now she'd been removed from that function and her father was locked away in a facility. Elizabeth was acutely aware of her lack of friends. It was to her disadvantage that she'd been somewhat antisocial growing up. It wasn't that she had a particular dislike of others, but more that she tended to entertain herself. Sketching her cartoons, or plunking around on computer keyboards, occupied too much of her time. Now that she was in dire straits, she suffered a pang of regret about not connecting with anyone else much sooner.

It hadn't been all bleak. Elizabeth had bonded with Amanda. On reflection, maybe she shouldn't have, as she was more and more convinced that her friend's death fell on her shoulders. She could have warned Amanda that hanging around with her could mean trouble. But in her wildest imaginings, Elizabeth hadn't dreamed such a relationship involved lethal peril.

The wind whipped across the terrace, and Elizabeth wrapped the jacket tighter around her. The transparent panels around the rooftop, intended to block the wind, were inadequate. There were heaters to handle the chill from the rapidly dropping temperature, but she couldn't muster the initiative to get up and turn them on.

With her feet on the chair, Elizabeth wrapped her arms around her legs and rested her chin on her knees. In the quiet of her rooftop respite, she dug deep for answers. Now that her father was incapacitated, her brother Kyle ran the operations at shipping company under her Uncle Martin's supervision. She had no issue with that, as she certainly didn't want the duty.

She didn't have any responsibility for medical decisions concerning her father either, as he had given power of attorney to his brother Martin. Once the illness had been diagnosed, her uncle had taken charge. Not that Elizabeth would have done anything differently. Her father was sick and needed expert care. He was better off in the facility, as he couldn't be properly cared for at home.

It didn't matter that no particular duties fell to Elizabeth. Her family had no faith in her, and hadn't for some time. Only her father gave her credit, probably more than she deserved, for her abilities. But now he barely recognized her when she visited.

There was no one to turn to. It was out of the question to go to her uncle with her dilemma. He wouldn't listen to her anyway. And her brother was well intended but naïve. The idea that he'd believe that her friend was murdered was ludicrous. He'd accuse her of imagining the whole thing.

Her friend had died, and if Elizabeth's theory was correct, the incident had some connection to past transgressions. But she had no idea what acts had been significant enough to provoke murder. Yet if the killer was after her, he would soon enough realize his error.

Her life was in danger. She'd told her attorney about the murder, but she'd kept silent about her concern that it was in some way connected to her. If she had breathed a word of that, Thomas would have insisted that she hire a bodyguard. In the past, she'd adamantly refused to be guarded like a prisoner.

Elizabeth had been safe enough in her daily life. But these were unusual circumstances. Hiring a bodyguard wasn't such a bad idea. The more she pondered it, the more it seemed like the right thing to do. She was in a tight spot and needed help.

There was no one she could turn to—except for *one man*. Elizabeth pulled out her phone and punched the button for the airlines, before she could change her mind. She booked an early flight for Los Angeles, then went downstairs to pack.

CHAPTER TWO

Wyatt Mercer could have had a cushy corporate position in his family's company, but he wanted no part of it. Sitting at a desk all day wasn't his style. When he retired from the Navy, he'd checked around for a career that suited him.

He'd kept in touch with some of his buddies, former SEALs he'd been deployed with, and learned that many had gone to work in security companies or paramilitary gigs. It was a way to use their carefully honed and hard-won skills in civilian life.

The pay was good, and Wyatt had pride in what he did. He'd been a protector in the service, and that hadn't changed. It was rewarding to assure a client's safety, plus he was good at it.

Sweat rolled down his chest as he pumped the barbell a few more times, just for good measure. He'd arrived at the gym early, as was his routine. A grueling workout was the way to start the day. Breathing hard, he lowered the bar to the floor and wiped off with a towel.

While swigging water from a bottle, he sauntered over to the window. The facility was on an upper floor, and offered a view of downtown Los Angeles from the wall-to-wall windows. Traffic moved like sludge along the streets between the office buildings rising up to the sunny California sky.

He'd grown up in New York, but didn't mind LA.

He didn't miss the snow, and had the luxury of going to the beach on his days off. Santa Monica wasn't far, and the boardwalk at Venice Beach was an option too. He'd even learned to surf.

After years on deployment, living in the city was like staying at a vacation resort. But Wyatt didn't allow himself to get soft, despite the good life. He lifted weights, and jogged daily, sometimes ten miles or so—unless duty called.

In the years he'd been with Stealth Security, Wyatt had been assigned various jobs. Each involved the protection of some VIP, a celebrity or business type. Not all challenged his ability. Sometimes all that was required was to escort a client to a seminar, or follow them around on vacation. There were worse things he could do.

The most excitement he'd had recently on a job hadn't been his own assignment. Wyatt had assisted his buddy Garrett Flynn in what turned out to be a life-and-death situation. But it had turned out well, and Garrett had lucked out on that one. His client had been Marlene Parks, the movie star. Now Garrett and Marlene were soon to be married. Wyatt couldn't be happier for him.

Stealth was a good company to work for, and since the men employed as bodyguards were all former SEALs, there was plenty of camaraderie. Even more important was the loyalty, as he knew he could count on his teammates, and that really meant something.

Wyatt rolled his shoulder to work out the kinks. It tended to get stiff, so he kept it limbered up as much as he could. Deployments over the years had resulted in lots of wear and tear on the body. No matter how strong Wyatt had been in basic training, the endurance and power required in battle had chipped away at his physical integrity. It wasn't just one thing, but more of an accumulation of various injuries, some of which hadn't quite healed.

It was his right shoulder that had finally folded on him. He'd had rotator cuff surgery twice, but it remained an issue. Maybe it had been weakened, since he'd overused it playing baseball in college. Whatever was the reason, it was a problem. Fortunately, it didn't inhibit his duties as a bodyguard. Most of the time, he hardly noticed the stiffness or soreness.

Wyatt threw the towel into a basket and headed for the showers. A couple of other guys, the regulars, were pumping iron and grunting. His passing didn't even get a glance. He took a hot shower and dressed for the day, then texted the office to see if Tessa wanted coffee.

Tessa Pate was the receptionist at Stealth, although that was really a misnomer. The woman knew as much, maybe more of what went on there than the guys did. She was sharp, and a looker, too. Not really Wyatt's type, but he liked her. They'd become friends, and he often picked up coffee on the way in.

She texted back: *YES*. Wyatt laughed. Must be a rough day already; she needed her caffeine. He took the elevator down and exited the building. October boasted some of the nicest weather so far. Winters had been cold, even if there was no snow and too little rain. And summers were bloody hot. But this time of year, the air was cool, and as fresh as it could be in a smog-filled city.

He strode to the coffee shop at a brisk pace. Downtown thrived with activity, but it didn't compare to New York. The East Coast vibe was just different from the west, more intense or something. But no matter: LA was just fine with him.

Wyatt yanked open the door, and the aroma of freshly ground coffee filled his nostrils. He took a deep breath. A good cup of java was just what he needed. The line wasn't very long, and he had the two coffees without much delay. He kicked the door open and dashed out to the sidewalk to navigate the few blocks to Stealth.

Once inside the building, Wyatt took the elevator up. He wondered what Travis had in store for him. The last job had been wrapped up, so he'd had the weekend off. Monday morning would bring more clients, new jobs. Maybe his boss would dump something interesting in his lap. But whatever his assignment, it was about protecting the client, not about fueling his adrenaline pump.

Yet once a SEAL, always a SEAL. Wyatt thrived on danger and survival of the fittest. But he was a civilian now, a condition he still had to get used to. As such, he couldn't expect to defend his life and those of his team at every turn. This was normal life, and he just had to cope.

The elevator doors opened, and Wyatt walked up to the marble desk. Tessa grinned at him. "You got me an extra shot like I asked?"

"I'd be taking my life in my hands to come in here without it."

"You got that right, Mercer." It hadn't taken long to figure out that Tessa could take care of herself. She was brilliant, and could likely out-think him. Plus, she'd taken self-defense classes and God knew what else. It was common knowledge among the guys in the office that if some bad-assed dude messed with Tessa, he'd regret it.

Before engaging in further conversation, Tessa took a couple of sips of coffee. She was dressed in business attire, since clients had an open invitation to the office, should they want to deal in person. Often the contracts were brought to them. VIPs expected service in line with their status.

"Mmm, that's what I needed." Tessa placed her coffee next to the phone and tossed her wavy blond hair over her shoulder. "You better get in there. Travis has been waiting for you."

Wyatt gave her an inquiring look, hoping for some inside scoop, which he had no doubt she possessed. But Tessa didn't take the bait. Her expression gave away that she knew something, yet she didn't offer him any crumbs of information. She waved him past her desk. "Go see for yourself."

Now curious, Wyatt hustled down the hall. It wasn't wise to keep Travis waiting, even for a couple of minutes. Operations ran on schedule; his boss made sure of that. Clients were attended to promptly, and Stealth had gained a reputation for being the security company to go to for dangerous situations that needed defusing.

When Wyatt sat in the chair across the desk, Travis looked up from a report. "Don't sit down," he said. "You have a client waiting on you."

"You could have warned me."

"No need. You were due any minute. And Tessa's not a patient woman when it comes to coffee delivery."

Wyatt couldn't argue. "So who is this client?"

Travis looked at him, but didn't spit it out. "She wants to tell you herself."

"*She?*" Now Wyatt was more than curious. "Do I know her?"

Travis stabbed his finger toward the door. "She's waiting. Go find out."

The mystery irked him. *Why not just say what the assignment is?* Sure, he'd hoped for some excitement, just not in this form. Wyatt anticipated bad news. Otherwise, Travis would have just told him straight out who the client was.

The conference room was soundproofed, with no windows looking out to the hallway. It was designed for maximum privacy. At the moment, Wyatt would have preferred a trendy glassed-in deal, placing the client in full view. Then he would have been able to get a look before walking in on her.

But that was not to be. Wyatt opened the conference room door and stepped inside. The room was quite large, designed to accommodate meetings with the staff, and clients as well. Wide windows looked out on the city below, and a woman sat in one of the chairs at the far end of the table, the bright outdoor light illuminating her like a spotlight.

She might as well have been in the dark, because Wyatt hadn't a clue who she was. The woman was small, just over five feet tall, at best. Her petite stature seemed deceptive, because there was something about her attitude that put him on guard.

The new client wore dark glasses and a black silk scarf over her hair, so Wyatt didn't know what color it was—or if it was long or short. Plus, he couldn't look into her eyes, so he began guessing. Blue eyes, brown, hazel?

This was ridiculous. Why disguise her appearance inside a conference room? Wyatt was the first to agree to a client's privacy, but this was going a bit far.

The woman swiveled the chair and stood up. There was something about her mannerisms, the way she moved, that was familiar, but he couldn't place it. Wyatt should know her; he was sure of it. Yet he didn't.

When she walked toward him, it struck a chord, as if she was an old friend. But that wasn't possible, was it? Then she pulled off the scarf and tossed it onto the table. Short, dark hair, some kind of punk style, shaved on one side and spiky everywhere else. He definitely didn't know any punk-rocker babes.

The woman removed her sunglasses, holding them in her hand. Brown eyes, big, large, and thoughtful. That was the best description. She tipped her head to the side in greeting, and the diamond studs lining the curve of one ear sparkled under the fluorescent lights.

Then it struck him. She looked so different. This was not how he remembered her—not at all. But then, even as a young girl she'd been a rebel.

Wyatt looked into her eyes. "Elizabeth?"

"Hello, Wyatt."

She was the last person he expected to see. When he'd joined the Navy, she'd been in New York—where she should still be. That was where she'd grown up, where her family was.

"What are you doing here?"

Elizabeth didn't smile. In fact, he didn't sense any warmth in her greeting. "Is that any way to speak to an old friend...a childhood friend, I might add?"

Her unexpected appearance in Wyatt's life threw him off balance. Any semblance of professionalism went out the window. He wanted to know what was going on, and he wanted to know now. When he retired from the service, he'd made a point not to return to New York. He had no use for his family, and he certainly had no reason to reunite with *her*. When they'd parted, it hadn't been on good terms. She seemed to overlook that fact.

It annoyed Wyatt that she had the nerve to show up in his life. He didn't need this, nor did he want it.

"I need to hire a bodyguard," Elizabeth said.

"Travis will take care of that for you. We have a lot of guys working here. They are all highly trained—"

"I want you. I don't know any of those other guys."

"Elizabeth, be reasonable."

"It's Beth to you. I insist that you not call me by my given name. That's reserved for my father. To my *friends*, I'm Beth."

So now they were friends again. "Okay, Beth. I don't know why you've come here or what kind of situation you've gotten yourself into, but I'm not your man."

"Oh, but you are." She glared at him. "And how dare you insinuate that I've gotten myself into a situation. That's insulting."

Wyatt knew from experience that trouble found *Beth*, whether she looked for it or not. But as he recalled, she'd done her best to find it.

"I don't like being here any better than you like having me here. But I have nowhere else to turn. As distasteful as it may be, I'm counting on you. So I ask that you hear me out." Beth went over to the drink station and poured a glass of water.

As much as he wanted to send her packing, Wyatt couldn't turn away a woman in need. It wasn't in his makeup. He may not be comfortable with the circumstances, but it was his duty to make sure that she was okay. Friend or not, she deserved that much.

Wyatt plopped into a chair some distance from hers. "I'll hear what you have to say, but I don't guarantee anything."

"Fair enough." Beth sank back into her chair by the

window and took a sip of the water.

Wyatt leaned back in the chair and crossed his arms over his chest. "I'm all ears."

"A lot has changed since you've been away. I'm alone in the house now. My father is ill, and he's in a nursing home."

"I'm sorry to hear that." That part was sincere. Wyatt thought highly of Stephen Foster, and considered him one of the few honest men in the business.

"My brother runs the company with my Uncle Martin's assistance, but when my father was still in charge, he hired me to help in accounting."

Wyatt raised his brows.

"Don't look so shocked. I'm handy with computers, and bookkeeping software isn't all that sophisticated."

"You do have talent with computers."

Beth brightened slightly, taking in the unintended compliment. "Anyway, to get to the point...I've been accused of embezzling funds, and, as a result, kicked out of the company."

"And did you steal the money?"

The easiest thing to do was raise Beth's ire. It had been that way since he'd known her, which was most of her life. And why wouldn't he ask that? She'd been in trouble more than she was out of it. He wouldn't put much past her. Although he wouldn't have dreamed she'd graduate to criminal activities. Pranks were one thing; time in prison was another.

"Oh, that's just great." Beth propelled herself from the chair, shooting up like a rocket. "I come here in good faith, and you readily believe the worst of me, just like all the others."

"I didn't say that. I'm just asking."

Beth huffed and sat back down. "Well, no, I didn't

25

do it, if you must know. But that doesn't change anything. My brother and uncle are convinced that I did. So I'm banned."

"Did they file charges?"

"No, they didn't. You must realize that it would look bad for the family. They prefer to keep it quiet. It's enough to disown me."

"Won't your father stand up for you?"

"He would, but he can't. That illness I mentioned is Alzheimer's. He's not in his right mind." Beth paused. "I'm on my own."

Wyatt furrowed his brow. "Why come to me?"

Beth hesitated, then took a breath and continued. "The onset of my father's illness was so sudden, and I'm all alone now. I'm certain my brother's aim is to inherit Foster International, every dime, if he can. And my uncle Martin is on his side. He's conspiring to have me written out of the will."

"So it's the money you're concerned about?"

Beth shook her head. "Not in the least. I didn't manipulate things in order to scoop the family fortune, even though I was my father's favorite."

"Well, what has you worried, then?"

"I'm treated like an outsider. My uncle will do anything to see that I don't get my inheritance...and more. But as you might recall, he has a temper. And, well, I've decided that I need some security."

Wyatt knew her too well. There was no question that she hadn't told him everything. Beth was strong-willed, and not easily bullied. She'd stood up to her uncle for years. Had something changed while he'd been away?

Wyatt leaned forward, resting his forearms on his thighs. "Do you think that your brother or uncle wish you harm?"

Beth seemed to ponder that question a moment longer than necessary. "I don't know," she said, without much conviction.

"Then why hire a bodyguard?"

Beth shrugged. "Just in case." When he didn't offer to take the job, she added, "I'll feel better."

Wyatt wasn't anxious to get involved. He was under no delusion; he would be stepping into a bad situation. Whatever it was that Beth hadn't told him was going to come back to bite him. Yet she was a woman alone.

Sitting across from him, dwarfed by the plush office chair, she looked small. In her jeans and cotton shirt, Beth didn't look any older than early twenties, although she had to be twenty-eight. He was five years older than she was. The woman was an enigma. Her petite size gave her a vulnerable appearance. Yet she carried herself with a don't-mess-with-me attitude, and the new punk look she'd acquired lent credence to that.

Beth waited for his reply. There was no way in hell he would send her back to New York by herself, into a situation that could be dangerous. He didn't understand how her family posed a physical threat, but the fact that she was concerned for her safety was enough for him.

Wyatt would do it, but he didn't have to like it. "I'll take on the duties as your bodyguard, but just until the issue is resolved and you're out of danger. Then I'm done. Agreed?"

Beth's smile lit up her face, and she looked quite pretty. "Okay, agreed." She stood up. "Travis mentioned there's something I need to sign."

Wyatt nodded, then went over to the door and opened it for her. "After you," he said.

CHAPTER THREE

The paperwork took a while, since Beth was asked in-depth questions to enable Stealth to set up security for her. The head of the team Travis Hewitt orchestrated the proceedings and the financial agreement. He was a family man, judging by the photos of his wife and daughters on his desk.

Then a guy in a ponytail, introduced as Rip, filled in a detailed questionnaire on his computer while he interviewed her. Beth tried to answer the questions honestly, knowing that the company could and probably would find out anything they wanted to. But she didn't volunteer more than she was asked for.

While Wyatt met with their computer expert, Beth lingered in reception and got to know Tessa. The woman was friendly, straightforward and not pretentious. Since Tessa had been to New York, and knew a bit about the city, she asked lots of questions. It seemed like questions were part of the Stealth culture.

Beth updated her about the shopping scene, some new restaurants, and other trivia. But she skipped over anything personal. After all, she'd just met the woman, even if she did work for a team of ex-SEAL bodyguards. It paid to be careful.

Wyatt returned, interrupting before the conversation got too interesting. "I think we're done here," he said.

"Then take me to lunch." Beth winked at Tessa, who

smiled. "I'm starved. Personal history questionnaires wear me out."

Wyatt stood next to Beth, but the top of her head barely reached his shoulder. *Was he that tall before?* "Where do you want to go?"

"I'm new in town," Beth said. "You'll have to pick the place. But no green smoothies or tofu, all that health food stuff."

"You have something against health?"

"Just the food, if it's extreme. Isn't California known for the yuppie, trendy, healthy lifestyle?"

Wyatt lifted his hands. "Burger and fries?"

Beth grinned. "Lead the way." She waved at Tessa on the way out.

In the elevator, Beth leaned against the opposite wall to get a good look at her new bodyguard. It had been over ten years since she'd seen him, and he'd definitely changed—for the better. He'd been handsome as a youth, but maturity suited him.

"Looking at something?" Wyatt said.

"You've filled out. Where'd you get all that muscle?"

"It was required in the line of duty."

Beth couldn't imagine what he'd experienced as a SEAL, but it must have been demanding. That much she could guess about special ops. Yet she had no personal knowledge of the rigors he'd endured. Whatever he'd been doing had sculpted him into a solidly built specimen—a sexy one, at that.

Yet she didn't want to go there. This bodyguard arrangement was temporary, and solely for her protection. She had no designs on a guy she'd known most of her life, even if he had morphed into some sort of Adonis. Her memories of him largely involved arguing, and judging by their unplanned reunion, that hadn't changed.

The elevator door opened, and Wyatt followed her out. "We can walk. It's not far."

The weather was unexpectedly pleasant, so Beth took off her jacket. "I'll have to get used to so much sunshine this time of year," she said. "It must be part of the attraction."

Wyatt glanced over. "That, and the beaches, the food, the—"

"Women?"

"That too."

"You said that just to annoy me."

Wyatt motioned for her to turn the corner. "Which is not difficult to do. But you asked the question. I didn't start it."

Beth would have taken issue, just on general principle, but the restaurant was a few steps away. Wyatt strode up to the door to open it for her. He was such a gentleman.

The place was very LA, with polished wood floors, and chrome and glass tables under pendant lighting. Sheer fabric was tied back from the windows to reveal the view of downtown. Beth favored New York, but she could appreciate the local ambience.

The greeter escorted them to an open table along the bay of windows. Beth slid into the tangerine-colored vinyl booth, and Wyatt took the chair across from her. While studying the menu, she noticed him staring. "What? Is my hair out of place?"

"You just look different, that's all," Wyatt said. "I'm not sure what I expected. Well, actually, I wasn't sure I'd see you again. But since I have...what's with the new look?"

Beth made a face. "It's not a look." Having him around was going to be a challenge. "It's my style, and it hasn't changed much since I've been an adult. You just haven't been around to see."

"Hmm, that's right. You turned eighteen right before I left."

"I'm aware." Beth put the menu on the table, and when the waitress glided up to the table, she placed her order.

"I'll have the same," Wyatt said, "but with cheddar on the burger."

"You didn't write to me while you were away?"

"You didn't either."

Beth sighed. "That's no answer. And anyway, I wouldn't have known where to send a letter to you."

"Is that still in fashion...writing letters?"

"You're changing the subject." Beth studied him, a man she knew so well yet didn't know at all. "Why did you leave?"

The waitress came by with the iced teas, giving Wyatt a chance to come up with his answer.

"I joined the Navy."

Beth dumped a packet of sweetener in her drink. "I know *that*. But why? You were so good at baseball."

Wyatt shrugged. "Not really. I fancied that I was, and the sports scholarship boosted my ego. But it takes more than that. I just didn't have it, not for pro ball."

"So how do you go from baseball to boot camp?"

Wyatt took a gulp of tea. "You ask a lot of questions."

"I just answered more questions than I have since you left, so it's your turn."

"My father wanted me to take over the family business. Since I'm the eldest, he considered it my duty. We differed in that opinion—strongly. So I left. The service called, and I had the physical abilities required. End of story."

Beth huffed. "Men."

"What did I do now?"

"You summarize ten years and a major life-changing event in three sentences. That was three, wasn't it?"

"Talk to your girlfriends, then."

Beth didn't have any girlfriends, really. And the one friendship she'd begun to form had ended abruptly, as of the day before. Quickly she blocked out the unwelcome memory. Arranging her napkin on her lap, Beth avoided Wyatt's eyes.

He might be perceptive enough to notice her discomfort. That would not do. Beth had purposely skipped telling him about the subway tragedy. Eventually, Wyatt would find out, but she preferred to keep it quiet for now.

The entire incident unnerved her. There were too many unanswered questions, too much mystery. Beth had seriously considered the murderer had been after her, that Amanda's demise was a case of mistaken identity. But on the flight to California, she'd begun to doubt it.

Despite her family issues and the animosity toward her, Beth had difficulty believing that someone wanted her out of the picture, as in dead. It went beyond her reality. Sure, she'd been privy to crimes of a sort, deeds that the wealthy didn't give a second thought to.

But homicide had not been a part of it.

So Beth didn't want to draw attention, and had gone quiet about her theory that the subway killer had pushed the wrong woman. It was best to wait and see, considering the incredulity. If a cop didn't believe her, then why would anyone else?

She needed to see how things played out, and now, with Wyatt's protection, she was safer. Yet he'd been reluctant to accept the role of protector, and suspicious of her allegations. If she'd confessed her fear of being the target of a killer, or shared her suspicions of what took place in the subway, Wyatt might not have agreed to take the job as her bodyguard.

Beth hadn't wanted to take that chance, and still didn't.

Wyatt leaned back in his chair. "You seem thoughtful."

"Just hungry." As if on cue, a busboy delivered the meals. Beth cut her burger in half and took a big bite. It was especially good, or maybe she was more starved than she'd thought.

Wyatt doused his fries with ketchup then stuffed a wad of them in his mouth. For the moment, he was distracted, which offered Beth a reprieve from revealing her thoughts.

After a few more bites of her hamburger, Beth nibbled some of the fries. Then her phone vibrated and she pulled it from her pocket. It was a text from Thomas. She held the phone up so Wyatt couldn't read the screen from across the table.

It was an update on the legal process her uncle had initiated to have Beth removed from her father's will. And her attorney mentioned the subway incident, assuring her that the press hadn't gotten wind of it yet.

Wyatt continued chewing. "Anything important?"

"A text from my attorney."

"Thomas Stapleton?"

"You have a good memory."

"He probably still represents my family in business

matters, too."

Wyatt's statement was a reminder of how intertwined their lives had been. Growing up, their wealthy families had been friends, and attended many of the same events. Since he was five years older than she, Wyatt had tended to look out for her. "My uncle is pressing to get the will changed. But my father is unable to sign right now, or the deed would be done."

"Your father wouldn't cut you out of your inheritance, unless there's something I'm missing."

"Uncle Martin has undue influence over him. He'd use it to force the signature. Even though it's not legally valid for my father to sign under duress, there's no way to prove it. So my uncle would probably get away with it." Certainly, no one would believe Beth if she made that claim.

"When did that change? Your father used to be his own man. He wouldn't have let his younger brother push him into anything he didn't want to do."

"It's a long story," Beth said.

"Now who's summarizing information into a couple of sentences?"

If only Wyatt knew all that Beth wasn't telling him. "What can I say?"

Wyatt finished his burger in silence, and Beth pushed her plate aside, no longer hungry. "I hope you get travel pay, because I have to fly back to New York."

"I figured as much." Wyatt wiped his greasy fingers with his napkin. "When?"

"It's my brother's birthday, and my uncle is throwing him a big party Friday night. I'm planning to be there, if for no other reason than it will irritate my uncle. I have a right to be there, but I have a hunch that he hopes I won't show up," Beth said. "And there's no better time to face the enemy."

"How will you explain my presence?"

"We've known each other...like, forever. I'll just say I knew you were out of the service and looked you up. It's not strange to invite you to the party with me."

"How did you know I was out of the Navy?"

"Your sister told me."

Wyatt went quiet then, making the point that he wanted no part of his family. Yet Beth had a relationship with his younger sister Jessica, and happened to know that she hoped to reunite. The falling out between Wyatt and his family didn't make sense, but now was not the time to bring it up. She'd pressed her luck enough for one day.

"Where are you staying?" Wyatt said.

"At the Omni."

Wyatt widened his eyes. "Nice."

"I'm not poor—yet, anyway. If my uncle has anything to say about it, I will be, so I might as well enjoy it while I can."

"I'll escort you to your suite," Wyatt said, tossing some money on the table.

Beth nodded at the cash. "I can put it on the tab."

"No need to." Wyatt stood up and reached for her hand.

"I can get to the hotel on my own."

"That's not how it works. Until we take off for New York, I'll guard you."

The bodyguard situation may be too confining. Beth hated to be closed in, and hadn't expected Wyatt to watch her every move. All she'd wanted was for him to be around, in case she needed protection. "I'm not sure I like this arrangement."

Without flinching, Wyatt said, "You came to me,

remember?"

Beth stood and allowed her new bodyguard to follow her out. Now what had she gotten herself into?

*****

Once he'd seen Beth to her hotel suite, Wyatt had gone home. But not before checking the place for bugs and looking around to be sure it was safe.

Beth had glared at him with her arms crossed. "It's the Omni."

"I know what hotel we're in."

Wyatt ordered her to lock the door behind him, and not open it until he returned. She swore that she looked forward to a long soak in the tub and a good night's sleep, since she was travel-weary. He didn't trust her any more than he had to, and planned to be at the hotel by the time she was ready for breakfast.

The next morning, Wyatt went to the gym very early. He pounded out the miles on the treadmill, mulling over his current assignment. He wasn't sure what Beth was up to. He believed that she was concerned for her safety, he just didn't know why. Her uncle wouldn't physically harm her in order to write her out of the will. There was more to the story, and Wyatt intended to find out what.

It wasn't surprising that Beth had come to him. Wyatt had protected her many times in her youth. One time in particular, Beth had gone swimming in a restricted area. She'd pushed the envelope by jumping off a bridge into the water, which was deep enough, but the fall could have been the end of her. Her brother had snitched, aware that Wyatt tended to look out for her.

Wyatt had arrived in time to see Beth perched high on the bridge, teetering toward the dark water. "Beth, don't!" But his shout didn't stop her. She was fearless and, with a wave at him, she'd propelled her small body toward the water.

She'd screamed all the way down and splashed into the glassy surface. At the time, she'd been eight years old, but already defiant. Wyatt had torn off his shoes and jogged to the water's edge. She hadn't surfaced, so he dove in. Luckily, he'd found her beneath the surface. A bump on the head had knocked her out.

Beth had lived to see another day. Wyatt had made sure she was breathing, then run home with her in his arms. And that hadn't been the only time he'd run interference between Beth and disaster. After all these years, he'd hoped that she'd outgrown her propensity toward accidents.

From what Wyatt could tell, Beth hadn't reformed. She was still a rebel, a woman of her own mind, out to prove something. He just hoped that he could save her this time. For there to be a chance of that, Beth would have to come clean and tell him what was really going on.

A visit to her family was a step in the right direction. Wyatt could see her family and witness the interchange firsthand. If her uncle wished her ill, then there would be signs. It was a damned good thing Wyatt would be there with her.

Beth wasn't a child anymore. Her arrival had caught Wyatt off guard in more ways than one. It was a surprise to see her at all, but he couldn't have predicted his reaction to her. The constant bickering with her continued, as if he hadn't been out of her life for so long.

But there was something else. Beth had developed into an alluring woman. Was it just the mystery that surrounded her, the excitement attached to her? That was part of it. Yet underneath the thick, dark eye makeup, the tricked-out hair, and the ear piercings, Beth was attractive.

There had been chemistry between them before Wyatt had left for basic training, but he'd brushed it aside. Beth was a unique woman. For all the messes she'd gotten into, she was a good person. He couldn't have known her as long as he had without witnessing her good side.

But she persisted in being the tough girl, proving that she didn't care, that not much could get to her. At one point, Wyatt would have agreed. And he'd moved on with his life, committed his skill and talent to his SEAL team. Yet now Beth was here again.

The best course of action was to ignore any attraction. Beth was not the woman for Wyatt. He'd have enough of a challenge rescuing her from the tight spot she'd gotten into, much less getting personally involved. That wouldn't be good at all. He'd do his job, then let her get on with her life.

Drenched in sweat, Wyatt hopped off the machine. He toweled off and headed for the shower. When he got his bag from the locker, he checked his phone. There was a text from Rip:

Preliminary security risk analysis complete. Client has dysfunctional family. No other threat detected.

Wyatt replied: *Something has her worried. Keep looking.*

If Wyatt didn't uncover the truth soon, Rip would. His abilities as security analyst were akin to supernatural powers. More than once, he'd come through with vital info that had escaped the usual channels. Working in combo with Cooper, a computer tech who could hack into anything powered by electricity, unsavory types didn't stand a chance.

And that was what Wyatt counted on. For now, he'd do his part and accompany Beth to her brother's birthday party. It should be interesting, at the very least.

*****

Beth secured first-class tickets to New York, but the seats were cramped anyway. The plane took off, and Wyatt looked out the window. His thigh was pressed against Beth's. It wasn't intentional, and he would have moved, but there was nowhere to move to.

When the flight attendant came by, Wyatt ordered Coke and Beth had a glass of white wine. "I need the boost of courage," she said.

"Are you worried about seeing your family?"

"No, actually, I'm looking forward to it...but for all the wrong reasons." Beth held the plastic cup in both hands and took a sip.

"You haven't explained what you need me for," Wyatt said.

"Moral support."

Wyatt laughed. "That would be a first." He swished his drink around, melting the ice into the soda. "I've known your family for a long time. I can't get my head around any one of them wishing you harm. Oh, I'm aware of jealousies and the cutthroat tactics that your uncle or your brother would resort to. But hurting you is entirely different."

"I hope you're right," Beth said. She held a pencil and sketched figures on her napkin.

"You're still into sketching?"

Beth shrugged. "It's no big deal, just a way to pass the time."

"Why won't you admit how talented you are? I saw

your stuff, way back when. You're good."

"Shut up, Wyatt. It's none of your business."

Clearly, Beth turned a blind eye to her talent for cartooning. She should have been proud of her work, but instead, she hid it. As a young girl, she'd sketched with a passion, but refused to share. Wyatt had encouraged her, but it had fallen on deaf ears. Did she assume she'd be laughed at, that no one would take her seriously? Wyatt wanted to ask, but since she'd bitten his head off, he kept quiet.

Beth crumpled the napkin, then looked over at him. "Should we take a detour and visit your family when we arrive?"

"I'll skip that, if you don't mind."

"I don't get you, Wyatt. Your family cares about you. Why do you shut them out?"

Mercer Resources had holdings in oil and gas. His father Patrick Mercer had built the company from the ground up, which would have been a feat to admire, except that the man's ruthless tactics weren't. Any achievement had been blotted out by how the success had been achieved.

Wealth and power wielded over those less fortunate had left a bad taste in Wyatt's mouth. His father had pressed him to follow in his footsteps, but Wyatt hadn't been able to get the hell out of there fast enough. The college scholarship and living on campus had been a breath of fresh air.

His father had berated him for it, and harangued him to accept an apartment, fully paid for. Wyatt refused. He wanted no part of the ill-gotten wealth, and preferred the dorms. Then he'd gone into the Navy, welcoming deployment, as it put him beyond his father's reach. Even the wealth of Mercer couldn't penetrate the Navy SEAL organization. Thus, the awesome and powerful Patrick Mercer had been effectively cut off from his son.

"Okay, so I know you didn't get along with your dad," Beth said. "I get it. But your brother runs the company now, and Jeremy has different principles. He isn't a replica of your father. You should give him a chance."

"We'll see." But Wyatt doubted it. He had no reason to reconnect. All these years away had been good for him. His only regret was that he'd left his sister Jessica behind. It wasn't her fault that her dad was an ass. She'd been much younger than Wyatt and had looked up to him. At one time, he'd been close to her. Now he didn't even know how she was, or what she'd done with her life. He was a sorry example for a brother.

*****

The plane touched down early, and after checking into the hotel, there was plenty of time before the party. "We have a stop to make on the way," Beth said.

"Where is that?"

"Foster International."

"I thought you were booted from your position?"

Beth nodded. "But I'm going to hack into my brother's computer and see what I can find."

"I don't like the sound of this." Beth seemed to gravitate toward trouble. No wonder she was embroiled in some family situation. "If you get caught, your brother will have all the more reason to go against you."

"I won't get caught. I'll make sure he's not there. It's his birthday, so it's my best chance of getting in there when he's away." Beth scrolled on her phone then hit the button. "I'll check with Susan." She looked over at Wyatt. "His secretary. She likes me. We're sort of friends. She'll tell me."

Wyatt shook his head. As far as he knew, hacking a company computer was illegal, even if you were the owner's daughter.

"Susan...it's Beth. Yeah, I've been kind of tied up. I need to drop by, but you know that my brother is mad at me." Beth winked at Wyatt. "He gets in those moods. But I need to stop by and get something. It's best if he's not there." She paused. "Oh, he isn't? Perfect. I'll ring when I get there and you can buzz me in. You're a real friend...and Susan, it's probably better if you don't mention to anyone that I was there."

Beth put her phone down. "Susan says that Kyle hasn't been in all day. He told her it's his birthday and he has plans. She doesn't know about the embezzlement thing. I told her that he's miffed at me for some stupid reason, but he'll get over it."

"I should talk you out of this."

Beth grinned. "Have you ever been able to talk me out of anything?"

Wyatt expelled a breath. "You made your point. Let's go grab a cab."

*****

Foster International was as imposing as Wyatt remembered. The rambling four-story complex took up an entire city block. Beth led him around back and lifted a phone, then announced her arrival.

"It's the back way in," she said, looking up at Wyatt.

A buzzer sounded and the door clicked. Beth yanked it open. "Follow me. I'll try to be fast."

Wyatt followed her down a long hall, and past some glass windows. Beth gave a woman, who must have been Susan, a thumbs-up as she passed by. Then she shoved open the door to an expansive office. The desk alone cost a fortune. It was long enough to take a nap on.

"Don't gawk," Beth said. "We have a job to do. You keep watch and I'll get the data."

Wyatt stood by the door, prepared to block entry to any intruder. If it was her brother, he'd shove him in the hall and concoct some cover story. Beth went to work on the computer, but swore when she couldn't decipher the passcode.

"My brother's not that clever. Tech support must have set this up for him," Beth said. "That gives me an idea."

Beth clicked away on the keyboard, while Wyatt's anxiety built. He wasn't afraid of an encounter, since he was trained for defense. But if Beth was caught in her brother's office, she'd have more than a little explaining to do.

"Come on, Beth. What's taking so long?"

"Hey, you want to come over here and crack this thing? What kind of password could they have used?" Beth was talking to herself now, coaxing the computer system as if it might take pity on her and cooperate.

As the minutes ticked by, Wyatt lost patience. He was about to grab Beth and get out of there, when she had success.

"Got it. Now I'll transfer all the data to this drive. I don't have time to look it over right now."

"Damn right you don't. Copy it fast, and let's go."

The copying took a while. Apparently, there was a lot of data on her brother's system. Finally, Beth came over, holding up a small drive. "This is what we need."

"What exactly are you looking for?"

"I'm accused of embezzling, remember? Well, let's just see what's going on in this company. I didn't steal any funds, but if I can figure out who did, I can clear my name."

"It a start." Wyatt grabbed her hand, hauled her out of the office, and back down the hall without delay. The sooner he put distance between Beth and Foster International, the better.

CHAPTER FOUR

Beth slipped the tiny flash drive into her pocket, and Wyatt ushered her into the cab. There could be valuable information on there, evidence to shed light on the accusations against her. Later she'd have a chance to review the data and see what she could come up with.

"Where to now?" the driver asked.

"I have plenty of room at home, if you want to stay there," Beth said.

Wyatt didn't hesitate. "Give him the address. A hotel is out of the question. It's my job to stick close to you."

Beth gave the address to the cab driver. Then she leaned back to catch her breath. Breaking into her brother's computer had her nerves on edge. It was like a scene from a spy movie. She could have asked Kyle first, demanded that he confess his role in kicking her out of the family.

But Kyle could lie. It was better to get the goods, then see what he had to say. Unless her brother had wiped out anything incriminating, Beth would find at least a clue to the intrigue. She doubted he'd thought of safeguarding information, and probably considered a password sufficient. But with Beth around, such flimsy methods were inadequate. Luckily for her, Kyle hadn't figured that out yet.

On the way to her house, Wyatt didn't say much. That was just as well, since the cabbie could overhear any conversation. Beth glanced at her hunky bodyguard, wondering what he thought of all this. He hadn't been keen on sneaking into Foster, but she had a right to be in her father's company offices. Even if her uncle or brother would argue that she didn't.

Her home wasn't far, so Beth would have an opportunity to change clothes before going to the party. She'd lived alone for a while, and it would be different to have a man in the place—particularly Wyatt. He'd been a part of her life before, and now he was again.

Beth wasn't sure how to handle it. She couldn't pretend indifference. After all, Wyatt knew her better than most people did, and he was her friend. Or, at least, he had been. Many years stood between that friendship and whatever relationship Beth had with him now.

She needed to keep it light, treat him as a hired protector. That might not be easy. Wyatt was a hot alpha type. He'd been a SEAL, and the toughness showed, in his confident demeanor and his rugged build. Any flesh-and-blood woman, Beth in particular, would find a man like that attractive.

Beth resisted the chemistry, and steeled her resolve to focus on her dilemma. Once that had been handled, Wyatt would leave anyway. He had no reason to stay in the city, not even for his family. And his career was on the opposite coast. What did she care? Her life didn't include involvement with a former military man, not even one she knew well.

The cab pulled in front of her building, and Wyatt leapt out to jog around to open the door for her. She hadn't expected that. "The service had a good effect on your manners," she said. Wyatt ignored her comment.

When the driver got out and opened the trunk, Wyatt paid him. "I got it," Wyatt said, and lifted their suitcases out.

At the house, Beth punched in her security code and opened the door. She motioned toward the elevator, and Wyatt followed her through the marble lobby, wheeling the luggage.

"When did you move in here?"

Inside the elevator, Beth leaned against the handrail. "It's been a while. My father wanted to be closer to the office."

The doors opened and Beth stepped into the foyer. "I'll show you to the guest suite. You can settle in there. I'll get dressed and meet you in the library. I'm sure you can find it."

When her father had been home, a butler had seen to guests. But now that she was the only one living there, Beth saw no reason for such an extravagance. Plus, she preferred privacy.

After shedding her clothes, Beth took a hot shower, taking her time getting ready. She had neglected to RSVP to the party, unsure if she'd attend. Now she was glad her family wasn't expecting her. Her arrival would catch them off guard, and she would relish witnessing her brother's reaction.

Beth had gotten along with Kyle just fine. He was her younger brother, and she'd tended to look out for him. But once he'd gone to work at the company, he'd changed. Now he had an arrogant tone and an aloof manner, which hadn't concerned her until the false accusations had turned her life upside down.

It was important to discover Kyle's real intentions, and what part he played in the destruction of her family reputation. Certainly his role was integral, since he was the acting CEO. It annoyed her that her own brother behaved so badly towards her.

After she dried off and redid her makeup, Beth went to her closet to pick out an outfit. The party would be dressy. It would be a big deal, since it was her brother's birthday. If she didn't miss her guess, a lot of friends and business associates had been invited. It should be a real bash.

She opted for mesh stockings and a short leather skirt with matching jacket, over a crimson lace top. Her knee-high boots and chunky silver chains accessorized nicely, matching the silver studs that trimmed her jacket collar. Surely, Wyatt didn't expect her to emerge in a simple black cocktail dress, and her family would consider her outfit rather conservative, compared to some she'd worn.

Beth went to the library to find her date. Wyatt wore charcoal slacks that stretched over his thighs, showing off the lean muscle. He thumbed through some books on the shelf, providing her with a nice view of his firm ass, and her body responded.

"I'm ready," she said, walking over. Wyatt's musky cologne had an effect on her, but she did her best to conceal it.

Wyatt looked her over. "Leather suits you."

"Glad you approve. Did you find everything you needed in the room?" Beth struggled for small talk, not a skill she'd perfected. Yet it steered the attention away from the electricity radiating through her.

"Yes, the room was fine." Wyatt's deep brown eyes pierced into her. *What a heartthrob.*

"I called a cab. My uncle would have sent a limo to pick me up, but he doesn't know I'm coming to the party."

"That will be interesting."

"Very," Beth said. "The element of surprise will be

on my side."

*****

The driver pulled up to the residence. "My uncle has come up in the world since my aunt divorced him. He fancies that he's a billionaire, and if one is to go by appearances, he is."

Wyatt helped her out and looked up at the brightly lit mansion. "As I recall, Martin received half of your grandfather's fortune."

"One would think that would do it, but the divorce hit him hard. And I wouldn't be surprised if his extravagant lifestyle has drained a good part of what he had left." Beth took Wyatt's arm. "But who am I to say? I'm the black sheep of the family, so my uncle certainly doesn't confide in me."

Beth had taken care to arrive fashionably late. The party was in full swing. A uniformed butler opened the front door and allowed her to enter with her date. Inside was a crowded affair, but she didn't recognize many of the attendees, and assumed valued business contacts had filled out the guest list.

Kyle was nowhere in sight, so Beth followed Wyatt to the bar to get a drink. The bartender gave her a glass of champagne and handed club soda to Wyatt. "Can't drink on the job?"

Wyatt lifted his glass. "No alcohol. It's a bad mix with protection duty."

Music was playing loud enough to make conversation unnecessary. As Beth walked through with Wyatt in tow, she garnered glances from a few of the guests. Her style of dress was noteworthy, but she ignored the attention, intent on finding the guest of honor.

Walking down a carpeted hallway, Beth heard

voices. She looked up at Wyatt and nodded toward the open door. Then she strode into the room. Her brother stepped back from her uncle, tongue-tied. It appeared he'd been in the midst of a private talk. Beth was curious what it had been about.

Her uncle was not thrown off by the interruption, and went on the attack. "What are you doing here?"

Beth smiled and went over to give him a light hug. "I'm your niece, remember?" She laughed, more from pleasure at needling her uncle than from her lame joke.

"Yes, I'm aware of that," Martin said. "But you could have had the courtesy to respond to the invitation, so we'd know you'd be coming."

"Oh, I'm sorry. Are you concerned you'll run short of food? That the bar will be low on cocktails?" Beth shook her head. "You needn't have given it a thought. From what I saw, you'll have provisions for the next month."

Wyatt stood back, watching.

Kyle took a step in his direction. "What an unexpected pleasure," he said. "Wyatt?" They shook hands. "I didn't know you were in New York."

"I recently arrived," Wyatt said. "I heard congratulations are in order. It looks like quite the birthday party."

"Yes, Uncle Martin insisted."

Then Beth's uncle moved toward Wyatt like a vulture to its prey. "I thought you were in the Navy. When did you get out?" His questions were nothing more than accusations, making it obvious that Wyatt was unwelcome.

"I've been out for a while." Wyatt stood immobile, as if daring Martin to push it.

Beth caught her uncle's eye, and he glared at her.

"I see you two have reunited."

His harsh tone was typical. Of late, Martin had been irascible and borderline rude. Beth had grown to expect it of him. "I thought it would be nice to bring him to the party, considering that he's a family friend."

Martin motioned toward the door. "We should get back to the party. The guests will wonder what's happened to you."

Then Kyle followed him into the hallway. "I'll see you out there," he called back.

"And *that*...is my loving family," Beth said.

Wyatt's expression was serious. "Martin seemed to take issue with me tagging along tonight, or being with you at all."

"I'm sure he prefers to isolate me, all the easier to control matters. He's a bully."

"And Kyle...I don't know," Wyatt said. "He was friendly enough, just hadn't expected me to show up after so long."

"Yeah, well, we'll see about my brother. Success has gone to his head. Moving into the position of CEO at Foster has swollen his ego. He behaves as though he's entitled."

"He didn't seem much different than I recall."

Beth headed back to the party. "Stick around. You'll see."

*****

Wyatt followed her out, with his eyes on her hips. The tight leather skirt hugged her petite form, and it was a damn sexy look for her. He'd better stay focused on the task at hand. Tonight was a chance to see her family in their element, and determine what threat existed. Whatever urges Beth stirred, Wyatt didn't intend to do anything about it.

He planned to keep tabs on Martin and Kyle, just to satisfy his curiosity. Beth was convinced that one or both meant her harm. Yet on the surface, the situation involved no more than family squabbles—unsettling but not dangerous.

Wyatt accompanied Beth back to the bar for a refill. Then a late arrival to the party caught his attention, and his heart sank. His sister Jessica entered the room with a man he didn't know, clearly her date. Although Wyatt hadn't seen her since he'd gone into the Navy, she was still his younger sister. He had a surge of brotherly love, and looked at the guy she was with to see if he was acceptable.

Then Jessica spotted him and smiled. It was just like her not to hold his bad behavior against him. His sister crossed the room, went right into his arms, and gave him a big hug. "Wyatt, it's so good to see you. I didn't even know you were in New York." She put both hands on his shoulders and looked into his eyes.

A pang of guilt stabbed Wyatt in the gut. "I meant to get in touch." It wasn't true, but, seeing Jessica, he wished he had contacted her.

"You weren't very good at staying in contact," Jessica said. "I didn't hear from you while you were away. At least you let me know when you got out. Are you working?"

"I'm in the bodyguard business. I hooked up with some other SEAL buddies at Stealth Security."

"That suits you. So I suppose moving back to New York is out of the question?"

"Pretty much."

Jessica looked over at Beth. "You didn't warn me that Wyatt was coming to the party. You should have mentioned it."

Beth gave her a hug. "Sorry, I didn't have much notice."

"Well, you look stunning. Crimson is your color." Jessica introduced her date, who'd stood back from the fray. "Michael is an attorney. We met at work." She smiled up at Wyatt. "Oh, you don't know. I graduated law school."

"I'm impressed," Wyatt said, and shook hands with Michael.

"I'm parched," Jessica said. "We'll catch up with you later."

Wyatt's sister disappeared in the crowd, and Beth glared at him, as if he'd committed a crime. "At least I kept in touch with your sister."

"Don't rub it in," Wyatt said. "I already feel like a heel."

Food and drink flowed, and the noise level rose as the evening progressed. Beth ran into a couple of people she knew, and introduced Wyatt. But he could tell that she was no more interested in partying than he was. After a few bites of caviar, several glasses of club soda, and roast beef paired with unrecognizable side dishes, Wyatt was ready to go.

"I need to get my brother alone," Beth said. "I'm not leaving without some answers."

A birthday party didn't seem like the right time for true confessions, but that didn't deter Beth. She strode past a table laden with gifts, and plowed through guests in search of Kyle. Then she pointed to the terrace. Her brother was chatting with a small group, and Martin was among them.

If Beth intended to make a public challenge, the evening would get a lot more interesting. She walked outdoors with Wyatt a step behind. When Martin saw her, he furrowed his brow. "If you'll excuse me, I have an important call to make."

That left Kyle with his friends. He smiled at Beth. "Are you having a good time?"

Beth didn't respond. Instead, she plunged ahead with her agenda. "I need to speak with you, Kyle...alone."

The other guests took the hint and vanished inside, leaving Kyle to face his sister. "You are welcome tonight, Beth. I know Uncle Martin can be harsh sometimes. It's just his way. Don't take it to heart."

"Don't try to placate me," Beth said. "You know damn well that I'm upset. You conspired with our uncle to boot me out of the company and deprive me of my inheritance. And I want to know why."

Kyle flushed, and Wyatt wasn't sure if it was from anger or embarrassment. "You've got it all wrong. Just because you messed things up, you can't blame me. I didn't do anything."

"Oh, but you did. You set me up. It was you, Kyle, who had access to the books. You're the CEO, for Christ's sake. And you have a whole accounting team. Yet you were so quick to tout that I was guilty."

"What was I supposed to think?" Kyle said, raising his voice. "Uncle Martin is trying to look out for us now that Dad is sick. Would you have me call him a liar? He told me that he had evidence against you. I mean, embezzlement isn't hard to prove. The numbers don't lie."

Beth let out a heavy sigh. "It's that easy, huh? Martin tells you I committed a crime and you don't even question it?"

Kyle stared at her.

"Did you consider asking me if I did it?" Beth shook her head. "I guess that was too much to expect." She moved closer to her brother. "If the books have been tampered with and I didn't do it—which I didn't—then you better take a closer look, because someone committed the crime. Or maybe it was your doing, and you're pointing the finger at me to escape the guilt."

"You're assuming a lot."

"How would you feel in my place?" Beth crossed her arms. "Does an unconfirmed charge of embezzlement justify writing me out of the will?"

Kyle didn't reply.

"It hurts me to think that you'd conspire to gain the inheritance all for yourself. You're my brother, Kyle. It shouldn't be this way."

"You've got it all wrong. It's not like that."

Beth took Wyatt's arm. "Let's get out of here." She walked through the main room and out to the front steps, then asked the attendant to call for a cab.

Wyatt was unclear about the situation. Beth's relationship with her family was untenable, but he wasn't convinced that either her uncle or brother wanted to hurt her. The way she'd been treated was unfair, but not life-threatening—unless Beth knew something he didn't.

Once inside the cab, Wyatt broached the subject. "What did you gain by that encounter? If your brother wasn't against you before, you've given him reason to be now."

Beth glared at him, her brown eyes like daggers. "That's just great. You're the one person who is supposed to defend me, and you're on their side."

"I'm not on anyone's side," Wyatt said. "And it was a good thing that I was with you tonight. That's not the sort of thing you need to be doing alone." He took a breath. "But I don't get why you fear for your safety."

Beth stared at the back of the seat.

"Is there more? Is there anything you haven't mentioned, something that makes you think they mean you physical harm?"

"You wouldn't understand."

Wyatt closed his eyes and raked a hand through his hair. *Frustrating woman.* Why wouldn't she confide in him? After all, he'd accepted the role of protector. But he sure as hell couldn't do his job if Beth kept secrets from him.

The atmosphere was tense, and Wyatt couldn't wait to get back to her house. He was going to hash this out and get to the bottom of it. Or he was damn well flying back to California and putting this behind him. He wasn't about to follow her around, in the dark about the alleged danger—if there was any.

The cab pulled up to the curb. Wyatt checked out the lighting, not liking that it was so dark.

"I'll have to call maintenance. The outside light should be on. It must have burnt out," Beth said.

Wyatt was instantly alert. When a circumstance was unusual, there was often a reason. He scanned the building, but saw no motion. It was quiet. Yet it was too dark to see well.

"Driver, back up so your headlights shine on the entry." Then Wyatt took Beth's hand to help her out, watching for any disturbance.

Beth punched in her code and put her palm on the door to push it open. The cab rolled away, leaving them on the darkened sidewalk.

Wyatt stood close, wary. Then a stranger soundlessly emerged from between the buildings and came toward them. A glint of steel flickered, but before the man could draw his gun, Wyatt reacted. His training kicked in; defense was second nature.

With one powerful blow, Wyatt knocked the gun from the guy's hand and it clattered into the street. In a flash the attacker produced a knife, and crouched, ready to pounce.

Wyatt growled, "Don't do it, asshole." He stepped forward, just as the attacker dove past him toward Beth. She screamed, but the blade had struck fast. Blood spurted, and Wyatt couldn't tell how badly she was hurt. He yanked the bad guy's coat, hauling him back, then grasped his wrist in a death grip. The knife dropped, and Beth gasped.

There was too much blood. Wyatt's attention was riveted on Beth. The killer butted hard enough against Wyatt to knock him aside, then took off running.

"Beth..." Dropping to the ground to see how badly she was hurt, all he saw was blood. He looked closely to examine the cut. The knife had grazed her head, but the gouge wasn't too deep. It was a good-sized gash, though. "You'll be okay. It's a scalp wound. They bleed like a son of a bitch, but it's not fatal."

Wyatt helped her stand up, keeping his arm around her. He had to get her to a hospital. She might need stitches. Fortunately, cabs were easy to get in this town.

*****

At the hospital, Wyatt procured some gauze to soak up the blood, until the nurse took Beth back. He was allowed to go with her. The nurse cleaned the wound and the doctor took a look at her injury. "You are a lucky lady. If it had been any deeper you'd require stitches, but I can dress the area so it will heal up."

"That's a relief," Beth said. "There won't be any scar?"

"There shouldn't be," the doctor said. "But you need to file a police report."

"We'll take care of it," Wyatt said. "Right now I just want to get her home."

While the nurse gave Beth instructions and prepared her to leave, Wyatt called Stealth. After a few rings, Travis answered. "What's up, Mercer? I'm having a late dinner with Melanie, and the girls are sleeping over with a friend. So this better be good."

"Some idiot tried to kill Beth."

"Shit. How did that happen?"

Wyatt relayed the highlights, then said, "We're at the hospital now. It's fortunate that I was there. Beth wouldn't have stood a chance."

"Any theories on who is after her?"

"She's on shaky terms with her uncle and her brother. Until this happened, I couldn't make the connection between that and a threat on her life. But we just left a family party, where Beth confronted her brother Kyle on some touchy matters. Not an hour later, some asshole tries to kill her. So...you tell me."

"I'll fill the team in on what's happened. Killers attack for a reason. Somebody paid the dude, and we need to find out who did."

"The sooner, the better. Beth's life is at stake here."

"I'm all over it. Stick with her, and I'll contact you tomorrow."

When Wyatt hung up, Beth was waiting for him. "I heard you on the phone. Was that Travis?"

"Yes. I trashed his evening, but he doesn't mind. We're going to find out what's going on here," Wyatt said. "You were right all along. Someone is out to get you. And I'm damn sure going to see that they don't succeed."

Beth leaned into him, and Wyatt put his arms

around her. "I'm here to protect you. No one will hurt you again." He wrapped her in a strong embrace, and she hugged him tight. She'd been on her own, but not anymore.

CHAPTER FIVE

Beth pressed her cheek to Wyatt's hard chest and nestled into his embrace. For that moment, she was safe in his arms. Beyond just being her bodyguard, he believed her now, knew that she was in real danger. Wyatt's combat skill had saved her. Although intercepting the man from the shadows must have been child's play for him. Even as frightened as she'd been, she'd seen how Wyatt had dealt with the attacker.

"You're a good man to have on my side," she said, then looked up into his eyes.

Wyatt's dark hair was disheveled, and his brown eyes were filled with concern. "You made a good decision when you hired me."

That was all; they were client and bodyguard—even after tonight. Beth shouldn't have expected more. And when had she started expecting anything?

Slipping from his arms, Beth turned away, unwilling to have him see her expression. Wyatt was observant; she'd give him that. Earlier that evening his astute observation had averted a disaster. That was enough for one night. She wanted to get home and hide inside, away from intruders, to breathe a sigh of relief that she'd cheated death once more.

Wyatt put his arm around her, making this difficult. "Does it hurt much?"

"Not really, but the doctor gave me some pain pills, in case I need them." Beth didn't look up, unable to trust herself to peer into her bodyguard's caring eyes.

"It will be good to get you out of here," Wyatt said. "Hospitals aren't my favorite place."

"I could use some fresh air. I wish we could walk back."

Wyatt lifted her chin, so Beth had to face him. "No way; it's too dangerous. I don't know who's out there and I'm not taking any chances."

Beth couldn't argue with that, and wasn't sure how far she'd make it anyway. The adrenaline surge during the attack had kept her pumped up, but now she was beginning to fade. It would be embarrassing to collapse so Wyatt would end up carrying her. A taxi was a much better option.

The hospital entrance was a circular drive under a concrete overhang, reminding her of some fancy hotel. Yet it was far from that. Beth could still smell the antiseptic, and shuddered to think of the patients she'd seen in the emergency room. This was no vacation.

In the back of the cab, Wyatt put a hand on his knee, and she wanted to reach for it. Just for reassurance, she'd like to feel his big hand close over her smaller one, reminding her of his strength. Her imagination was out of control, a sign that she was a bit delirious from the injury. It was a bad idea to view Wyatt as more than a protector. Even the term *friend* meant more than Beth had a right to expect.

Wyatt leaned back in the seat and cracked his knuckles. "There had to be a motive for what happened tonight." He looked at her in the darkened back seat. "But what? That's what I can't figure out. What prompts someone to hire a killer?"

"Many things," Beth said. "Money, power,

greed...passion."

Wyatt raised a brow. "You have a lover that you haven't spoke of...a man jealous enough to want to kill you, as well as the other guy?"

"Very funny." Beth rested her head against the seat. "If there is, then where has he been? I don't recall eliciting such..." She caught herself. Did she really want to admit to Wyatt that there had been no man that sparked such passion? "Anyway, you can look elsewhere for the perpetrator. I haven't even dated anyone seriously in a while."

Wyatt's satisfied look irked her. Beth wished she'd had more dates to boast of, or more interesting ones. She'd devoted more attention to hacking computers, sketching, or shopping, than to starting a meaningful relationship. It was sad, really.

The house wasn't far, and this time there was no unwelcome greeter. Beth stabbed at the security pad and Wyatt shoved the door open. He flipped on a light and then pushed the elevator button. Once upstairs, he made her wait in the main room while he checked the house for intruders.

"I don't think anyone can break in," Beth said.

"Someone can always break in. It's just a matter of whether they have or not."

"I have a security system."

Wyatt didn't reply, just disappeared from view. It was a few minutes before he returned and assured her the place was secure. "I'll sleep with the door open," Wyatt said. "You lock yours behind you."

Beth understood his precaution, even though she didn't see how anyone could get past her bodyguard. The living space, including the bedrooms, was several flights up. So unless some guy scaled the outside of the building like Spider-Man, he'd have to come out in the open to get to her.

Once she was in her bedroom, with the door locked as instructed, Beth went into the bathroom to check out the damage. She couldn't tell how bad the cut was, since it was covered with a bandage. Other than a headache, she wasn't too bad off. It could have been much worse.

After getting ready for bed, she snuggled under the covers. As a young girl, there had been so many times that her father had tucked her in. A stressful night like she'd just had made her long for the past. There'd been a time when she hadn't feared, when she was confident that she was loved and cared for.

But now, her father couldn't help her. He needed her more than she needed him. It pained her that she couldn't rescue him from his nursing home prison. Stephen Foster had been a vital, productive man all his life—until the illness had taken hold.

Beth closed her eyes, struggling to process the past few days. It was notable her uncle hadn't mentioned the subway death, and her brother hadn't either. Neither of them had met Amanda, because Beth had made a point of keeping her newsroom connections separate from her family life.

It was her way of maintaining privacy. And her cartooning was her own business. She hadn't needed the ridicule from those that should have been supportive. Only her father had commended her for the talent she exhibited, but mostly, Beth had kept quiet about her passion. She didn't need to hear what her uncle or brother thought about it.

So far, her attorney must have been able to keep the press away from the Fosters, and from asking too many questions. That was a good thing, as it gave her a chance to discover the source of the attack before her family got involved. Wyatt had spoken of motive, but Beth was clueless.

She'd nearly been killed twice, yet had no idea why. Visions of the subway incident flooded her thoughts. Beth no longer doubted that she'd been the target. Amanda's only crime had been to wear the logo jacket, innocently so, and she had died as a result. Beth was consumed with sadness. She vowed to find out who had done the awful deed and make them pay.

*****

The next morning, Beth slept in. There was no place she had to be, and the rest had likely been good for her. She threw back the covers and got up, feeling pretty normal. In the bathroom, she carefully removed the bandage.

The cut was on the left side where her hair had already been shaved around the ear. It was convenient that it hadn't been on the other side where her hair was longer, as the doctor would have shaved that side too. That would have looked weird. She cleaned the cut as directed, then showered and dressed.

Revived from a good night's sleep, Beth went out to the kitchen with a renewed sense of purpose. She didn't like having to wonder when she'd be attacked next, cower at every corner, and hide behind her bodyguard. It was time to get to the bottom of this, and deactivate the deadly threat.

Wyatt was in the kitchen, scrolling on his phone and drinking coffee.

Beth poured a steaming cup of coffee and took a sip. "I see you figured out how to use the coffee machine."

"I couldn't find any food, though, except for a mostly empty bag of chips that I finished off." Wyatt tossed his phone on the table. "Don't you shop for groceries?"

"I don't cook."

"Well, I do. So we'll have to stock up."

Beth sat across from him. "You cook? Why didn't I know this before?"

"I suppose it didn't come up." Wyatt rocked his chair back and balanced it on two legs. "No wonder you're so tiny. You don't have any provisions."

"I'm not tiny; I'm just short...petite, if you will."

Wyatt grinned, and he was so darned handsome. She had to resist touching. She hadn't forgotten how good his arms felt wrapped around her. His longish, dark hair was messily groomed, dusting his collar seductively. His lips looked so kissable, and Beth imagined what it would be like to have his mouth pressed to hers.

"Forget the coffee," Wyatt said, and stood to reach for her hand. "We're going out for breakfast...lunch, or whatever meal it is. And I'll buy you a cup of coffee anywhere you want."

Beth took his hand. Why did this feel like a date? All he wanted to do was feed her, or he was starving and she was along for the ride. "I know just the place," she said.

A few blocks away, was a neighborhood cafe that specialized in comfort food. It had a rustic setting, nothing fancy, and tasty food. Beth figured the establishment could accommodate a hungry guy—one who hadn't eaten anything but caviar and thinly sliced roast beef since the day before, if you didn't count the stale chips from her cupboard.

Plus the coffee was good. Beth ordered an Americano

with cream and Wyatt had black coffee. After placing the food orders, Beth savored her rich drink and glanced across the table. She enjoyed watching Wyatt. "You know I'm still mad at you."

Wyatt put his cup down. "*I* should be mad at *you*."

Beth didn't see that coming. "Whatever for?"

"The way you treated me before I went off to the Navy." Wyatt narrowed his eyes. "What was it...some bitchy comment about me shirking responsibility?"

"Oh, that. Surely, you aren't still harboring a grudge?" Beth rolled a shoulder. "I was just miffed that you were abandoning me."

"How do you figure?"

"You, sailor boy, left home. You escaped without a thought for me." Beth crossed her arms. "I had to stay, deal with my family, and suffer with circumstances I couldn't do anything about."

"Hey, I had to go. There was no way in hell I would've followed in my father's footsteps. He was a conniving, cheating, power-hungry—"

"Bitter much?"

"You know exactly what I'm talking about. My father's methods were no secret. The man would do anything for a dollar...and you know it."

"I'm not saying he wouldn't." Beth sighed. "But you could have taken over the business, changed things. Instead you fled."

"I'd hardly call enlisting as a Navy SEAL *fleeing*." Wyatt drummed his fingers on the table. "I'm not my father's boy. I'll leave that to my younger brother. I'd shrivel up in an office like a plant without sunshine. My talents are physical, not administrative."

Beth couldn't believe how many years it had taken to get that out in the open. But then, she hadn't spoken to him after he'd left for basic training. It was good to clear the air.

The meals arrived and Beth shuffled her eggs around with a fork. Wyatt dumped syrup on a stack of pancakes, cut into it with his fork, then stuffed a huge bite in his mouth. Chewing, he glanced up at her. "Still mad?" he said through a mouthful of food.

Beth laughed. "I guess not." She wiped a glob of butter onto her toast. "Are you?"

"Naw, I wasn't really mad. I just thought you were stuck up." Wyatt held up his hand. "Settle down. I'm teasing you."

After breakfast, Beth coerced him into going for a walk. "I can't stay cooped up. It's New York; I'm used to walking. And I doubt anyone wants to mess with you, not when you can see them coming." She looked him over: wide shoulders, bulging biceps, chest as hard as a rock. "Nope. We're safe."

It was a pleasant day for late October, so Beth got her fill of walking. Wyatt had no problem keeping up. She guessed he could outwalk or outrun her without breaking a sweat. But it was good to get outside and clear her mind. She lifted her head and strode with confidence. With Wyatt on her team, she'd be able to conquer her enemies.

*****

With the sun still high in the sky, Wyatt led her back home to plan the next move. Now that he had food in his belly, he was ready for battle. It was good to see Beth smile, and the cut was healing well.

The elevator doors opened and Wyatt stepped out into chaos.

"Oh my God, what happened?" Beth raced inside, looking around. "How did anyone get in here? The place is a mess."

The home had been ransacked; a thief must have been looking for something in particular. At first glance, it appeared that expensive items had been ignored. Money couldn't have been the motive. The job had been quick and dirty.

Wyatt looked around, verified that no one was in wait for them, and made a preliminary assessment of the damage. He turned to Beth, who wasn't nearly as frantic now. "What's missing?"

"I don't keep cash here, except for what I had in my purse. I had my phone in my pocket and the flash drive in my jacket." Beth rubbed her temple. "Force of habit, I guess. I don't leave important information in my home."

"What about your laptop?"

Beth shook her head. "There was no vital data. I'm a hacker—well, in case you didn't know. It's foolhardy to store anything important on a laptop."

Wyatt widened his eyes.

"Because a thief can just run off with a laptop, and passwords aren't that difficult to crack...usually."

"So I witnessed yesterday."

"I'm guessing the thief got into my laptop, but quickly discovered there wasn't anything to copy." Beth fell into a nearby armchair.

"What else, then?" Wyatt asked.

"I'm not sure, but whoever did this left some pretty valuable items behind."

"Yeah, this was personal, not some random theft."

Beth got up to scavenge around some more. Wyatt dug through the wreckage, picking up stuff, and looking for any evidence. There was a framed photo of Beth and her brother that had fallen onto the tile floor, and the glass had cracked. Kyle had blue eyes and dark hair, like his sister. Her brother was younger, and Wyatt remembered him as a little tyke. It was difficult to get his head around Kyle wanting to kill his sister.

"Wyatt, my journal is missing."

He looked up to see Beth standing in the doorway. "You're sure?"

"Yes, absolutely. I kept it in the desk drawer and it's gone." Beth slumped onto the sofa.

"What was in it?"

"Just stuff. I goof off sometimes, write political commentary...things like that. It was a hobby. I scribbled lots of notes and did research." Beth looked up at him. "Over the years, being privy to the underpinnings of my family's company...I sort of started investigating."

"What do you mean, *sort of*? What did you plan to do with the information?"

"Nothing, really. I uncovered some dirt in my family's history. It intrigued me," Beth said. "After all, I haven't been treated well, so it made sense to know what I was dealing with."

Wyatt sat beside her. "What exactly was in there?"

"I made some discoveries that dismayed me, mostly power-play-type stuff. The usual...disregard for the rights of honest people, manipulating and doing anything for money." Beth sighed. "I love my father. It was a disappointment when I learned of these underhanded dealings. I can't imagine him condoning such activities."

"Maybe those events took place after he got sick, so he wasn't a participant," Wyatt said. "But in any case, someone doesn't want that information to get out."

"Most of it was easy to find, which is why I didn't hide it. Given enough interest, it's public knowledge."

Wyatt frowned. "Possibly someone was afraid of *what else* you might discover, if you were allowed to continue."

Beth looked thoughtful. "Or...whoever it is doesn't want *me* to have the information."

"And is prepared to kill to make sure you don't act on what you know."

Wyatt looked at Beth. Her life was at risk; the stakes in the game had just gone up. There was a motive to kill her. He didn't have it all figured out yet, but this was a solid lead. It was time to call in some backup.

Wyatt called a number and hit speaker. He set his phone on the coffee table.

"Cooper here...what's up?"

"Coop...I'm with Elizabeth Foster, at her home. While we were out somebody broke in and took a look around. He made a mess of the place."

"Doesn't she have a security system?"

"Yes, but it's about to be upgraded," Wyatt said. "Anyway, you'll be interested to know what was stolen."

"I can't wait."

Wyatt told him about the journal and its contents. "It appears that information wasn't meant for public viewing, and now someone intends to silence Beth before she reveals it."

"I agree. Elizabeth must have struck a nerve with her prying into company affairs, and it was enough to make her a target."

Wyatt glanced over at Beth. "That's why I'm calling. I need to know who wants her dead, and why."

"I'll follow the money," Coop said. "I'm betting that greed is involved here. And you should know that I did find out something about Martin Foster. It seems he had a gambling problem."

"That's not a crime."

"True, but if he gets in over his head..."

"What about her brother Kyle?"

"I'm digging, but so far he's clean as a boy scout," Coop said. "But I'm still looking; I don't rely on first impressions."

After the call ended, Beth said, "I knew my uncle liked to gamble, and wrote about it in my journal. In his younger days, he had some run-ins with the police. My father told me of it, but as far as I know, Martin reformed. He hasn't shared much about his personal life, so all I know is from other sources."

"So we know that he's capable of misdeeds. Maybe he's behind all of this."

"Since my father got sick, my uncle has been the head of the family. My brother is acting as CEO, but Uncle Martin has control of major decisions, and has a lot of influence." Beth looked thoughtful. "My uncle is a cold-hearted man, and he fired anyone who wouldn't go along with his redirection of the company."

"We need to look closer at your uncle," Wyatt picked up his phone. "For now, we should call the police, file a report. I doubt they will find the burglar, but still we should have the incident on record."

"I suppose so." Beth glanced at the wreckage. "I guess we should have left everything like it was."

"Probably, but at this point, it really doesn't matter. The question is: how much do we tell them?"

Beth paced. "We're only guessing at most of it. I say that we give the police as little as possible. It's safer that way, for now." She motioned toward his phone. "Go ahead and call, so we can get this over with."

CHAPTER SIX

The whole situation was unsettling. Every time Beth turned around, there was some other mishap. What next? Now she didn't feel safe in her own home, with security that she'd thought couldn't be broached. So much for security systems—although Wyatt assured her that Stealth would install a better one.

Beth's head was reeling. The innocent notes she'd scribbled in a journal about her family's history had garnered more interest than she'd imagined. She racked her brain to pinpoint what she'd said that had posed a threat. Yet without knowing who was behind all of this, or what the person feared, she was at a loss.

The police didn't take long getting there, or in looking around. The consensus was that it was an amateur burglary, though the cop in charge had no clue why valuables weren't taken. Beth didn't offer any theories, just answered his inane questions.

"I'm through here," the cop said. "I'll be in touch if we find anything."

Beth didn't hold out hope for that. She closed the door behind him. "I'll call the cleaning crew. This place is a mess." It looked like she'd had a wild party, and seeing her personal belongings treated with such disregard was disheartening.

"I'll text the office. Travis can have a local company install the new security system."

"Why don't I find that reassuring?" Beth stepped over things strewn about, and went to her office to get her laptop. While she was there, she grabbed a sketchbook partially filled with drawings and stuffed it into a satchel.

Wyatt appeared in the doorway. "That's taken care of." He walked over to her. "I'll carry that for you," he said, and reached for the laptop. "We need a quiet place to go. It's time to take a look at that data from your brother's computer."

"We can walk over to the Marriott. It's not far, and it has that great terrace that overlooks the park."

Wyatt motioned toward the door. "You lead, I'll follow."

"The cleaning crew has keys, so we don't need to wait for them." Beth didn't want to set eyes on her place again until it was in some semblance of order. A stranger had taken liberties in her private home.

Outside in the fresh air, Beth breathed deeply, striving to restore a sense of calm. She couldn't let this get to her. There were more important things to focus on—like staying alive, for one. She hefted her satchel higher on her shoulder and increased her stride; walking was a balm to the soul.

Glancing at Wyatt, she said, "What I want to know is why you didn't contact me when you got out of the Navy."

Without missing a step, Wyatt said, "How did we get on that subject?"

"That's not an answer."

"I was on the outs with my family, so I wasn't thrilled about a visit to New York." Wyatt looked over at her. "Besides, I thought you'd changed. After your antics before I left, I didn't think you were the same person anymore."

"What's that supposed to mean?"

"You want the truth?"

Beth glared at him.

"Okay, I thought you'd turned into a snobby rich bitch, and that you'd live up to your snooty name, *Elizabeth Marie*."

That was the ultimate insult. "Because I was snippy before you left, you thought I'd succumbed to the temptations of money, that I'd become one of them?"

Wyatt shrugged.

"And besides which...may I remind you that I didn't choose my name. I was named after my great-grandmother, *so there*." Beth stopped mid-stride, and Wyatt turned to face her.

"Is that what you still think...that I'm some spoiled brat who considers I'm better in some way, just because I was born into a wealthy family?" Beth narrowed her eyes. "You don't know me at all."

"I can see that now," Wyatt said. "I was a fool to think it."

"Damn right." Warmth filled Wyatt's chocolate-brown eyes, and Beth nearly kissed him. Where had that come from? She turned and started walking again, unsure how to deal with what had just happened between them.

Fortunately, the hotel was in sight, so Beth shifted gears. She wasn't out of the woods with the life threats, and should pay attention to gaining the upper hand with the enemy, not going all sentimental with Wyatt—even if he was unbearably handsome.

But Beth couldn't let it go, and once inside the hotel, she said, "Speaking of being involved with the wealthy, you're a bodyguard for VIPs...in case you forgot."

"I just guard them. I don't get involved with them."

Was that supposed to mean that Wyatt didn't intend to get involved with her either? Beth dropped the subject and headed toward the elevator to the terrace restaurant.

Wyatt picked a table that was nearest the wall, and had the best view to the park from above. It was also more private, so Beth could do her research uninterrupted. The waiter took drink orders and went off to get the iced teas.

Beth dumped her bag on an empty chair and pulled out her sketchbook, in case inspiration struck. When Wyatt leaned over the table so he could see better, she handed him the book. "Here, you can look if you want."

"I see you're serious about sketching. What are they of?"

"Oh, various things: satire on big business, wealth and greed, or political stuff."

"I didn't know you were interested in politics."

"I'm not, but I get a kick out of highlighting the absurdities."

"So you research the dirty deeds, keep notes in a journal—which is now stolen, I might add—and then create satirical cartoons."

"Something like that."

While Beth set up the laptop then plugged in the flash drive, Wyatt flipped the pages of her book. "These are really good. What do you plan to do with them?"

"I just sketch them because I like to."

"Why not sell them, and do something with your skill? Cartooning is a talent; it shouldn't be wasted."

"Why do you care?" Beth couldn't help it if she was sensitive about the subject. The less anyone else knew about what she was good at, the better. Once she allowed anyone to see her ability, expectations would follow. She didn't want that.

Once the data had uploaded to her computer, Beth plunked away on the keyboard, ignoring Wyatt. She was vaguely aware of him ordering food, but wasn't really hungry. The information on her screen absorbed her. Even Wyatt, eye candy that he was, didn't draw her attention.

As the data flew by, from one screen to the next, Beth was more intrigued. She scrolled through page after page, but no unusual facts or figures popped out. Her memory was good, and she had clear recall of what she'd seen of the Foster International accounting history.

Things seemed to match up, and most of what her brother did from day to day was thoroughly boring. "I'm glad I don't have to stand in as CEO. I don't know how Kyle takes it."

On the second pass, Beth spotted a few transactions that she'd missed. It was some sort of covert deal, not one that had been included in the regular books. She would have remembered. On the scent now, she used her brother's access to get into bank records.

At first, the details appeared straightforward, the entries normal. But when she followed the trail, it paid off. After a bit of effort, she was able to hack into older financial records that only her uncle had access to. A significant amount of liquidated stocks followed by heavy withdrawals were a red flag.

Yet her uncle had accused *her* of embezzling. It was more likely that he had been usurping funds. Even if he was the controller, the board of directors would look askance at such activity.

"I found something," Beth said.

Wyatt stopped eating to listen.

"I almost missed it, but my uncle has been draining money out of the company. He has very cleverly covered it up. And also, it looks like my brother has been doing his bidding."

"You think they're conspiring to steal money?"

"I can't be sure," Beth said. "No wonder my uncle accused me of embezzling and threw me out. I was the perfect scapegoat. Plus, he wouldn't want me digging into the books. While anyone else might view me as an airhead punk chick, no more than the owner's daughter who was given a job out of pity..." She looked into Wyatt's eyes. "My uncle knew better. He was afraid of what I'd discover, and he tossed me out before I could do any damage."

"Is there enough evidence there to go to the police and file charges?"

"It's a family matter, and I already know the police won't care about solving this crime more than I do. It's personal," Beth said. "We'd need additional evidence, anyway."

"Make copies of the documents, and email them to Cooper. I'm sure you can manage encrypting it before transmission."

Beth managed a smile. "You have a lot of faith."

"I'll give you his secure email and let him know that something is on the way." Wyatt scrolled on his phone to text Stealth, while Beth considered what would be the safest way to transfer the data. There were a couple of options, so she chose the quickest.

"Coop is watching for it," Wyatt said. "Now I'm wondering, what exactly did Martin accuse you of? Did he show these transactions to you, and allege that you were guilty of theft?"

"Nope, he revealed very little. And I was in no position to press for confirmation. Both my uncle and my brother claimed that I'd done the deed, and no one else at Foster would dare assume differently."

"Now we know why he wouldn't show you the evidence," Wyatt said.

"Yeah, it would have incriminated *him*, not *me*." Beth was puzzled. "Kyle must be in on it. These transactions were made from his computer."

"I'd say our next step is to have another chat with Kyle. That should give us more ammunition..." Wyatt's expression darkened, and Beth was instantly alert.

"Don't look over, but the dude that just walked in doesn't belong here. Something's off," Wyatt said. "Act like everything's normal, but stand up as if we're about to leave."

Beth's heart pounded. *Everything is normal...right.* She stood up and reached to the far side of the laptop. Then she removed the tiny drive and slipped it into her pocket, moving slowly so as not to appear alarmed.

A shadow blocked the sun, and Beth was afraid to look up.

"We're leaving, if you want this table," Wyatt said, and Beth stared at a man who was no more than a foot away. Her breath hitched.

The man appeared of Asian descent, and looked short standing next to Wyatt. But his meaty biceps bulged at the edge of his short sleeves, and flexed as he spoke. "I'll take the laptop."

"I don't think so." Wyatt looked at the man, tensed and prepared to fight.

"You should do this the easy way. You will hand it over, one way or the other."

Wyatt made a fist. "And why is that?"

"I'm with security at Foster International. It seems your little girlfriend here was snooping where she shouldn't have been."

The security cameras at the company, hidden discreetly, flashed in Beth's mind. She should have thought of that.

"The laptop is hers," Wyatt said, "so I'm afraid you can't have it."

Beth's mouth was dry. She dared not speak. Would the guy harm her in front of witnesses? Yet before she settled on an answer, the man lunged for the computer. In a blinding flash, Wyatt yanked it from the table and flung it over the wall.

Out of the corner of her eye, Beth saw her laptop soar into empty space, then drop like a stone. It was gone.

With a growl, the *supposed* security guard pulled a gun and aimed it at Wyatt's belly. In the same instant, Wyatt pivoted and trapped the guy's gun hand, driving the barrel toward the adversary's chest. He yanked the barrel over and pulled the other guy forward.

Before Wyatt could take the gun, the security guard leapt up, kicking both knees under the weapon. The gun flew out, over the wall, toward the treetops below. When the guy's feet hit the ground, Wyatt threw a punch, and his knuckles connected with the man's jaw.

There was a resounding thump, then the attacker fell back, hitting his head on the stucco wall.

"Run!" Wyatt shouted, then hit the man again.

The cries of other diners faded into background noise. The noisy pounding in Beth's chest filled her ears as she ran through the terrace, dodging tables and people, like navigating an obstacle course.

Then Wyatt was beside her. He took her hand and sprinted. Beth glanced back and spotted the attacker, already up and headed their way. She slipped the flash drive from her pocket and dumped it into a pink cocktail perched at the edge of a table. That should wipe out the data.

She didn't believe for a second that this dude worked for Foster. But if he wanted the information, that was reason enough to get rid of it.

Wyatt raced out of the restaurant, down the hallway, and across the lobby while Beth tried to keep up. She whipped around the corner of a pillar, sliding on the polished marble floors, and caught sight of the guy in hot pursuit.

Without wasting a second, Wyatt dragged her to the stairwell and started taking steps two at a time. Out of breath, Beth doubled over. Wyatt wrapped his strong arm around her waist and lifted her off her feet. He carried her one more flight, then burst through the door to whatever floor they were on.

Beth's feet hit the floor, and she jogged around a corner with him. Stopping at a room, Wyatt took out a slender instrument and jiggled the lock. Magically, Beth was inside, and he shoved the door closed.

Panting hard, Beth managed to ask, "Whose room is this?"

"No idea."

Wyatt stood by the door, ready to nab any man who dared cross the threshold. There was nary a sound, nor any motion to indicate any unwelcome entry.

Pacing the carpet, ready to bolt again if she had to, Beth said, "What if someone had been in here?"

"I guess we would have improvised." Wyatt put his

hand on the doorknob. "You wait for me. I'm going back out to put that guy out of commission."

"Wait!" Beth reached out. "You can't leave me. If you're going, then I am going with you."

"Not a chance. It's too dangerous. I would have pummeled the guy already, but I had to get you to safety." Wyatt stood in front of the door, ready for battle. Sweat glistened on his forehead, and his chest was pumped like he'd just had an encounter with a set of barbells. He was a warrior, and dammit, he'd stolen her heart.

"You saved me," Beth said, stepping closer. "That's enough. That guy doesn't matter. If we wait it out in here, he'll leave."

"I'm sure he'll leave," Wyatt said. "He wanted that laptop. There's no reason to stick around now."

"Then why was he chasing us?"

"Maybe he hoped you had the data on a drive...just like you do." Wyatt held out his hand. "Where's the flash drive?"

Beth smiled, despite her trembling body. "It's now an ice cube in some lady's cocktail out there."

"You didn't."

"I did; it's all I could think of that fast."

Wyatt laughed. "That's pretty good," he said. "I'm not sure I would have thought of that."

With a mock pout, Beth said, "And, you know, that was a perfectly good laptop you pitched over the wall into Central Park."

"It was better than having our *friend* walk away with it."

Beth was confident the data had been transmitted to Cooper's computer, so all was not lost. "What do you say we use the room phone and call for backup? This hotel must have security, don't you suppose?"

81

"I'll call." Wyatt strutted over to the phone. His stride was reminiscent of his baseball days, when Beth had seen him walk off the field after a win. He did a lot to boost a woman's confidence. With him in tow, it had given her attackers more to deal with than they'd expected.

While waiting for security, *real security*, to arrive, Wyatt sat in an armchair. Beth slid onto his lap with her arms around his neck. "You have a talent for saving my life."

"So far."

Wyatt's body was warm, his breathing still elevated from the chase. His muscles were hard, and his arms were strong. Beth mused that it might have been worth nearly dying, *again*, to be in his protective embrace. When he looked into her eyes, Beth glanced away and stood up.

What in the world was wrong with her? Did a near-death experience make her hot for the nearest hunky male she could get her hands on? No, that wasn't it. Wyatt had a certain charm, a definite hero/protector image that had gotten to her, despite her vow to keep this business only.

. When there was a knock on the door, Beth nearly jumped out of her skin. It had been that kind of week.

"It's security," Wyatt said, and went to let them in.

"I sure hope so...because I've reached my limit of surprises for one day."

When two guards stepped inside dressed in hotel uniforms, Beth relaxed. Once more, she'd had a reprieve from a fateful end. It wouldn't last long, though. She had to figure out what was behind all of this. And who wanted her dead. Plus, she needed to do it soon, because delaying would surely get both of them killed.

CHAPTER SEVEN

The world of container shipping played a vital role in commerce, yet few people knew what really went on in the business of transport. The industry fascinated Martin Foster because of its potential, such as accruing immense profits from drug smuggling.

Martin rocked in the oversized executive chair, the very chair his brother Stephen had occupied for years. Now it was his. The private office accommodated his needs, when he bothered to come in. The weekend had been brutal, but he'd managed to arrive at Foster before lunch. He got up to lock the door, then opened his briefcase.

Most of his life, Martin hadn't needed to work, and it annoyed him that he did now—all the more reason to foist the majority of duties onto Kyle. He was the only son of Stephen, and had been groomed to take over the family's shipping business.

That was all the better, as it made things easier. Martin maintained control, had access to funds, yet had no function in daily operations. Any misdeeds, mistakes, and even crimes could be blamed on someone else. After all, Kyle was the man who handled the majority of transactions, even if he wasn't always clear about what they were.

Kyle was in his late twenties, anxious to do well in business, and loyal to the family. His trust and optimism worked in Martin's favor, and directing him posed no barrier. His nephew had accepted Martin's sudden involvement with company affairs, attributing his interest as willingness to support the family in a time of need. Without his father Stephen to guide him, Kyle seemed grateful for his uncle's presence.

That part was manageable, in contrast to other things. Martin sat in the leather chair and dumped a bit of the white crystalline powder on the glass tabletop. With a small blade, he scooped it together and placed a silver tube over it. He sniffed the powder up one side of his nose, then the other.

He leaned back in the chair, more alert. The pep was just what he needed. He relished the euphoria, and walked over to the window, feeling the high already. His mood was better; it was time to chat with Kyle. After locking up his stash, he exited the office.

The cocaine was pricey but worth it. If things went as expected, Martin would be able to pay for all the drugs he wanted, without concern. He went down the hallway, his heart pounding a staccato rhythm in his chest, and a spring in his step. He found Kyle at his desk, hard at work, and took the chair across from him.

Kyle was the spitting image of his father, just a younger version. It was eerie how much his nephew looked like Stephen. Martin squirmed in the chair. It didn't matter that his brother was in a nursing home; there were more urgent matters to attend to.

His nephew looked across the desk. "Uncle Martin, good to see you're in today."

"I'm sure you'll manage without me later, as I do have some meetings." Actually, Martin made a point to avoid attending board meetings, or any other type of meetings. "But I'd like to know what Beth said to you Saturday."

Kyle frowned. "It was nothing."

Martin exuded kindness, hoping he didn't come across as fake. "It must have been *something*. After all, it was your birthday party. After I went in to make my phone call, I returned and saw Beth with Wyatt, coming in from the terrace. Judging by your expression, she'd upset you. But I waited to ask until now."

"Beth had questions about the embezzlement charge. Actually, I'm not sure that I understand it. You discovered the missing funds, but you didn't show me, or Beth, the evidence. It's somewhat confusing."

"Of course I didn't," Martin said, his voice sterner. "That would be unwise. Beth is family. I certainly don't want to produce evidence against her, and be forced to press charges. You wouldn't want that, would you?"

"Since you put it that way... But you really should talk to her. Beth claims the situation is unjust," Kyle said. "Surely, if faced with the truth, she would make good...pay back the money."

Martin narrowed his eyes, in an effort to intimidate his nephew. "How would she do that? Beth has been supported most of her life. She had no initiative to get a real job, so your father saw fit to find a place in the company for her."

"Uncle Martin—"

"I opposed the suggestion, but your father wouldn't listen. He was adamant that Beth should be given a chance. Well, you can see what she did with the opportunity presented to her. As predicted, she was unreliable. Until she reforms, I'm afraid I can't allow her to have influence on you, or this company."

"It's overly harsh to write her out of the will."

The lie flowed off his tongue. "That's not my doing. It was your father's wish. Even he, as good-hearted a man as he was, got fed up with Beth's shenanigans. It's my duty to see it through."

"I'd like to hear *him* say that, because I find it difficult to believe. Father loves Beth; I don't see how that could change."

"Beth has only herself to blame. And unfortunately, your father is in no condition to tell you personally of his wish to disinherit her. My understanding is that he felt she would only waste the money, that only if forced to do so, she would finally make something of her life."

Kyle's expression was unsympathetic, but Martin didn't want to mess around with this foolishness. Beth had been a pest from the start; she had to be dealt with.

"I'll be out this afternoon," Martin said, then got up to leave.

Kyle didn't respond, didn't even look at him again. He resumed whatever he'd been working on, leaving his uncle to find his way out. Martin took issue with such rudeness. After all, he had stepped in as head of the family, and deserved some appreciation.

Martin went straight home to a limestone mansion on the Upper East Side that he didn't own, strictly speaking. In the divorce settlement, the properties had been divided, and he'd been deeded the residence. Yet with his funds dwindling, he'd mortgaged the place to the hilt. And now he had no way to pay it off.

But circumstances would soon change. Martin would see to that. He had no choice, as he couldn't let his life just go down the toilet. Yet it worried him, as it seemed he'd been caught unsuspectingly in a web.

His ex-wife Leila had incessantly nagged him about gambling during the marriage.

When he'd refused to forgo visiting the local casinos, his wife demanded that he request voluntary self-exclusion from all New York gaming facilities. He'd flatly refused. Such a request would have banned him from all casino activities, and would have prohibited him from collecting any winnings or recovering losses.

It was the most emasculating idea Leila had proposed to date. Yet when he wouldn't go through with it, she'd left him. It had been the last straw. Martin could stop gambling if he decided to, but the fact was that it was the one thing that made him feel alive. He'd won big a few times, and that high had been addictive.

He might have taken it too far of late. His losses had mounted, and drained his available funds. After the mortgage money had sifted through his fingers, he'd obtained what he needed from Foster's bank accounts. His father had inherited the company from his father; the shipping money had passed down many generations.

Yet control of Foster International had gone to Stephen. At the time, Martin hadn't let on that he cared. He'd been content to live off the sizeable inheritance, without having to maintain a schedule or hold down employment. And Leila had come from money, as well, so it had been most agreeable to marry her.

Now she was gone, and so was the money.

Martin went to change clothes. The sooner he got to the casino the better—more opportunity to make up some of his losses, and to escape his mundane life. Problems were mounting, and he needed to clear his head.

His shoes clicked over the marble hallway, and at the bedroom door he kicked them off. His feet sank into the thick, creamy carpet, his wife's choice, and he made his way to the closet. He scanned the double racks of shirts and pants, opting for comfort. It might be a long night.

His phone vibrated on the nightstand before he was able to make his escape. Glancing at the caller ID, he swore, then picked up. "Chen, why are you calling? We are still in preparations. I told you I'd get back to you."

Chen was a hotshot at the local casino, with ties to the Asian mob. If Martin had known that, he wouldn't have gotten involved with him. It was just that he'd needed some fast cash, unaware that he'd entered into a loan agreement with a dangerous group.

"It's *Mister* Chen to you, and you'd best remember who you're talkin' to." After a moment of silence, the gangster continued, "I've called to tell you something important."

Martin waited impatiently.

"There was an incident in the subway a week ago. Elizabeth was with some lady, and a mistake was made. If all had gone well, your niece would be dead, but our guy shoved the wrong woman in front of the train. The news on it hasn't been released for some reason, but I expect it to come out soon."

Martin was stunned...*dead*? "What are you talking about? You were just supposed to scare her. Who gave the order to kill anyone? We agreed that no one was to get hurt."

A soft chuckle on the line was his answer.

"I didn't mean for you to kill her. I told you that she knows too much, but the point was to make her stay away."

"She won't bother you when she's dead."

Control had slipped through his grasp, and Martin wasn't sure where he'd erred. "You've botched the job now. Beth will be on the alert; she won't let it go. I know her."

"My guy will handle it," Chen said. "He tried to fix it right after that party at your place."

"Kyle's birthday?"

"It seems there is some guy hanging out with Elizabeth, and he's fairly handy with street fighting...maybe ex-military or something."

Martin closed his eyes and rubbed his temples. Could it get any worse?

"A bullet to the head would have done the trick, but her escort intervened."

"Oh, God...was she hurt?"

"A cut to the head, that's all."

"Christ. You have to stop. This whole affair will fall apart the instant murder is involved."

"Our mistake was doing it the American way. Back home we would have ended this on the first try."

Martin shuddered. The Asian mob's preferred weapon was a meat cleaver. The stories he'd heard had made him nearly retch. It was a horror, and he'd blocked it out. Reminded of what the mob was capable of, his stomach churned.

"It's time for you to meet with the boss."

Martin cringed. "What for?"

"That's for him to say. You have a lunch appointment tomorrow at the Cave. He'll send a guy to pick you up."

Even the name of the establishment was repulsive. Martin was sinking fast. He had to do something to turn this around, so maybe it wasn't such a bad idea to meet with the guy in charge. He had to get his new partners on the same page, and disabuse them of the idea of murder as a solution.

"I'll be ready."

The siren call of the casino drew Martin, with its bright lights, strong drink, and perfumed women. That night he planned to get lost in the culture where he was most at home, and do what he was best at. A big win would do a lot to boost his morale.

Martin called a cab. The days of taking the limo were past; he couldn't afford the limo, or the driver. If traffic cooperated, he'd be at Empire City in less than forty minutes. He needed a drink and another snort before long. Then he'd hook up with a woman for good luck.

Sex and drugs had been a potent combo for years, even when he'd been with his wife. Lately, not so much. He'd allow the woman to hang on his arm for the evening and bring him luck. But he wasn't confident about performing. It wasn't likely he'd take her up to a room anyway, since he planned to gamble all night, especially if he was on a roll.

In the cab, Martin closed his eyes and leaned back, while the driver negotiated the route. *Murder.* It sank in that it had been real. Those creeps might have killed Elizabeth were it not for unforeseen circumstances. Taking out his niece would come back to haunt him.

The others would vanish, leaving him to answer for it. He had to persuade them that there were better ways to deal with the threat. He regretted telling them about Beth's curious mind, and her persistence in uncovering the truth.

Martin would spend time in a prison cell or worse if he didn't get a grip. What else had he told them?

This should be a lesson to keep his mouth shut, and deal with matters personally. In the long run, he'd be better off. But they'd demanded assurance that the plan would go off without a hitch.

Couldn't they see that these tactics put it all at risk?

He had a vested interest in seeing that it all went as planned. His debts were an anchor pulling him to the depths. The burden of owing the Asian mob fell heavy on his shoulders. But Chen had promised the full amount would be forgiven.

Then Martin would continue to profit from the new arrangement. His spirits lifted. Most illegal drugs were moved via container ships, some in sailboats or fishing boats. The drug traffickers' fast boats could even outrun law enforcement on occasion.

Martin had been enlightened on the subject. The cartels were innovative and reaped substantial profits. It was a sweet deal, and now Martin was part of it. He had control of a major shipping line, and his services were in demand. Such an arrangement offered salvation—if only his new associates didn't blow it.

*****

The next day, Martin was back in the city in time for his lunch engagement. He had no big winnings to boast of, just a doozy of a headache. His body was heavy, his limbs leaden. And his brain was dull. He'd have to snort a line before facing the imposing man he was scheduled to meet.

Martin hadn't heard of the Cave before, and suspected it was privately owned. A limo with blacked-out windows was sent to pick him up, but he didn't appreciate the amenity. He suspected that the mode of transportation was to set the tone of the meeting, not for his comfort.

The restaurant was tucked away off an alley, but it was by no means a dump. Dim lights lent an ominous mood to the encounter, and muscular personnel stood at the ready, in case Martin should become a problem. He got the message.

The mobster was short and fierce. His dark hair was thinning on top and his eyes appeared black in the low lights. His short stature did not diminish his imposing presence. He stood up, and Martin got a good look at his attire. He wore a designer suit and leather boots, and had diamonds on his fingers.

"Welcome, Martin," the menace said. "I'm Mr. Zhang."

Martin bowed, assuming that was appropriate. That seemed to please his companion. "Mr. Zhang," he said, "finally we meet." He wouldn't have addressed the man by first name even if he'd known it.

The full impact of the situation became clear. Martin faced a deadly foe, one who would snuff him out at the least provocation. It was abundantly obvious how the Asian mob had acquired its reputation.

Martin sat across the table from the man. "I assume Chen brought you up to speed?"

Zhang didn't smile; he didn't even move. "Before we eat, there are a few things we need to go over."

Martin swallowed hard. His hands sweated, and he wiped them on his pants.

"Your niece has evaded us, but not for long. She will regret taking an interest in your affairs, now that your company has been allied with ours." The man's expression darkened. "I fear that she has information that could be an issue—merely a nuisance, probably. But it's unwise to take chances."

Zhang proceeded to detail some of what he feared Beth had possession of. "We have the journal that you spoke of."

"You stole it?"

"If you wish to view it that way. We have a right to see what she has uncovered." He paused. "You've been careless."

Martin held his breath.

"We will take care of it. Her laptop is no longer functional," Zhang said.

Christ, what have you done now?

"It's likely she has a backup source, but we'll ensure the information doesn't leak." The man leaned forward. "It's her connections to the press that concern me. She has to be silenced."

Martin didn't venture to point out that attempts thus far had been failures. Dread filled him. What was next?

There wasn't a lot more to discuss. Zhang set the rules, and Martin had to abide by them. He was backed into a corner. Opting out of the business arrangement wasn't a choice; he was in over his head. The mob would see that he made good on his debt, one way or the other.

Martin hadn't gotten a fair shake. Life was against him. But that would change. Once Zhang got his money, any additional profits would be shared. The income from drug smuggling would set him up nicely, and he could have the lifestyle he deserved.

*****

The following afternoon, Martin went to the assisted living facility. He had to make sure that all was under control. He couldn't risk Stephen interfering, not now. Upcoming events had to roll out without a hitch; Martin's future depended on it.

He walked up the stone path to the entry, and a pang of guilt struck him. He brushed it aside, as the accommodations weren't bad at all. The multistoried building was beige stucco, looking more like an exclusive hotel than a medical facility. The upper floors were for residents with Alzheimer's, while the other levels were for a variety of types of care. With supervision, his brother could move about the facility, join in group activities, and even go outside to the gardens.

The care facility was one of the best, and Martin had employed a private nurse to care for his older brother. Martin spotted her writing notes in a chart. Irma was mid-forties, short brunette hair, and wore glasses. Her demeanor and motherly look inspired faith that she would see to Stephen's care properly. He spoke with her first, checking that the medication was being administered as prescribed. Assured that there had been no deviation, he entered the room.

Stephen sat by the window, staring into space. All around him, the area was orderly. The bed was neatly made, personal items were arranged on shelves, and the room had a fresh scent. His brother wore casual slacks with a polo shirt and running shoes. By first appearance, he was the same as he'd been.

Then Stephen looked up, but didn't recognize his own brother. Martin took a nearby chair, yet didn't speak immediately. He studied his brother, considered handsome by many. With his good build and strong jaw, he probably was an attractive man even in his fifties. It had saddened his friends to hear about the early onset of Alzheimer's.

Stephen had been charming enough to win Evelyn, the very woman Martin had hoped to gain the affections of. Evelyn Mayes, with her amber eyes and deep brown hair, had been a stunner. She'd had the figure of a goddess and the voice of an angel. And she should have been Martin's.

It was probably the only time that he'd truly loved a woman. At first, she hadn't realized it. Evelyn only had eyes for Stephen, and they'd married after a short engagement. Martin hadn't forgiven him for that. Their first child Elizabeth Marie had arrived within a year, and Martin had despised even looking at the baby. His attitude towards Beth had wavered little since.

Of course, he'd pretended to have affection for his niece and was cordial to his sister-in-law, as he'd had to. But he hadn't forgotten. Stephen had garnered all the good fortune. He'd done well in school, had many friends, and seemed to attract admiration without effort. Then their father had put the family's shipping business in Stephen's hands. That had been the ultimate insult.

"It's different now, isn't it?" Martin managed a wry smile. "You don't control it all anymore, do you?" There was a sense of satisfaction in that.

Stephen gazed into the distance, seemingly unaware of Martin's questions.

"You know, I didn't tell you this before...but I once tried to steal Evelyn away from you." Martin chuckled. "Oh yes, it's true. I confessed my love and offered her the world. I was wealthy in my own right, then."

Stephen's eyelids fluttered, as if he might drift off. Then he looked over at Martin, and his mouth moved as if to say something. But no words came. His expression was childlike.

"Do you know what she did? She mocked me...sweet Evelyn thought she was above consorting with me. She laughed in my face." Martin clenched his fists. "She was loyal to you. Imagine that. She could have had so much if she'd accepted my offer." He let out a heavy breath.

"Instead, she made me promise not to tell you what I'd proposed. 'You're brothers,' she'd said, 'and I wouldn't want this to come between you.'"

Martin tossed his head back and laughed. "She was so good, better than any woman I'd known before or have met since. When she died..."

Martin put his hand on his brother's knee. "You always had the best of everything. Now...it's my turn."

Stephen found his voice at last. "Who are... Do I know you?" His features clouded with confusion.

"I'm on my way out," Martin said. He would make something of his life, and for once, his brother would be jealous of him. The fact that Stephen was disconnected from reality didn't detract from the prospect. Over the years, Martin hadn't received love from his family. His wife had abandoned him. No one had cared what happened to him. He'd had to make his own way, and that was exactly what he intended to do now. He was finished with settling for second best.

CHAPTER EIGHT

Hotel security assured Wyatt that the cameras hadn't recorded any footage of the attacker, or captured any scenes that corroborated the incident. "We don't video in the stairwells, so any activity there wouldn't be on record."

Beth was interviewed and a report was made; the authorities would be informed. Calm had been restored to the premises. The bag that Beth had left in the empty chair on the terrace was miraculously returned to her undamaged.

The head of security guaranteed that it was safe now. Then the hotel concierge offered complimentary drinks at the restaurant, to express regret for the earlier inconvenience. Wyatt believed that the man who'd chased them was gone, at least for now.

A two-man security team served as an escort to the restaurant, then left Beth and Wyatt to enjoy the rest of their day. "A drink sounds pretty good right now," Beth said, and took his arm.

"I'm all for unwinding while we let the crisis pass. It can't hurt to delay going back outside. I'm confident we're okay in here, and you could use the break." Wyatt spotted a table near the back wall, where he'd have an unobstructed view of the entrance. The waitress followed with menus in hand.

This time there was no scenic view of the park, which was just as well. The table was in front of a wall decorated with cracked gold mirrors. It gave the illusion of space, but with the security of a solid wall to protect them. Beth sat in the padded leather booth, and Wyatt slid in across from her.

"A glass of Chardonnay, please," Beth said.

"Coke for me." Wyatt could use the caffeine.

When the waitress left, Beth let out a sigh. "I need that wine. My life is altogether too exciting at the moment."

Wyatt admired her. Beth looked innocent enough, despite the ear piercing and the spiked hair. But she was strong-willed, a personality trait that hadn't changed. "You're still as tough as you were when we were teenagers."

"Is that a compliment?"

"That's how I meant it." Wyatt liked being around Beth, and it reminded him of when they used to hang out together. "I remember that no one could bully you."

Beth glanced away and ran her fingertips through her hair. "But someone would try, just like now. Either I appear to be an easy target or I'm a magnet for trouble."

Wyatt wanted to put his arms around her, and tell her how great she was. "Neither one, as anyone coming after you gets more of a fight than anticipated. And you didn't bring all of this on yourself."

"How can you be so sure? You haven't been around in a while."

"I just know; that's all."

The drinks arrived and Wyatt pulled out his phone. "I'm going to check with Coop about those documents." He sent a text, then received a quick reply that the encrypted documents had been securely delivered.

"We didn't lose any evidence," Wyatt said, and took a gulp of Coke.

Beth sipped her wine and looked over at him. Wyatt vividly recalled being alone in the hotel room, and the feel of her on his lap, with her arms around his neck. If she hadn't leapt up, he might have kissed her. He glanced away, lest she sense his mood. Beth's feminine scent had intoxicated him, and she'd still been breathing deeply from the run up the stairs. The physicality of it had turned him on.

"What are you thinking about?"

Wyatt turned to face her. "Just...things. I wondered why we didn't do anything when we had the chance, before I went in the Navy."

Beth twirled her glass. "As I recall, we chose to bicker or give each other a hard time—whenever you weren't occupied with saving me from disaster." She smiled. "Then you went off to college. I didn't see you much."

"I thought when I got out of the service that you'd be *involved*."

Beth laughed. "But you didn't call or anything."

"I just assumed you'd fall into the hands of some wealthy guy." Wyatt studied her.

"You're hung up on the money." Beth blushed. "I'd only marry for love."

An awkward silence followed, and Wyatt couldn't think of what to say.

Beth furrowed her brow. "So what's your take on that fake security guy?"

Wyatt was glad for the change of topic. "Who hired him is the question."

"I agree. I should have considered the surveillance system at Foster. My brother probably knows I was in his office with you copying data from his computer."

99

"Or he was informed," Wyatt said. "I doubt he reviews the recordings personally. But I'm sure it's no secret that you obtained damaging evidence."

"There's a concerted effort to make sure I don't make use of it." Beth drained her glass and lifted it to signal the waitress for more. "It makes me curious about how much more there is to find out. So far, what I have wouldn't be enough to motivate my relatives to bump me off."

"I can see wanting to keep you quiet, but there are less risky ways of forcing you to back off. Murder is a final solution. Whoever is willing to go that route is serious."

The waitress dropped off a fresh glass of wine, and Wyatt ordered nachos with a Coke refill.

Beth smiled. "I'm glad you're keeping your strength up." She took a few sips of wine. "My uncle is up to something. He has been bleeding funds from the accounts, or as much as he probably thinks he can get away with."

"So where is the money going? From what I saw of his house, he's rich, same as he has been since I was a kid."

"Things can change. Even a billionaire can go broke if investments are mismanaged. There's definitely something we don't know," Beth said. "Our next step is to have a visit with my brother. He's more likely to spill secrets. Then we'll have more ammunition against my uncle."

The nachos arrived and Wyatt dug in. Intrigue worked up his appetite.

"I wish my uncle hadn't gotten involved at Foster. He can be intimidating, and I don't think Kyle can stand up to him."

"If Kyle knows we're on his side, that might boost

his confidence," Wyatt said, and scooped a chip laden with cheese into his mouth. "When you talk to him this time, let me join in. You can press him, and I'll be the good guy, understanding, sympathetic. We'll work him until he folds and tells us what we want to know."

"Uncle Martin made me look bad to Kyle. Now my own brother suspects me of embezzlement, but I can prove I didn't do it. I didn't have access to that stock account." Beth looked thoughtful. "What I can't figure out, though...is who wants me dead?"

*****

The stroll back to Beth's house was uneventful. "The cleanup crew should be finished," she said.

Wyatt stayed alert, but saw no one suspicious, nor any movement that was unusual. Tourists and locals filled the sidewalks, seeming intent on their destination. It was light outside, and it wasn't far to her place.

There had been enough drama for one day. Wyatt wanted to get Beth home unharmed. He would have preferred to put his arm around her, even hold her hand, just to keep her close. But he didn't have such privileges, and shouldn't get distracted from the business at hand.

Beth walked next to him, barely reaching his shoulder. She was petite in stature, but strong in spirit. She was the kind of woman he was drawn to, one who wasn't easily cowed, a woman who could stand up for herself. Yet he hadn't met any such woman except Beth. She was special, but unfortunately, she wasn't his.

At the residence, Wyatt shielded Beth while she opened the door. "I'd point out that you're being overly cautious," she said, "but I know better."

The elevator opened onto the foyer and Beth stepped out. Order had been restored, leaving no sign of the earlier intrusion. "Thank goodness," she said. "I feel better already." She looked up at him. "What about that new security system?"

"Travis will have it installed tomorrow," Wyatt said. "But I wouldn't worry. The thief took what he wanted, so I doubt he'll be back."

"Well, I'm going to take a hot shower. All that running made me sweaty," Beth said. "Then later we can go out for groceries and you can cook for me."

Wyatt raised his brows.

"You claimed that you know how to cook, so I expect a delicious homemade dinner." Beth disappeared down the hall to her room.

Wyatt could use a shower too, but delayed. There was no rush. Beth was bound to take longer to get ready than he would.

Grabbing the remote, Wyatt clicked to the news and plopped onto the sofa. He mindlessly watched as the newscaster droned on. He crossed one ankle over his thigh and leaned against the cushion, content to find out what was going on in the world.

He was about to switch to the sports channel when an image caught his eye, so he turned up the volume. The anchor reported on a recent subway accident. The police had just released the details.

Wyatt uncrossed his legs and leaned forward to get a good look. A blowup of one of the scene photos filled the screen. A woman had died after falling in front of a train, but that wasn't what had his attention. The deceased wore a pink satin jacket, the type Beth was fond of. A close-up of the back showed a logo of an eagle. It was a vector image in gold, with rhinestones outlining it.

That eagle was the same as the one on the front of Beth's sketchbook; Wyatt even remembered when she'd come up with the idea and what it symbolized. The reporter talked about the jacket and mentioned that it had belonged to Elizabeth Foster, heiress to the Foster International fortune. Then a photograph of Beth appeared on the screen.

Long after the reporter moved to other current events, Wyatt stared at the TV. Why was a dead woman wearing Beth's jacket? It was too coincidental. His suspicions were confirmed. Beth hadn't told him everything, not by a long shot.

Beth bounced back into the living room fully clothed, but barefoot, with her hair still wet. She opened her mouth as if to say something, then took a look at his face. "Did something happen? You have a strange expression."

Wyatt was pissed. He'd done his best to keep her alive, yet she'd neglected to tell him the truth. "I'll tell you what happened." He stood, towering over her. "I just saw a dead girl on the subway tracks, wearing *your* jacket."

Beth stiffened.

Wyatt leaned closer. "Would you care to explain that to me?"

Beth slumped into an armchair, looking defeated. "I didn't know how to tell you. I guess...I was afraid that you wouldn't help me."

That made him more furious. "You were afraid that if you told me there had been a murder, I'd turn the other way?"

"I just... It was all so confusing." Beth put her hand over her eyes. "I wasn't sure *what* to do."

Wyatt sat on the ottoman in front of her. "I'm listening."

Beth uncovered her eyes and looked directly at him. "I'd just been defamed by my uncle, booted from my job, and then...Amanda gets killed. It was terrifying." She proceeded to relay every detail, focusing on the stranger who followed her and pushed her friend to her death.

"Why did the police take so long in reporting it?"

"The police were there right away, but Thomas met me at the station and did his best to keep the media out of it."

"I'm amazed that he kept the press quiet this long," Wyatt said. "So who wanted to kill Amanda?"

Beth shook her head. "That's what I thought at first, too...or tried to believe. But we looked so much alike. With my jacket on, I think the killer made a mistake. He'd really been after me."

Wyatt's blood boiled. "*Damn*...you were in lethal peril and you chose not to share that information?" It boggled his mind.

"My friend died." Beth was choked up. "I feel so guilty; it should have been me." Tears rolled down her cheeks, and she wiped at them with her sleeve. Wyatt pulled her into his arms, and let her cry until his shirt was soaked. He was furious, but he couldn't stand to see a woman cry.

When Beth calmed down, Wyatt released her, and she slumped against the chair.

"I flew to LA the next morning," Beth said. "I couldn't process it all, so I decided to keep quiet until I could figure something out. You were the only person I could turn to. I didn't know if I could trust anyone else."

Wyatt shook his head. "This amps up the danger. If your brother or your uncle were involved, broadcasting the incident makes it worse. The reporter didn't give specifics of your involvement, but flashing around a picture of Amanda wearing your jacket is enough. It's not much of a leap to make the connection."

Beth wrapped her arms around her waist. "I'm glad that you finally know about the accident. I asked Thomas to keep it out of the news as long as he could, but I knew that wouldn't last. And I was terrified of what would happen."

"Now it's out. The press will be after your family for a statement," Wyatt said. "What a mess."

"It won't be any surprise to the man who is after me. He must have known right away that he'd killed the wrong woman."

"Yes, that explains the knife attack; the killer intended to finish the job." Wyatt let out a deep sigh. "And he won't stop now, whoever it is."

Beth looked up, her eyes dry but a bit red.

"Don't keep anything from me again," Wyatt said. It was damned important that he knew everything.

Beth stood up and glared down at him. "The next time some creep kills a friend of mine...*right in front of me*...I'll be sure you're the first to know." She stomped off and slammed the bathroom door.

She still had a hot temper, but Wyatt didn't care. Her life was at stake and he wasn't sure he could trust her. Agitated now, he paced the floor. He had to be more alert, more on top of things. A mistake could get Beth killed.

While Beth finished getting ready, Wyatt snooped around. Maybe the intruder had missed something. What else was Beth hiding from him? He was ticked off that he'd been left in the dark. Beth could be difficult to handle sometimes; that was one thing that hadn't changed. He lacked confidence that she would confide in him from now on. He imagined the worst, but couldn't help it.

The place was orderly now, with magazines stacked neatly and items arranged on shelves. Wyatt didn't spot anything that looked out of the ordinary; it was all normal household stuff. He went to the library and searched her desk drawers. Mostly it was papers, pens, and paper clips, some junk.

What was he doing? What could he possibly hope to find?

Then he tried the bottom drawer. It stuck at first, but he jiggled it. Inside was a small leather-bound book, closed with a clasp. It wasn't locked, and easily snapped open. Further inspection revealed that it was Beth's diary. For a second, Wyatt gave in to guilt; he shouldn't be looking at her personal stuff.

To hell with it. This was important. Wyatt flipped through the pages. The entries had no connection to recent events. Beth had written about her personal feelings, and about her passion for cartooning, or interactions with friends that had affected her, plus a variety of other topics—all just girl stuff. He marveled at the types of things a woman found important. He tossed the book back into the drawer and shoved it closed.

Wyatt went back to the other room and glanced at the hallway. No sign of Beth yet. Her bag had been dumped beside the sofa. She carried that thing everywhere, and he wondered what was in there. Setting the bag on the arm of the sofa, Wyatt dug around.

Aside from her wallet, along with items such as a comb, makeup, and mints, there wasn't much. She'd left her sketchbook inside, but he'd already looked through that. Wyatt propped the bag against the back of the sofa and tried to think.

He stared at the shiny gold emblem on the purse that said Prada, tagging it as a designer purse. His eyes locked on to an imperfection in the leather beneath the emblem. Wyatt sat on the sofa and put the purse in his lap. The emblem appeared slightly misaligned, as though it had been removed and put back imprecisely.

Not a man to ignore inconsistencies, Wyatt fiddled with the Prada label. It was loose, and that piqued his interest. Moving it back and forth loosened it more, then it came off in his hand. Inside the metal covering was a tracker.

Wyatt took out the tiny device and rolled it around in his palm. That explained a few things. He didn't disable it just yet. Wyatt had checked Beth for trackers when she'd hired him, and he'd scanned her belongings at the first opportunity. So the tracker had been planted since then.

Beth reappeared, then walked over with a puzzled look. "What's that?" she said, staring at the item he held. Her earlier anger had been replaced by curiosity.

"It's a tracker."

Beth glanced at her bag, with an empty space where the Prada label used to be, then back at the small tracker. "It was in my purse?"

Wyatt looked up at her without comment.

"That sure made it easy...the guy who greeted us at my door the other night...the burglar who knew just when to break in...it all makes sense." Beth looked at him with wide eyes.

"I'd like to know when they had the chance to plant it on you...whoever *they* is." Wyatt left the purse, but kept the tracker. "How long has your enemy been following you?"

. "And how did they get it in there? I carry that bag around with me." Beth pointed a finger at him. "*Except*, I remember at my brother's party, I put it behind the bar so I didn't have to lug it around. It was a private event at my uncle's home, so I didn't keep my purse with me."

"It would have been a simple task. It could have been your brother...your uncle...or anyone, really."

"What are you going to do with it?"

Wyatt put it on the coffee table. "For now, leave it here. Eventually, whoever is monitoring you will figure out that you must have gone out. But for a bit, it will serve as a decoy."

Beth pursed her lips. "I think it's time to have that chat with Kyle." She grabbed her phone and hit speed dial, then listened. After ending the call, she said, "We missed him. His voicemail says he's out of town."

"For how long?"

"I'll find out." Beth made another call. "Hey, Susan, how are you?" She listened. "That's good to hear. We'll have to grab lunch sometime. By the way, do you know where Kyle is? I tried his phone but it says he's away." She wrinkled her brow. "Oh, I see."

When she hung up, Beth tossed her phone onto a cushion. "No luck: he's in Boston on a business trip. Susan says he's negotiating a contract with some new importer. Must be a big deal, or he wouldn't have gone to handle it personally."

"When will he be back?"

"She wasn't sure. Kyle said he'd stay until the deal was wrapped up—a few days, maybe." Beth sighed. "I can't do this over the phone. I have to see his face, so he can't blow me off."

Wyatt sensed her frustration. "There's not much

you can do until he gets back in the office." He looked at Beth, dressed in black jeans and a tightly fitted sweater. "I guess that's my cue to make dinner." For the evening, danger was on hold. He may as well enjoy the company.

Beth ordered groceries delivered, and Wyatt was just as happy not to go out. He had a hankering for a juicy, flavorful steak, and since Beth preferred real food over diet fare, he pan-seared filets. He procured her assistance to prep the asparagus and red potatoes, then set the table.

For a woman who didn't cook, Beth seemed at home in her kitchen. This domestic side to her attracted Wyatt, and he imagined having other meals together. It was cozy, and when she wasn't looking, he ogled her fine figure. Beth couldn't be described as voluptuous, but she had curves, and Wyatt's urge to explore nearly overpowered him.

The wine, the smell of fine food, and the sway of Beth's hips as she moved about the kitchen were enticing. Any threat had been held at bay, for a while, anyway, leaving Wyatt to spend a few hours with a sensual woman. How could that be bad?

It was one thing to appreciate good food, and the agreeable sight of the woman sharing it, but Wyatt cautioned himself not to take it further. The enemy wasn't breathing down Beth's neck right then, but was near enough, waiting for the next opportunity to attack.

And just because Beth had gotten over being mad at him, and he'd forgiven her for keeping secrets, it didn't mean the relationship was going anywhere. Beth's mood could change in an instant, and often had. Having dinner was one thing; getting personal was another thing entirely.

Wyatt filled the plates with steaming food and carried them into the dining room. He entered to find Beth sipping wine, and his eyes went to her luscious lips.

"I like this arrangement, of you cooking for me," she said, and smiled at him. "Everything smells so delicious."

Wyatt took his seat. "You haven't tasted it yet."

The steak was as juicy as it looked, and Beth made a deep "Mmm" when she took her first bite. Wyatt scarfed his meal, washing it down with a few sips of wine. Beth looked thoughtful as she ate.

Leaning back, Wyatt said, "I won't leave your side, so I don't want you to worry."

"I'm not concerned about that," Beth said. "It's just annoying to have to wait. I'm anxious to get to the bottom of this. I don't like being hunted...or tracked like some animal."

Wyatt pushed his plate aside. "It's interesting...I would have been in New York now even if you hadn't hired me."

"How come...to see your family?"

"No, for my buddy's wedding. Garrett is marrying Marlene Parks."

"*The* Marlene Parks, the movie star?"

"Yes, that's her. You'll like her; she's really nice."

"What do you mean *I'll* like her?"

Wyatt grinned at her. "You're going to the wedding with me."

"Oh, no," Beth said. "I don't do weddings."

"Well, now you do...because I'm not leaving you behind. And the whole team is flying out for the ceremony. I wouldn't miss it."

"And I'm supposed to attend as your *date*?"

"Why not? I dress up pretty nice in a suit," Wyatt

said. "And no one has to know I'm your bodyguard. Of course, the guys will know, but I mean the guests or the family."

"You ask a lot of a girl, Wyatt Mercer."

He figured it was a bit soon to talk about weddings and such. He got a kick out of Beth's reaction, though. It was still so easy to get her riled up. He didn't envision his own wedding, not for some time, anyway—and certainly not with Beth. She was attractive, but marriage was a whole different deal. He could only imagine how much bickering would go on if they lived together.

"It's just my friend's wedding, that's all." Wyatt thought she'd look good in a dress. "I'd appreciate it if you'd accompany me." Beth didn't readily agree, but he'd won that round. She really had little choice—besides, she'd probably have a nice time.

CHAPTER NINE

Martin padded across the carpet in bare feet, the luxurious softness making him sick to his stomach. The residence had cost an obscene amount of money, and payments were coming due. If he couldn't make good on the loans, he'd be out on the street.

He stepped onto the cool bathroom tile, the globes of light over the mirrors blinding him. Leila had always wanted the best. She'd had the fixtures imported from Italy, and hired an interior designer to decorate the place. It was fancy enough to be in one of the home magazines his ex-wife had liked so well.

The place wasn't the least bit masculine, so it served poorly as a bachelor pad. Martin hadn't minded at the time. Heck, he'd had plenty of money then. But his wife had taken him to the cleaners in the divorce, and he'd had to live on what was left.

If he'd done better at the casino, things might be different—in many ways. Martin got into the shower with two massive showerheads pouring out hot water. He stood under the massaging one, letting the pulsating spray knead his tight muscles.

He closed his eyes, but relaxation didn't come. His level of frustration blocked out any sense of calmness. There would be no peace until all of this was over. He'd hooked up with the Asian mob, for Christ's sake. You'd think they could do their part without mistakes.

Yet Chen must have hired a bunch of amateurs,

some local gangsters who'd muffed the job. Martin hadn't wanted his niece killed, but it was worse to bungle several attempts. It was downright embarrassing, as well as dangerous.

The losers hadn't been able to bump off a slender young woman, not much over five feet tall. Hell, the would-be killer probably could have picked her up in one hand and squeezed the life out of her. Yet Beth continued to evade them.

Martin would have to take matters into his own hands, if this kept up. But he hoped it didn't come to that. He had a distaste for murder, and preferred not to get his hands dirty. It was better to keep his distance as much as possible, so he could claim innocence.

He was a smooth talker, one attribute that had saved him more than once. He cringed to think of what he might need to finagle his way out of this. If Beth had reported the attempts on her life to the police—which she certainly must have—then inquiries would be made.

Martin needed to cover his tracks, so the path wouldn't lead to his door. On one side, the mob pressured him to do their bidding, and on the other was law enforcement. Being stuck in the middle was uncomfortable, as whichever way he turned was threatening.

It would be advantageous to have Beth out of the way, permanently, as long as Martin could escape any guilt for the deed. He washed and turned off the water, then got out to dry. Since he had to make a trip to the office, he dressed accordingly. There was no dress code, but he wanted to give the impression of respectability. It was part of the image he had to maintain.

While Martin was still in stocking feet, his phone rang. It was Chen, probably checking up. Apparently, his neck was on the line too, unless the strategy went off without a hitch. Zhang wasn't the type to show mercy for screw-ups.

"Chen, you're up early." It couldn't hurt to be friendly.

Pleasantries were apparently beyond the gangster. "I'll be at the casino tonight. Don't make yourself scarce. We need to talk."

"What about? I've got things in motion," Martin said. "Kyle won't be a problem." It was good that his nephew was so trusting, and blind to the undercurrent of the company's affairs. "I arranged a trip to Boston, and he won't return until the deed is done."

Martin was proud of pulling that off. He might be in a tight spot, but he wasn't without resources or connections.

"And the rest of your family?"

"I checked on Steph. There's no change." Martin had considered including his brother in the scheme, but he'd tested the water a couple of times. His brother wouldn't go along with anything that wasn't above board. He was too bloody honest, even when there was substantial profit to be made. But he was out of the way now.

"It seems that if your niece hadn't nosed in where she doesn't belong, our plan would have rolled out smoothly."

"I booted her out before she learned too much. Stephen put her in accounting, the worst choice. But that's long since been taken care of."

"It's not enough," Chen said.

Martin's gut twisted; the mob seemed to have a taste for blood. Yet he dared not argue. It would be

114

better to bide his time and see how things unfolded.

After the call, Martin finished dressing and walked a few blocks to a café. He hadn't eaten in a while, nor did he have much of an appetite. But the strong coffee perked him up. The shop was pleasantly warm and plenty busy. He sat in an open booth and carved a hunk of syrup-soaked pancakes that he didn't eat.

If Chen and his crew had backed off and let Martin handle things, there would be a lot less potential for disaster. Drug smuggling could be done in a clandestine manner, with no one the wiser—and certainly no feds breathing down his neck.

But when you added in a couple of attempts on Beth's life, matters got messy. It made what should have been a quiet operation way too high profile. And it would be worse if the mob succeeded in killing her. That blasted news release might be enough to pull Martin in for interrogation.

When he'd watched the coverage, he'd groaned. The media thrived on controversy, and what better than an accident scene? It was bad enough killing the wrong woman, but the victim just happened to be wearing Beth's jacket.

It was just Martin's luck. And now what was he supposed to do? It was a damn good thing his attorney could run interference. That prompted him to make a call for confirmation that the whole incident wasn't about to blow up.

The law firm's secretary was on a first-name basis with Martin, and put him right through. Thomas Stapleton had handled family matters for years, and he'd been a reliable bloke. "Stapleton...Martin here. That news story is on CNN; it's been broadcast coast to coast."

"I couldn't help that," the attorney said. "I kept a

lid on it for as long as I could. It was only out of respect for Foster that the producer held off at all. He wanted to make sure he had his facts straight, and didn't want to mention Elizabeth's name until the details had been substantiated."

"So why was that woman wearing her jacket?"

"According to Beth, they traded. It was as simple as that."

Of course, Beth would have gone to Thomas right away for protection. Sometimes the family attorney knew more about what was going on than Martin did. "My phone has been ringing off the hook, and the same at the office. I refuse to speak publicly. I didn't know the woman who died, and if Beth did, then she can take the heat."

"I've advised her not to speak to the press. It's a sticky situation. It's wise that you stay away from them too. This will lose steam after a few days, if there's no more information to fuel interest."

After the call, Martin left his uneaten breakfast and went to Foster. Susan greeted him cheerily, oblivious to anything untoward. She was a fixture at the company, and did her job efficiently. Plus, she was smart enough not to meddle.

Martin gave her a cursory nod and headed off to see the head of security. He'd requested surveillance recordings for the past week. The guard set up the viewing and left him alone with it. It didn't take long to spot Beth in her brother's office.

She had no business at Foster, not since he'd fired her. He could have pushed the embezzlement charge, and likely should have. But it struck too close to home. Martin had liquidated those stocks to bankroll his gambling, but the money had slipped through his hands. Lately, fortune hadn't been on his side.

At Martin's request, Kyle's computer had been monitored by the IT department. He didn't completely trust his nephew. The setup had worked to Martin's advantage, because when the hard drive had been copied, IT had been alerted.

Of course, Martin had shared that knowledge with Chen. It wasn't wise to keep secrets from the mob, as a man could be killed for betrayal. The best course was to be open with any information he garnered. When he'd been told about the computer tampering, Martin had called security and learned that Beth had been in that day.

But he wanted to see for himself, and note anything else his niece might have done while at Foster. There on the screen was Wyatt Mercer. It was annoying that the guy was hanging around, a bit too close to Beth. The fewer allies she had, the better.

Plus Wyatt had buffed up a lot since Martin had known him years back. There was no question that his presence offered Beth protection, making him another obstacle. Martin shook his head. His niece should have just let it go.

Now she knew about the stock liquidation. Beth was sharp, and she wouldn't miss something like that. She'd see right through the embezzlement charge that he'd trumped up, and know that he was the real culprit. She couldn't prove anything—yet. But she'd butted in where she shouldn't have, and Wyatt was along for the ride. Both of them would live to regret it.

Before leaving, Martin went to his office and accessed his accounts. He'd drained all the funds he could from Foster for now, without attracting the attention of accounting. But he had one more option. It was a bit of a risk, but by the time he had to answer for the withdrawal, he'd be flush.

It wouldn't be long before he had plenty of cash, but until then he needed some for his visit to the casino later. He completed the transfer, then snorted a bit of cocaine to boost his mood. Life was overly stressful, and it would help him get through the day. Then an evening at the machines would raise his spirits.

*****

That night, the casino was buzzing. Martin's veins were pumped with enough drugs to blot out his worries. He was the king of the mountain, and he couldn't lose. For a while, he was on a roll, but didn't cash in his chips. There was more to be won.

Then Chen strolled up to the table, ruining the evening. Tattoos covered both his arms like sleeves, and his biceps flexed when he leaned on the table to speak into Martin's ear. "I need to see you alone."

What a depressing thought. It brought reality crashing back. Even if Martin kept winning that night, it wouldn't be nearly enough. And it was unlikely the mobsters would let him off the hook, debt or not. He'd made the agreement with them, and wouldn't allow him to bow out.

In a secluded alcove, Chen confronted him. "You're out there gambling like you don't have a care in the world. You'd better snap to, because there's no room for error."

The drugs and alcohol had taken control, and Martin spoke without considering his words. "How in the hell can I make sure there's no errors if you guys blow it for me? If you keep hiring misfits to do your dirty work, we're all going to be in a world of hurt. I'm not sure I should continue with this fiasco."

With a meaty fist, Chen slammed Martin against

the wall, his black eyes blazing. "Oh, you'll continue." He stabbed his other finger at him. "Let me tell you a story…"

He released Martin, but didn't step back.

The tale was sobering. Chen told of the vindictiveness of the Asian mob, widely known as the Triad. The story was of a reporter who'd had the gall to publish an article that regaled their activities in vivid glory. Far from being flattered, the gang leader back home had ordered retribution.

Meat cleavers were weapons that were not soon forgotten. As the story went, the reporter lived to tell another tale—minus his fingers on both hands. Martin shuddered. "I've heard enough."

Chen was in his face. "So, you'll continue, my friend…or we'll go after your family and carve them up, one by one." Martin choked on the man's stale breath. "And then…we'll come after you."

*****

The next day, Martin met with a representative who was used to doing business with the mob. He hired out boats used for drug smuggling. It could be arranged for a healthy fee, and Martin paid with company funds. He'd taken care to meet surreptitiously, and hoped to God that no one saw him.

He'd worried unnecessarily, or so he attempted to convince himself. The meeting took place at a restaurant, some dive not far from the docks. The guy was dressed in boating garb, complete with deck shoes, and looked exceedingly normal. No one would have suspected his true intent. For all appearances, he was there to set up a pleasure cruise.

Money changed hands as it was supposed to, and

the man politely assured Martin that the boat would be there on schedule. Despite the pretense of normalcy, the encounter unnerved him. Martin had personally hired a boat with its captain for the sole purpose of smuggling.

He'd committed a crime, and not a white-collar crime for which he'd be slapped on the wrist and told to reform. The DEA wouldn't look the other way about drug running. Martin would have nightmares about getting caught. With the way this whole business was going, the FBI and even Homeland Security would probably be after him.

What had seemed like an advantageous arrangement had turned out to be a trap. Regret seized Martin's chest, and a wave of nausea washed through his belly. Drug smuggling was an activity that might drag him to the depths, where it seemed he was already headed. Like a horror story, events unfolded before his eyes, and he was unable to stop before it was too late.

To listen to his new pals, Chen and Zhang, smuggling was purely business. The mob took what they wanted and dared anyone to challenge their authority. It was one more day in a life of crime, yet it certainly didn't seem that way to Martin. Stepping off a cliff, and plummeting to his death, was a more accurate description of the sensation that riddled his body.

*****

On a dark evening later that week, Martin made a trip out to the Port of New York. He wore all black clothing, with a knit cap and sunglasses, his best attempt at disguise. It wasn't likely any business connections or family friends would cruise the harbor in the dead of night—but he was in a cautious mood.

The momentous event drew ever closer, circumstances constricting around Martin like a snake intending to wrap tighter until it crushed the life out of him. When he arrived, Chen was already there with a couple of other thugs. Martin approached, and the guards stayed in the shadows. If their presence was to intimidate him, it worked.

Martin walked over to Chen. Together they gazed out at the black expanse of ocean. Somewhere out there, a container ship approached. It would be there by morning, just before dawn, to make the delivery. The ship carried cargo of all sorts, transported in containers to be unloaded at the dock.

For some reason, Chen had insisted on a final meeting. It wasn't like Martin hadn't gotten the message. Once the drop had been set up, it went through, or somebody died. It wasn't that hard to understand, and repeating it wasn't necessary.

Chen stuffed his hands in his pockets, taking a casual stance as if chatting with a friend. "You have confidence that your ship will be on time?"

"I checked the schedule. There's no reason to think otherwise."

"And the speedboat? It's arranged?"

"I paid enough, it damn well better show up." Martin glared at the mobster. "Besides, you assured me you'd worked with the company before and the service could be relied on."

"I set you up with the best, but the outcome is on your shoulders."

"Yeah, I don't need to be told." There wasn't much else Martin could do. He'd set things in motion, and the only thing to do was wait. He had no experience with this kind of thing; he was out of his depth. He prayed there wouldn't be a screw-up.

Chen patted him on the back and flagged his men, then disappeared into the night.

Martin shivered and wrapped his scarf tighter. He stepped to the edge of the water, and looked out. He understood what was about to take place, knew each step by heart. The Foster International ship would slow to a crawl, well before entering the main harbor.

One of Zhang's men was on board, undercover as a crew member. He'd blow the horn at the right moment, signaling the speedboat. The boat captain would navigate out to the ship and retrieve the package. It would be a special bag with the drug shipment.

The term that Chen used for the maneuver was *fly-by*. It was a standard maneuver where the shipping line would have the ship swoop closer to shore than it was supposed to, blare the horn, then sail on. The guy in the speedboat would zoom out to where the ship had been and pick up a floating bag full of drugs.

Martin didn't want to know what was in there. It could be marijuana, heroin, or another drug, depending on where the ship had come from. In this case, it had come from Hong Kong. Already, Martin knew more than he wanted to.

He preferred to take drugs, not handle smuggling them into the country. Chen had bragged about how easy it was, and so it seemed. Sure, it was simple, provided the authorities didn't catch on—then it would be a disaster. Another contact, a professor at a well-respected university, was the distribution point for an affluent area around the school. Chen hadn't shared his name, which was just as well. As university staff, the man was beyond reproach, the last person who would be suspected. It was all so clever.

Yet Martin felt as though he stood beneath bright lights, as if any moment the cops would scream up to the dock, sirens blaring, and arrest him. He wasn't cut out for this sort of stuff. He trudged away from the water, hoping the cab he'd paid to wait for him was still a few blocks up. He wasn't anxious to scare up another one, since cabbies didn't tend to hang out at the harbor.

Fortunately, his driver had waited, and when he spotted his fare striding toward the vehicle, he turned on the headlights. Once in the back seat, Martin asked to be taken home. All he wanted was to lock his door and curl up in bed, praying that he'd sleep until the drop had been executed. Yet he feared he'd pace the floor most of the night instead.

Desperation clawed at Martin. He was on his own, beholden to a ruthless group who placed zero value on his life. His wife wasn't at home to comfort him, or to tell him that she'd be there, no matter what happened. And the childless marriage had left him utterly alone when they'd split up.

Leila would be more inclined to side with the mob. After the cutthroat divorce, there was no love left. She tolerated him at best. After pleading with him to reform, she'd given up. What would she say if she knew of the situation he found himself in now?

Over the years, his brother had tended to side with him, due to brotherly love and all. Yet Stephen was incapacitated and locked away, of no use to Martin. Given the opportunity, his brother wouldn't have supported such a sordid affair anyway.

Beth's life was in peril, and the first person the law would pursue if anything happened to her was Martin. However innocently, she'd made sure of that with her stupid journals and satirical cartoon sketches. If she met with an early demise, there would be a lot of questions.

Yet there was no going back. Martin was immersed in events no longer under his power to control, and he was unable to extricate himself from the underworld, even if he wanted to. It was too late for that.

Plus there was no other option for wiping out his debt to the mob. He had nowhere else to obtain the funds. On the bright side, it wouldn't be long before he was in the black again. Then he'd see some real profits and his future would look much different.

Martin would be able to stop the bleeding of his finances, patch up the debacle of his life, and regain his respectable status. With Foster International at his disposal, a limitless supply of drugs could enter the country, greatly benefiting him.

It was all going to work out, once he got past this rough patch.

The driver dropped Martin in front of the mansion, and he paid with a generous tip. His cash was dwindling, but it wouldn't be long before he was back on his feet again. Once inside, Martin flipped on some low lights and turned on music.

He shed the black garb, then put on sweatpants and a shirt to settle in for the night. He sloshed a thimble of bourbon into a glass and gulped it. The burn in his throat relieved some of the tension, but not nearly enough.

From a wall safe, Martin retrieved his stash. With the doors locked, he settled into a padded chair and sprinkled the cocaine on the glass coffee table. He snorted, maybe a little extra, then leaned back. That was much better. His heart sped up, and his outlook instantly improved.

Martin refilled the bourbon and settled back into the chair. Sometime later, he woke up on the bathroom floor without a clue how he got there. He must have passed out. Nausea gripped him, and he hurled into the toilet. Then he rolled back onto the floor, the cool tile soothing his aching head. He'd lost track of time, and honestly, he didn't really care.

CHAPTER TEN

Beth wasn't used to having a man around all the time, even if he was her bodyguard. She had difficulty relegating him to that duty. Although she had her separate suite and plenty of privacy, more often than not Wyatt was with her.

She'd seen him first thing in the morning with scruff on his chin, and hanging around in jeans with a t-shirt, showing off his chiseled physique. Wyatt had strong thighs and a nice butt, not that she stared. But it was impossible not to notice.

When they stayed in, Wyatt was more than happy to cook, and Beth had even tried her hand at scrambled eggs for breakfast this morning. She'd added some secret ingredients to make them especially fluffy and tasty, and Wyatt commended her for her effort.

Beth sat across from him at the dining table near the spiral staircase. The slate-gray table sat on a wool carpet over the wooden floor, providing a warm feel. She sprinkled some pepper on her eggs and stole a glance at the beautiful male specimen, so close she could touch him.

And she wanted to touch him. By some miracle, Beth had held back, but in such close quarters the temptation was great. She wondered how Wyatt fared under the circumstances, not that he'd come right out and said he was attracted to her.

But a woman can feel things, and Beth's intuition

told her the chemistry was mutual. Wyatt was all male, and her hormones were going wild. It was terribly inconvenient, because danger loomed and Wyatt wasn't dating her, just protecting her. Why was that so damn sexy?

Wyatt leaned on the table, his biceps flexing with the motion. Beth shifted in her seat. He was fresh from the shower, and his damp hair dusted his neck. He smelled of soap and cologne, making her breathe deeply of his maleness.

When Wyatt's dark brown eyes met hers, Beth glanced away. She didn't know how much self-control she possessed. "I'm surprised you agreed to let me go shopping today without you."

"It's not as though you won't be guarded. After all, my sister is a criminal lawyer, and, as such, makes enemies. She guarantees that the firm's security is top notch."

"And you believed her?"

"No, I had Travis check it out. He did backgrounds on the guys that will be with you ladies today, and they check out. With his stamp of approval, I'll deliver you into their hands, but only for a few hours."

"You're the one who coerced me into going to the wedding. I don't have anything to wear. Jessica offered to assist, and that requires shopping."

"I'll be meeting with the team anyway. They arrive later, so I'll connect up with them at the hotel," Wyatt said.

"Who's coming?"

"It's a good turnout, as a show of support. Travis will have the honor of giving away the bride; his wife and daughters will be at the wedding with him." Apparently noticing Beth's expression, he paused. "Marlene's father died in battle."

"Oh, I see," Beth said, moved by the situation.

"Cooper will be the best man. Rip broke down and rented a suit for the occasion." Wyatt pushed his plate away and tipped back in the chair. "Even Tessa is coming."

"I like her," Beth said, admiring the camaraderie of the group. She doubted that she could get more than two people together, even for her birthday. A wedding would be a sad affair. "You're lucky to have such friends."

Wyatt's expression was kind. "You'll fit right in. You already met most of the team out in LA."

"True, but not at a social event."

"Garrett and I go way back, went on plenty of missions together. When he got out of the service, I hooked him up with Stealth. He was looking for a career, and Travis has put together a tight group."

Beth studied Wyatt, his face lightly tanned, with a few lines of maturity. She thought of what he must have experienced when on deployment, but it was probably best not to ask. There was wisdom in his face, goodness in his eyes that reflected character.

"If everyone is here, who will run the office and take care of clients?"

"Travis has staffed well; there's a pretty large crew overall, and he left Hunter Davis in charge. You haven't met him, but he's loyal and can be trusted."

Beth sipped her orange juice then grinned.

"What are you smiling about?"

"Oh, just that with that many former SEALs present, the wedding is likely the safest place for me."

"You got that right."

Beth looked forward to meeting the bride and groom, plus seeing the others again. She'd do her best to fit in, but was nervous. Weddings were so formal, and this was a movie star wedding, as well. Wyatt didn't seem bothered about it, so she'd try to assume his relaxed attitude.

*****

Jessica Mercer lived in a condo in East Village, conveniently located to the firm in the financial district where she practiced law. Beth had been there before, since she'd had a friendly relationship with Wyatt's sister for a long time.

When not tied up at work, Jessica was usually game for shopping and lunch. She was like the sister that Beth hadn't had, and she was a woman that could be relied on in a crunch.

The red stucco building didn't look exceptional from the outside, but the interior was classy. "You're going to be impressed with your sister's place," Beth said. It seemed odd that he hadn't visited in so long and hadn't seen where she lived.

"I'm sure I will be," Wyatt said. "She's a big-time lawyer now." Beth didn't detect any resentment in his voice, and was sure he loved his sister despite having been apart from her for years.

Jessica greeted them at the door and ushered them inside. She wore wool slacks with a creamy sweater that set off her eyes. She had soft brown eyes, which reminded Beth of Wyatt's. His sister was attractive, and had a friendly, easygoing personality. She had her long brown hair tied back at the nape of her neck, a casual look.

Wyatt gave her a hug. "Good to see you, Jess." He held her at arm's length. "You look great. I'm sorry we didn't have much time to talk at the party."

Jessica stood on tiptoes and kissed him on the cheek. "Well, I hope to see more of you." She guided them through the foyer into the main room. The window along one wall had an expansive view of the East River. The place was decorated in earth tones with wood tables and plush furniture, giving it a welcoming feel.

There was a narrow staircase leading to the second floor, and the upper wall exhibited a geometric modern painting. Seated on one of the sofas was Wyatt's younger brother. When Jessica entered with company, he stood up. "I didn't expect to see you."

Jeremy Mercer was as tall as Wyatt, but leaner. He lacked the rock-hard muscle that the Navy required, and looked like more of a jogger. He had short-cropped brown hair, brown eyes, and was handsome. He fit his role as the CEO of Mercer Industries, and was plenty charming when he chose to be.

Wyatt patted Jeremy on the back, then gave him a quick brotherly hug. "How are you these days?"

"Good, real good." Jeremy shifted from one foot to the other. "We'll have to get together for a beer or something while you're in town. I'd stay, but I'm on my way to the office."

"Sure," Wyatt said, "we'll do that."

"Nice to see you too, Beth. I hear you need my sister's fashion advice."

"Yep, I sure do." Jeremy worked long hours, so Beth didn't see him as often as his sister. But she'd frequently run into him at family get-togethers or at his sister's place.

Jeremy kissed his sister on the cheek. "I'll call you," he said before he left. "And thanks for the legal advice."

Wyatt plopped into a chair. "He seems to be doing well."

As she took a seat, Jessica gave Beth a knowing

glance. Obviously, she'd planned it so the brothers were there at the same time. "Yes, he is doing a great job. And he's made some good changes," she said. "Ones that I think would meet with your approval."

"I'm not in charge there, nor do I plan to be," Wyatt said. "So whatever he does, I'm in no position to be critical."

His sister continued, "He's donated to a variety of environmental programs, and supports charities. And he is determined to run a business we can all be proud of."

Wyatt crossed his arms. "And Dad lets him make the decisions?"

"So it seems. Once he retired, he didn't interfere. Not that he wouldn't, but he's been traveling a lot. I guess he has other interests now. I get postcards from him."

"Where is he currently?"

"In Florence—enjoying the wine and women, no doubt," Jessica said.

Beth clasped her hands in her lap and looked over at Wyatt. He and Jessica had lost their mother when they were still in grade school, a result of a drunk driver hitting her vehicle head-on. It had happened so long ago that Wyatt didn't talk about it.

"How is the *old guy*?" Wyatt asked. The chasm had developed between Wyatt and his father, far before his joining the Navy had become an issue.

"Mean as ever." Jessica laughed, and the others joined in.

"Where's Michael today?" Beth asked, referring to Jessica's recent heartthrob.

"He's at the office. I took a personal day to go with you." She looked at her brother. "You didn't give Beth much notice to come up with an outfit suitable for a celebrity wedding."

"I didn't know she was going to show up in LA, or that she'd be my constant companion," Wyatt said. "Anyway, I should head out and let you women get to shopping." He stood and looked at his sister. "Where's your protection team?"

"Out in front in the bulletproof car," Jessica said, and held up her phone. "I got a text from Leo when he arrived; he's served as my bodyguard before."

Wyatt gave his sister a quick hug and headed for the door. "I guess criminal law can be a dangerous career."

"Defense work has its risks. I've heard about a home break-in by the friends of a disgruntled client who had been recently imprisoned. Plus there are plenty of death threats. I don't take most of them seriously, but I'm not foolhardy. If I need protection, I hire it," Jessica said. "However, today was at *your* request, for Beth's safety."

Wyatt looked at Beth, and she said, "Yeah, I'll have to fill you in...when your brother leaves."

"I'm gone." Wyatt lifted a hand and strode across the room. "Text when you get home later and I'll come pick you up," he said to Beth.

A well-built guard named Leo, dressed in khakis and a dark jacket, escorted Beth and Jessica outside. A driver was visible behind tinted glass. "Two guards?"

"Sure, you get only the best," Jessica said, then told the driver where to take them, before raising a privacy panel. "Now that we're alone, tell me everything."

"I hired your brother as my bodyguard."

Jessica looked crestfallen. "That explains why he didn't kiss you goodbye. I really hoped there was something between you. You've known Wyatt most of your life, and if you got together it would be so...romantic."

"You can get the stars out of your eyes. We are friends, and the current arrangement is strictly business." Beth spoke with more certainty than she felt. Why did she feel like what she had with Wyatt was more than a work relationship? The stressful situation had jumbled her mind.

Jessica's slight smile unnerved her. "All right, I'll accept that for now. But I can envision Wyatt falling for you."

Beth was uncomfortable with that. "For now, you need to envision that he keeps me alive."

Jessica widened her eyes. "I saw the news. What was the deal with that woman wearing your jacket? Does it have something to do with why you need protection?"

"Yes, it does. And so much has happened." Beth launched into a recounting of recent events. It was a relief to tell Jessica, unburdening as a friend. When she confessed her guilt about Amanda, fear spiked through her. If Beth was unable to stop the threats against her, the same fate awaited her. The harsh reality of it was sobering.

She told Jessica about the attacks, and shared her thoughts about her journal being stolen. "There's something to that. I'd been digging around without any focused purpose. I used the material for cartoon ideas, and just researched out of interest."

"Whoever is doing this doesn't see it that way," Jessica said. "You pose a significant threat. There must be something you're missing, something that is worth killing over."

"I wish I knew what it was." Beth rubbed her

temple. "The ways both our families have run companies, the questionable tactics were no secret. Hell, that's part of why Wyatt left, why he wanted no part of running Mercer. I'm not sure what I found out that has made me a target."

"You need to think, because something has."

"I have thought, but my journal was pages and pages of all kinds of stuff." Beth told her some of what she'd written about, and talked about doing some cartooning for the paper Amanda had worked for, then digressed into ragging on her uncle.

"I haven't gotten along with Martin either," Jessica said. "He's an arrogant ass."

"I'm used to that. I just wish he hadn't decided to step in when my father got ill. Kyle could have handled things without him nosing about," Beth said. "Some uncle...he is out to get me...I swear he is."

"He accused you of actions that I know you aren't capable of," Jessica said. "The whole situation is unbelievable," Jessica said, "not to mention *scary*."

"Very scary. You just get death *threats*; I've had actual attempts on my life," Beth said. "Without your brother looking out for me..."

"I dread to think. Will Kyle talk to you...tell you what you need to know?"

"It depends; I'm not certain how he's involved or what he knows. But whatever information he has, I intend to pry it out of him."

The car had reached Fifth Avenue and had been cruising, waiting for instructions. Jessica hit the button and spoke into the intercom. "Let us out in front of Bergdorf Goodman." The driver navigated through the congestion, and when near the store, Leo hopped out and opened the back door. "He'll handle the car. I'll stick with you," he said.

Jessica and Beth entered the store, bodyguard in tow. "What do you wear to a movie star's wedding?"

"Nothing you have," Jessica said. "Black makes the wrong statement. It's supposed to be a joyous occasion."

"I'm not the bride."

"You don't have to be. But you asked me to help you find a dress, so that's what I'm going to do."

"It just can't be anything too..."

"Conservative?" Jessica smiled. "I'm aware. Have faith. We'll check out designer dresses. I'm sure there's some trendy stuff, and the clerks are fashion experts."

Beth followed, counting on her friend to make her look good. "I don't want to feel like I'm wearing someone else's clothes. I'll be self-conscious enough as it is."

"You worry too much." Jessica was at home with fashion. Beth normally was too, except that her idea of fashion included lots of leather, lace, and metal. A new look was in order.

Jessica enthusiastically embraced the task of finding the right dress. After trying on half a dozen garments, she gave up. A variety of other stores along Fifth provided no better options, so Jessica dragged Beth over to Broadway. "There's a bunch of small boutiques. That's what we need."

Beth was exhausted. Who'd think that trying on clothes could be such work? Jessica scrutinized each selection. "You're petite, so we don't want too much material; you'll be lost in it." Another choice disappointed her too. "It's too...pastel. You have such good skin. That color washes you out."

The afternoon sped by, and Beth was inclined to go with black after all. She was comfortable with it, and it matched her hair. "Absolutely not," Jessica said. "You're not giving up. I won't let you. The perfect dress awaits...I just know it."

And she was right. At a small boutique, Beth's hopes rose. The clothing was edgier, but not too dark or punkish. The dresses were more fitted, tailored for a smaller figure. This just might work.

The clerk looked Beth over with a critical eye. "You have flawless skin, and with those dark eyes and black hair...I have a couple of suggestions."

On the first try, Jessica approved a sheath dress that fit Beth's delicate curves. The material was soft and flowed with her when she walked. The satin material was covered with lace, and the bodice had a modest line. Beth didn't have the cleavage to show off a low-cut design.

The satin was deep crimson, and curved over her bosom. The see-through lace extended up to her collarbone and the cap sleeves were made of the same lace. The look was classy, sensual, yet different. It suited Beth.

At the car, the bodyguard let them in the back, then slipped into the front seat. The driver glanced back. "Where would you like to go?"

"I could use a drink," Jessica said. "You wore me out."

Beth laughed. "It's the other way around. You wore me out. I'd have quit while we were still on Fifth."

Jessica said to the driver, "Take us to PDT." That was Please Don't Tell, a cocktail lounge they frequented in East Village. The place had delicious drinks and specialty hot dogs.

The entrance was through a phone booth, with a red telephone. A note said the phone was the doorbell: *Dial one and someone will be right with you.* The door buzzed open then Beth and Jessica went inside with the bodyguard close by. The brick interior was pleasantly dark.

A waiter provided a table then handed over menus. Beth chose a Scandinavian-style hot dog, complete with pickles, coriander kraut, and mustard greens. She paired it with a Manhattan, a drink the restaurant had on tap. Jessica ordered the same. The drinks were promptly served.

While waiting for the food, Beth sipped her drink. "Ah, this hits the spot." On an empty stomach, she felt the buzz quickly. "So, is it serious between you and Michael?"

Jessica shrugged. "It's hard to say. He's a great guy and all, but *serious*...that's a big commitment. I'd like to marry, but I'm not sure if hooking up with another attorney is smart. It's a high-stress field."

"You can't pick who you fall in love with."

"Speaking from experience?"

"Nope, I've just watched lots of movies." Beth wondered if love would catch her off guard.

"You mentioned your cartooning. Has Wyatt seen your stuff?"

"He flipped through one of my sketchbooks."

"What does he think? He must have noticed how talented you are."

Beth wrinkled her nose. "Wyatt is a nag. He says the work is good, and that I should *do something* with it, make something of my life—as if it's any of his business."

"He has a point; you are good."

"Maybe, but I sketch because I want to."

Jessica didn't belabor the point. "My brother seems intrigued by you."

"I'm not sure how intriguing it is to rescue me

137

from being killed...*repeatedly*."

The food arrived, and Jessica moved her plate closer. "I meant how he looks at you. It's different than how he used to look at you."

"I don't think he looks at me any differently, except our bickering has toned down a bit."

"Yes, you and Wyatt did get into it, didn't you?" Jessica took a bite of her hot dog.

A flash of honesty overcame Beth. "I do kind of like him, though. He changed when he went away...matured. Those shoulders..."

Jessica laughed. "See, I knew it; you and Wyatt could be an item."

"*If* I live through this, and *if* we're still on speaking terms when it's over...Wyatt will go back to LA."

"And you?"

Beth shrugged. "I'm a New Yorker." She bit into her hot dog. The place sure had good food.

*****

When Beth got back in the car, she noticed that she'd missed a text. It was from Thomas Stapleton, an update on the inheritance dispute. The case was stalled because of her father's illness. Even with a power of attorney, it wasn't simple to change a will. Uncle Martin had reached an impasse.

"Anything important?" Jessica said.

"On top of everything else, my uncle wants my money. He's brought a legal action to change the will and write me out."

"That won't be easy."

"So it appears, but he won't give it up. I suspect he hopes to gain the money, and not allow it all to go to Kyle." Beth frowned. "He's become a sponge for money."

"He's had those tendencies for a while, so I'm not surprised. Sounds like it's worse than it used to be."

Beth sighed. "This whole inheritance issue is depressing. It's morbid to fight over who gets my father's money." She paused. "I love my father so much. My wish is for him to get well and live many more years. I'd trade all the money just to have him around."

Jessica didn't say anything, but Beth was sure she understood.

Later, back at Jessica's place, Beth went over to the window and gazed at the river. Talking everything over had provided new clarity, and one thing stuck in her mind.

"I'm glad you told me what's going on," Jessica said. "You shouldn't be alone in all of this. You have to let me know if I can help."

Beth sat down and crossed her legs. "You know...you just might be able to."

"Let's hear it, then."

"You work with criminals, so you must conduct investigations."

"Sure, we have a team that handles that," Jessica said. "What do you have in mind?"

"Cooper, the computer tech at Stealth, spoke with Wyatt. He specifically mentioned my uncle's gambling addiction. I'd thought he'd given that up, but I'm pretty sure he hasn't. And if he's racked up debts...that might explain a few things."

"Sounds like Stealth is already working that angle."

"Yes, but I have an idea," Beth said. "I'm trying to make the connection between mounting debts and killers coming after me."

"Hmm, I see your point. He might have hooked up with some pretty shady guys," Jessica said. "I know that crowd well. A multitude of crimes come out of the world of gambling and to the underworld connected with it." She furrowed her brow. "Especially gangsters who prey on losers."

"Gangsters who wouldn't think twice about bumping off a young heiress?"

"Exactly, and one of the most notorious gangs happens to be the Triad."

"The Asian mob?"

"A ruthless bunch, if there ever was one. I'll have my team lean on some connections, and see what can be learned. Word gets around when big money is involved."

"But you have to be discreet." Beth was playing with fire. "I'm already in someone's sights, because of what it's assumed that I know. If rumors surface that I have someone probing for information connected with the mob, the situation will be deadly."

"It already is," Jessica said. "Some very bad people might be after you. I'm afraid for you."

Beth shuddered. It was very possible that her uncle had fallen in with the wrong crowd. "You have to help me," she said. "I need to know what's really behind all of this."

"I'll do my best," Jessica said. "I promise."

CHAPTER ELEVEN

The wedding was twelve floors up on the Tribeca rooftop, with amazing views. The bride and groom had chosen the New York City skyline as the backdrop for the ceremony. Rows of chairs were set up on both sides of a white carpet overlaid onto the tile terrace. Vases of white roses lined the aisle, and at the far end was an arch-shaped trellis covered with flowers woven through green vines.

Beth wore the crimson dress, and had done her hair in a softer style. The shaved part had grown out some, so had a wispy look, and her longer hair had settled into gentle waves. She'd toned down the dark black around her eyes, and had chosen a deep red lip gloss. Along the rim of her ear, she wore a row of diamond studs that she reserved for special occasions.

Wyatt stood next to her by the wall, looking out at the view. Beth pointed out the Empire State Building as if she was a tourist, and marveled over the Hudson River below. "From up here, it feels like we're on top of the world. What an ideal venue for a wedding. It's like being up in the sky among the clouds, with the high-rises close enough to touch."

Beth looked at Wyatt, taken with his good looks; he could steal a woman's heart. He was cleanly shaved, except for the neatly trimmed mustache. The dark suit was tailored to his athletic form with not an inch to spare. The jacket was open, and she glanced at his solid chest filling out the starched white shirt, her fingers itching to feel the rock-hard muscle underneath.

Wyatt's dark eyes gleamed, and he fingered the lace of her dress. "You look beautiful."

It had been a while since a man had said that to her. Maybe he was the first—it seemed like he might be. Beth lowered her lashes. "You flatter me, but I rather enjoy it. And you look incredible in a suit. Aren't bodyguards supposed to wear suits?"

"Don't get any ideas," Wyatt said, and his hand dropped back to his side.

Beth took his arm, wishing to be close, and a bit out of her element. Guests had arrived steadily, and the rooftop was a buzz of activity. She spotted a few familiar faces, as Wyatt had, because he led her over to the Stealth group.

Cooper was the first to see them walking over. He beamed, flashing a charming smile, his eyes as blue as the sky above. He was devastatingly handsome, and likely women were easily attracted to him. He shook Wyatt's hand then patted him on the back. "Mercer...you made it," he said.

"Nice to see you again," Beth said, accepting a kiss on the cheek.

Beth took in the group at a glance. The guys looked impressive all dressed up. Even Rip was all decked out. He had his dark hair tied back in a ponytail, silver rings on two fingers of his right hand, and a silver hoop in one earlobe. His attire showed off his well-developed physique to best advantage.

"You remember Rip," Wyatt said, giving his teammate a bear hug.

Rip nodded at Beth with a warm smile, and she lifted her hand in greeting.

The guys talked about the city, places to see on the short visit, and sports. Beth leaned against Wyatt, content to let them carry the conversation. Then Travis entered with a beautiful middle-aged woman who had to be his wife.

Greetings were given all around, then Travis said, his voice laced with love and admiration, "This is my wife Melanie." His wife had chin-length dark hair, dark eyes, and a lovely smile. "Mel, this is Elizabeth Foster; she's here with Wyatt."

That might give the wrong impression, but she was sure Wyatt would set the record straight later. "It's a pleasure to meet you," Melanie said. "I'm glad to see you joined us."

Beth had been allowed entrance into the inner circle of the Stealth team. The exchanges were casual and friendly, as she'd expect of such a group. Yet it was a novel feeling, not one Beth had experienced before. Without voicing it, the team members showed respect for each other, and there was a bond that seemed unbreakable.

Standing with Wyatt, silently watching the interchange, Beth was a part of it all. She was safer than she'd been in a while, if ever. Among so many former Navy guys, SEALs made of tougher stuff than she could imagine, she was completely protected.

"Did you know that Beth's a cartoonist?" Wyatt said, out of the blue. His chest was puffed up and he had a silly grin. Apparently, he was proud of her. "And she's quite good; I've seen her stuff."

Beth's cheeks warmed. "Wyatt is overplaying it," she said. "I enjoy sketching, but I'm not well known or anything."

"Well, you should be." Wyatt put his arm around her shoulders, and for a fleeting second Beth wished she could boast such success.

Melanie disappeared for a few minutes, and she returned with two exuberant young girls. They looked identical, dressed in light blue satin dresses and white shoes. Each wore a crown of blue and white flowers. "I found them in the bridal suite," Melanie said. "They were being little pests, and the bride is trying to get ready."

Both girls danced about their mother on tiptoes, full of energy. "She said it was okay. She likes having us around," one girl said. "She said so."

Reaching for the girl who had spoken, Melanie said, "This is Abigail."

Sudden shyness overcame Abigail, who shrank behind her mother, then peeked around and in a soft voice said, "Hello."

"And this is Brianna."

Both girls had long brown hair that fell below their shoulders, and big brown eyes. They looked so much alike that Beth didn't know if she'd be able to tell them apart later. "It's nice to meet you both."

Brianna was more extroverted than her sister, and she danced over to Beth. "We get to be the flower girls," she said. "Marlene said we could." She looked up with a wide smile, then did a pirouette.

Beth had seen the photograph of Melanie and the twins when she'd been at Stealth. Plus Wyatt had told her a bit about Travis and his family. It seemed that Melanie hadn't been able to conceive for the longest time, then ended up getting pregnant with twins.

Beth stooped down to eye level with Brianna. "What kind of flowers are you going to throw?" And the young girl breathlessly told her all about it. She raved about the petals to be thrown, the colors, the bride, and many other details. Without further prompting, she entertained Beth for a while, but Abigail watched from the safety of her mother's skirt.

Then Abigail reached a small hand up to Travis. "Daddy," she said, "pick me up...please."

Travis was mid-forties, a rugged sort, build as solid as brick. His blue eyes could be intimidating; Beth had noticed when she'd met with him. He swept his daughter into one arm, and she clung to his neck with her head nestled against his neck.

Then the groom came out to visit with the group, and Beth was introduced. Garrett Flynn was in a tux with a white rose in his lapel, and he radiated joy. His blue eyes shone when he spoke of his bride. "Marlene is still getting ready, and I'm not allowed in there."

"That's the way it works, buddy," Wyatt said. "You're better off out here."

"You have the rings, Coop?"

Cooper laughed. "Yeah, yeah, just like the other three times you asked me."

"I just don't want you to screw it up," Garrett said. "I can't stand up there at the altar empty-handed, dude."

The initial flurry of attention to the groom faded, as conversations started up again. Melanie left with the girls, probably to let them burn off some energy before their wedding duties began. Garrett stood next to Wyatt, and Coop started talking to Beth. He knew of her affinity for technology, computers in particular, so they had something in common.

Cooper assured her of his backup with her current situation. "Sometimes these cases take work to crack, but there's always a way...if you keep at it."

Beth heard the groom speak in a low voice. "Is she your date?"

"A client," Wyatt said. "She lives in New York."

145

"The way you two look together, I'm thinking you consider her more than a client."

Beth's heart leapt, as if Wyatt might confess hidden feelings to his friend. "You're love-struck, buddy. Getting married has you all romantic and shit."

There was no reply, so Beth kept her attention on the casual discussion with Cooper. She was eavesdropping, but didn't have to be obvious about it.

"Okay, dude, Beth and I are friends. I must have mentioned her before. I knew her growing up," Wyatt said. "There, are you satisfied?"

Out of the corner of her eye, Beth saw the groom wink, but all he said was, "Sure...I'm satisfied."

All was disrupted when Tessa swooped in. "There you all are. I came out to check. The bride is doing fine; she'll be ready in plenty of time." She pointed a finger at Garrett. "And no peeking."

"How could I?" Garrett said. "The damn door is locked."

"And it's going to stay that way," Tessa said, then looked at Beth. "You're all alone out here with these muscled heroes." She linked arms. "Come with me; I could use a break and a glass of water."

There was a drink station just inside, and Tessa poured two glasses of water. "One for you." She handed one to Beth, then took a sip of hers. "I'm parched. Wedding preparations are nerve-racking...and I'm not even the bride."

Beth was glad to see Tessa. She was definitely a kindred soul.

"While I'm in the city," Tessa said, "I'm going to check out one of those new restaurants you mentioned...exotic hot dogs or something?"

"I ate there the other day. I think you'll like it. And

the place has the best Manhattans."

"I'm in, then," Tessa said. "Of course, I won't be here long, but I do have to eat."

Beth drank half of her water, thirstier than she'd realized. "I was happy to hear that you were flying in for the wedding."

"I wouldn't miss it. I've gotten to be friends with Marlene, and Garrett is...well, *Garrett*. I like the guy."

"It's quite a company...Stealth is."

"More of a family," Tessa said. "And I wouldn't miss a wedding of one of our own." She tipped her head. "Besides, somebody has to keep these alpha males in line."

Beth laughed. "You're the only woman who could."

Tessa raised her glass. "Damn straight."

It was too early to file into the seats on the rooftop. Beth spotted chairs meant for hotel guests, and walked over to sit down. "My feet are killing me," she said. "I don't wear heels that often."

"I'm with you there," Tessa said, and took a seat. She kicked off her shoes, and Beth did the same. "Ah, that's better."

"Wyatt said you took care of the wedding gift. I didn't know what to get," Beth said.

"I checked the registry and picked something for you. It will be on your tab." Tessa crossed her legs. "But you can donate if you like. Garrett and Marlene sent notes with the wedding invitations that instead of buying a present a guest could donate to the warriors' fund."

"She's known for her work to support veterans. I'd love to contribute," Beth said.

"There will be cards at the reception, so you can fill one in then, if you like." Tessa smiled. She chatted about the Stealth team and told a couple of funny anecdotes. It was apparent that she thought the world of the guys, and Beth couldn't blame her. Her fondness had grown, and she'd only recently met them.

Tessa had an air of confidence that Beth admired. She looked like a woman who worked out regularly, and had an attitude that showed she could take care of herself. It was a unique type of woman who could work with a bunch of ex-SEALs, and Tessa fit that image.

"I better check on the bride, see if she needs anything," Tessa said, and slipped her shoes back on. "Come with me; I'll introduce you."

"Are you sure? I don't want to intrude."

"It will be fine." Tessa headed for the elevator, and Beth followed.

The bridal suite was a hub of activity. If Marlene had wanted Zen-type relaxation before the big moment, she was out of luck. Classical music played in the background, but was drowned out by all the talking. Beth stood back from the fray, not quite sure if she belonged there.

A woman with wavy brown hair and stunning gray eyes wiped a stray lock of hair from her forehead. "Tessa, you're back. Have you seen the garter? She's going to need it in a minute, and I can't remember where I put it."

Tessa grabbed Beth's wrist and pulled her forward. "I brought Beth; she's with Wyatt." She nodded toward the woman. "This is Anna Tucker, the maid of honor."

Skipping the introduction, Anna said to Beth, "Oh, wonderful. Can you refill the water glass? I'm afraid the bride is going to get dehydrated."

Beth was happy to be useful, and saw to the task

right away. She handed the refilled glass to Anna, just as Tessa retrieved the blue garter from a drawer. "It was right where you put it."

"Of course it was." Anna took the garter and the water, then motioned for Beth to follow her. Across the room, Marlene Parks sat on a stool in front of a bay of mirrors. She wore a white bridal robe and slippers.

Anna put the water next to her friend. "Keep drinking water. You won't bloat. I promise." She put an arm around Beth to pull her closer. "And this is Beth. She's with Wyatt."

Marlene Parks was more beautiful in person than in the movies. Her blond hair was twisted up into a fancy style, with a few tendrils escaping down the neck. Tiny flowers were placed inside the curls, and diamonds sparkled on her earlobes. Her makeup was good enough for *Vogue*. Her skin was unblemished, and someone had taken great care with her foundation. Her cheeks blushed light pink.

"Oh, I'm so glad that Wyatt brought someone. And you're just in time."

Beth couldn't imagine what for. Gazing at Marlene, she was star-struck. It was really her.

"I need an objective opinion. I can't make up my mind," Marlene said. "The diamond tiara is gorgeous, and Julie says that she can work it into my hair so it will look good." She turned on the stool to look at Beth. "But I'm not sure. It's seems a bit overdone." She wrinkled her brow. "What do you say, Beth? Should I stick with the flowers or go with the tiara?" She sighed. "I just don't know. And there's a whole team of photographers out there. Whatever I decide, the image will be immortalized."

Beth took a closer look at Marlene's hairstyle.

149

"At least the media won't be at the ceremony or the reception," Marlene said. "That would be too much. This is a special day. It belongs to Garrett and to me, not to the public. Don't you agree?"

Beth nodded.

"But some of the pictures will be published, and I don't want the critics to write about how I was over the top with the diamond tiara...like I'm some princess or something." Marlene waited for her to speak.

"You wouldn't be some princess," Beth said. "You are the bride, and you can wear whatever you choose." *Spoken by a woman who has made a habit of defying fashion traditions*. "Why not wear both?"

After a moment of silence, Marlene grinned. "Can you do that, Julie?" she said to the hairdresser standing by with hairpins.

"It's all a matter of balance," Julie said. "I can make it work."

A lady with blondish hair and the same emerald-green eyes as Marlene mouthed, "Thank you." She sat in a chair off to the side. "I'm Cynthia Parks," she said, "the mother of the bride."

Marlene interjected, asking more questions, apparently willing to rely on Beth, although they'd just met. After a few minutes, Beth relaxed under the glow of the bride-to-be. Marlene wasn't a bit snooty, even though she had every right to be, and before long, Beth was her new friend.

Chatting away as if she'd know Marlene far longer than she had, Beth said, "How did you decide to get married in New York?"

"I've always loved New York." Marlene smiled at her mother. "This is closer, since my mom lives in Boston. And I was out here filming, so I just decided that this was where I wanted to get married."

Anna interrupted. "It's almost time..."

Marlene had more than enough assistance, so Beth excused herself. "You look amazing," she said, then headed for the door, leaving Tessa and Cynthia to oversee the process of getting the bride into her dress.

*****

The wedding was as enchanting as a fairy tale. Bouquets of flowers decorated the rooftop, and soft white clouds floated across the robin's-egg-blue sky. The minister waited with the groom under the arbor. The seats were filled on both sides of the walkway. Wyatt pointed out the groom's sister Adele in the front row with her family, seated next to his parents. And Beth saw Cynthia Parks seated on the bride's side.

"Glasgow Love Theme" played in the background, filling the rooftop with romance. Beth was moved to tears before the procession began. Wyatt's knee pressed against hers, and he glanced over with a barely visible smile.

Garrett Flynn proudly waited for his bride, his blue eyes bright. His expression was filled with anticipation, although he showed no outward signs of nervousness.

The flower girls entered, measuring each step to the music as best they could. Brianna walked with a bounce, as if she might skip or run down the aisle. Her shyer sister Abigail kept pace, but concentrated on each step as she careful navigated the carpeted runway. She glanced to the side as she passed, and Beth gave her a smile of encouragement.

The wedding procession followed, and each bridesmaid entered with a groomsman. As each pair reached the altar, the women lined up to the left, with the men to the right. The last to appear was Anna the maid of honor, with Cooper the best man.

All eyes turned toward the walkway, and Travis stepped onto the carpet with the lovely bride on his arm. Marlene was truly a princess. The tiny white flowers adorned her hair, set off by the sparkling tiara. Her green eyes gleamed, accented with dramatic shadow, and her skin glowed.

The sleeveless white satin dress was overlaid with beaded lace appliqués covering the bodice to below the waist. The skirt flowed around her, with the length of it dragging behind. Marlene stepped past, showing the sheer fabric back of the dress, also adorned with beads and lace. The appliqués cascaded across the gorgeous hemline, creating an enchanting look.

Beth's heart seized when the bride and groom looked into each other's eyes, love's strong bond apparent in their gaze. The ceremony was elegant; Marlene and Garrett each recited a short poem, specially written for their betrothed, then took their wedding vows.

Cooper produced the rings, and the diamond on Marlene's finger glittered in the bright daylight. Joy filled the room, with not a dry eye in the crowd. Garrett pulled his new bride into his arms and kissed her deeply, then the newlyweds turned with smiles to face the audience.

Amidst cheers, clapping, and tears, the couple strolled back along the carpet, to Ray LaMontagne singing the love song: "You Are the Best Thing." Beth watched, swept into the magic of the moment. She dabbed at her eyes with a tissue and rose from her chair, unsure if she should look at Wyatt or not.

It took a moment for Beth to catch her breath. She was in love with being in love, smitten with the romantic couple, and decidedly a convert to weddings—other people's, anyway. Wyatt took her arm, and she risked looking up at him. Emotion welled in his expression, and seeing his heart touched in that way, something changed for Beth.

She hadn't thought of Wyatt as sensitive or emotionally vulnerable, yet he'd been moved by the ceremony. "They deserve happiness," he said, his momentary lapse of self-control passed. But Beth had witnessed what he held inside. A macho, alpha warrior he may be—but he had a heart.

*****

The reception was held in a ballroom with a dance floor. Bouquets of white roses adorned the tables; food and drink were abundant. Beth had several glasses of champagne, and thoroughly enjoyed the toasts to a happy marriage, followed by the cake cutting.

The newlyweds danced their special dance, then the guests crowded onto the floor. Travis and Melanie danced tirelessly, as did Tessa, who had no problem finding dance partners. The twins Abigail and Brianna paired up with Cooper and Rip and giggled their way through a few songs.

For a while, Marlene stuck close to Garrett, then circulated to hug family and friends. Beth grinned at her. "You look gorgeous; the ceremony was perfect. And you have to keep that dress...*forever*." Marlene laughed with her. "Are you off on your honeymoon after this?"

Marlene beamed. "We are...Garrett is taking me to Madrid. Imagine weeks of tapas, Spanish wines, and live flamenco dancing. Not to mention the luxury

hotel suite...where I plan to spend plenty of time."
She gave Beth a quick hug, before heading to the next
table.

Beth accepted Wyatt's offer to dance, even though
it was a slow number. In a partying mood, she didn't
want to miss out. She let him guide her, with one
strong arm around her waist. She draped one arm
around his firm shoulder and took his hand.

Wyatt had removed his jacket and tie, then rolled
up his sleeves. His dress shirt was a little crumpled
now, all the more touchable. His broad shoulders and
well-developed pecs strained under the thin fabric, and
Beth imagined what he would look like bare-chested.

Beth shouldn't let her mind go there, but it was
happening anyway. The faint scent of Wyatt's
cologne, mingled with his own male scent, was a
potent aphrodisiac. She closed her eyes, and glided
over the floor in his powerful embrace.

There was something primal about the encounter.
To all appearances, Wyatt danced her around the
polished floor, but sparks of electricity radiated
between them, making her tremble. Beth had danced
many times before, but not with a man who had such
an effect on her.

She wished...for more than she should wish for, for
more than was possible. This day was special, a brief
respite from harsh reality, and the fantasy had
captivated her. Wyatt pulled her closer, and she
pressed against his chest. The nearness of his body
took her breath away.

Given the opportunity, Beth wouldn't be able to
resist his allure. Wyatt was handsome, charming, and
all male; he was a temptation that she couldn't turn
away from. She didn't want him to let her go, and she
rested her cheek against his chest, her head under his

chin.

One song flowed into another, and Beth wasn't inclined to pull away. It seemed that Wyatt wasn't either. Dance after dance, he held her close, until it felt as though they were one. The noise of conversation and laughing was a din in the background, leaving Beth with Wyatt, in a world of her own.

The dance floor was crowded, and Wyatt bumped into one couple, then another. No apology was given, since no one cared. The dancers were enthralled with the music and with their respective partners, paying little attention to anyone around them.

It was as though Beth was alone with Wyatt in the midst of a crowd. Her heart throbbed to the rhythm of Wyatt's movements, responding to the beat of the music. When he hugged her tighter, Beth nestled against him, wanting his touch.

Wyatt slowed his step; the music and the crowd still swirled about. With one arm around Beth's waist, he held her tightly against him. Then he lifted her chin, until she looked into his soft brown eyes. All seemed to still, except the drumming of Beth's heart.

Then Wyatt leaned down and touched his lips to hers. Beth made a tiny sound in the back of her throat. The feel of his mouth on hers was better than she'd imagined, more intense than she'd experienced before. The unspoken attraction strengthened, pulling her to him.

Wyatt dug his hand in her hair and covered her mouth with his. He took her, drinking her in, kissing her hard. Beth kissed back, needing more, craving his taste. Then he slowed, kissing her long, sweetly yet fiercely. She had no thought of resisting, only fear it would end—that Wyatt's warmth and earth-shatteringly sensual kiss would vanish forevermore.

CHAPTER TWELVE

Wyatt wasn't sure when he'd crossed the line, when fantasy had become reality. The wedding had transported Beth, and he'd sensed her falling under the spell of romance. It had touched him, and where before he hadn't dared hope she'd respond to his advances, he felt her open up to him.

Meeting with friends, being part of a storybook wedding, drinking and dancing at the reception—events had cascaded forward, bringing Beth closer. Wyatt had danced with her, felt her heart beating next to his, her warmth in his arms, and he hadn't wanted to let her go.

He hadn't let her go at all. He'd kissed her.

He doubted anyone had noticed, with all the drinking, dancing, laughing. But Wyatt had tasted Beth's sweet lips, pressed her luscious body to his, and was unable to put aside the feeling. He couldn't forget it, couldn't ignore it. And the worst part was that he wanted her, more than ever.

After the dance, Wyatt had escorted her back to the table. He hadn't spoken of the intimacy, and Beth hadn't either. The rest of the reception had been uncomfortable, until the bridal bouquet had been thrown and the radiant couple escaped to be alone.

Wyatt had taken Beth home. Last night had been awkward and each had retired to bed alone. Wyatt had agonized, wanting to go to her, fighting the urge to wrap her in his arms, to have her for his own.

But it was not to be.

Wyatt had been hired to do a job, and he'd crossed the line, violated boundaries. How was he supposed to keep her safe if he'd failed to protect Beth from *him*? He'd taken advantage of the moment, of her emotional state, and her trust of him.

A killer was after her, Beth's very life on a precipice, and all Wyatt had thought of was his own need. How far would he have taken it if she'd let him? It wouldn't work anyway. Beth would know that too, once she thought about it.

Wyatt's life was with Stealth. Beth's was in New York. And she was an heiress, part of a world that he'd long since relinquished. It was one thing to share a kiss, as deliriously sexy as it had been. It was another to share his life with a woman. He had to get it together, and focus on what was best for Beth.

*****

After a night of agonizing, Wyatt was the first one up, drinking black coffee at the breakfast table and planning the next move. It was time to thwart the attacks on Beth's life, and put her enemies out of action for good.

Beth came out with her hair tousled from sleep, wearing jeans and a fitted sweater. Wyatt wanted to sweep her up and take her back to bed, only this time he'd be with her. But he kept his mouth shut. It was best to feel things out.

"Good morning." Beth went straight for the coffee pot and poured a cup. Wyatt couldn't read anything in her expression. Maybe she wasn't awake yet.

Wyatt went to refill his cup and stood right next to her. The aroma of perfumed soap and a warm feminine scent made his blood heat and his pants tighten. It didn't matter that it was early; his body responded to Beth's nearness.

He backed off and sat down in his chair. Beth sat across from him and sipped her coffee without looking up. This wasn't good. Was she mad that he didn't make a move last night? Didn't she know how much he'd wanted to—and still did?

Wyatt wasn't good with words; he wasn't sure what to say. There was no way to broach the subject, so he'd have to be patient. Beth had to look up sooner or later. Then he could gaze into her eyes, and know.

He was halfway through his second cup before Beth set hers down and looked at him. Her brown eyes telegraphed a multitude of emotions, and he couldn't decipher what she felt. He dared not ask. His gaze locked with hers.

Electricity sparked across the table, as if he still held Beth in the sensual embrace of a slow dance. Wyatt's lips burned to kiss her, and his body was on fire. What this woman did to him was...hot. And all he'd done was kiss her. Taking it further would ignite a flame in his heart that he might not be able to put out.

In a sexy voice, Beth said, "You really know how to kiss."

That was it? His body was amped up like it might explode, and Beth talked about a kiss. Hell, he'd show her kissing. Next time...

There wasn't going to be a next time.

"So do you," Wyatt said. How lame was that? But he was unable to think of any clever response. He just stared at Beth in that sexy sweater, craving to reach underneath and cup her soft breasts in his hands.

The spell was broken when Beth pulled her phone

from her pocket. She glanced at Wyatt. "It's my Aunt Leila. I better take it."

She hit speaker so Wyatt could hear the conversation. "Hi, Aunty, it's good to hear from you."

"I'm glad I reached you, Elizabeth. It's been too long. I haven't been to New York in a while. If I make it there, we'll have lunch."

"That would be wonderful. Is everything okay?"

"I was going to ask you that," Leila said. "I saw the news. Your picture was there, and that woman was wearing your jacket."

"It's a long story."

"I'm sure it is, honey. I'd rather hear it in person anyway. But I'm worried."

"The media thrives on controversy; they blow everything out of proportion."

"I don't mean that," Leila said. "But I am concerned for you, Beth, especially with your father away, because there's no one to keep Martin under control. And I don't trust him."

"You did divorce him, so I'm not surprised."

"I had good reason for that divorce, and from what I can tell, the man hasn't changed."

Beth looked over at Wyatt. "In what way?"

"His gambling, that's what. I know he told the family that he'd given it up. I'm sure he wanted Stephen to believe that," Leila said. "I knew it was a lie, but it wasn't for me to say. I was out of it and I've moved on. I don't want anything to do with him. But..."

"But what?"

"As part of the divorce, we divided the assets, but there was one mutual account that remained. It didn't matter that much to me, so I just left it," Leila said. "But a few days ago, Martin cleaned it out, without a word."

Beth widened her eyes.

"He needed money, or he wouldn't have bothered. That tells me that he's at it again. And if I know Martin, he will be looking for more."

"I understand," Beth said. "I appreciate you telling me. Kyle's running the company now that Father is unable to. I'll be sure to warn him."

"You do that, honey. I worry about both of you. I wish... If only Stephen was in good health. He's the only man who had influence on your uncle," Leila said. "How is your father?"

"There's not much change."

"I'm so sorry. Well, take care of yourself. I'm here if you need me."

Beth ended the call. "That backs up what we already know. Martin liquidated stocks and stole the funds. Not long after, he cleaned out my aunt's account."

"He can't seem to get his hands on money fast enough."

Beth stood up. "I have to finish getting ready. Didn't you say we're meeting the guys before they fly back to LA?"

"That's the plan."

*****

Wyatt and Beth arrived at the Starbucks close to the hotel. The guys had shoved two tables together that were loaded up with coffee, sandwiches, and pastries. Travis waved them over. "Help yourself if you're hungry. I bought extra."

Beth sat next to Coop, and Wyatt sat across from her, then unwrapped a sausage and egg muffin. After a couple of big bites, he said, "Any updates?"

160

Rip slid a black pen across the table to him. "Consider it a gift."

Wyatt smiled. It was a classy pen, complete with a laser beam that activated when the button was pressed. He didn't need to test it, as he'd used one just like it before. It wasn't powerful enough to cut a man in half, like in a James Bond movie, but it wasn't a classroom pointer either. It could do some damage, and at least temporarily blind the enemy.

"In case you need to slow someone down," Rip said. "By the way, I looked into that subway accident. The perp was a hired killer—not a very bright one, at that."

"He didn't earn his fee, did he?" Wyatt said.

Rip chuckled. "Looks like he didn't, since Beth is still very much alive."

Coop slid a large brown envelope over to Beth. "Here are the documents you asked for." Then he leaned onto the table. "Also, I did some digging into your uncle's affairs. It seems his gambling problem is serious. He has a reputation for huge losses, and rumor has it the guy can't pay his debts."

"That could be dangerous," Wyatt said.

"Yep, it can be hazardous to the health," Coop said. "I'm following the money trail. The dude has to come up with more cash soon...a lot of it."

Beth frowned. "He's drained a few sources we know about, but it's not nearly enough if what you say is true."

"He'll need to get his hands on a sizable sum with the way his debts are mounting," Coop said. It impressed Wyatt how much Cooper could find out about a person. It was amazing what could be accessed via computers, especially if hacking wasn't an issue.

Travis swigged his coffee and leaned back. "The question is how Martin will make good on what he owes. Where will he get that kind of money?"

"That's what we intend to answer. It could explain a lot," Wyatt said.

"Well, we're heading back, but keep me updated," Travis said. "I can pull in backup for you...just say the word."

Wyatt held up his hand. "I'm good for now, but I'll let you know if that changes."

"Where's Tessa this morning?" Beth asked.

"She's staying in the city an extra day," Travis said. "I guess she has friends here."

The team left to catch the airport limo, and Wyatt stayed to finish eating. He slipped the gadget Rip had gifted him into his pocket and watched Beth sip orange juice.

"Something has to break loose soon," Beth said. "Jessica has put out some feelers too; criminals are her field. She might come up with some information for us."

"We could use it."

Beth glanced at her phone, then picked it up. "It's a text from Susan. My brother got home last night, and will be in the office tomorrow."

"Speaking of information..."

"Yes, I'm not waiting any longer." Beth stood up. "It's time to pay him a visit. At home is fine with me."

Wyatt called a cab and slipped into the back seat with Beth. He was worried about her. Whoever had tried to kill her would try again, and all he had to go on was a few gambling debts, however sizable they were. Gamblers racked up debts every day without killing anyone.

A piece of the puzzle was missing, and Wyatt

hoped that Kyle could shed light on it. Desperate men did desperate things, and time was running out. Beth had to find out the truth behind all of this, and she needed to find out now.

Wyatt fingered the laser pen in his pocket, glad he'd come with Beth to confront her brother with what she knew. Kyle hadn't struck him as the violent type, but this was a volatile situation. A man could be pushed into actions he wouldn't conceive of under normal circumstances. Wyatt had seen it on deployment, witnessed how a man could react under pressure—and it wasn't always predictable.

*****

The cab dropped them in front, and Wyatt told the driver not to wait. He wasn't sure how long they'd be. The brick building was in a good area, but the place wasn't as pricey as his uncle's mansion. But no doubt Kyle had a good income as Foster's acting CEO.

Beth hadn't bothered to call, as she didn't want to warn her brother about the visit. The large envelope was under her arm. Wyatt rang the bell, unsure what to expect. He'd scanned the environment, but all appeared quiet—just a sleepy morning in an upscale Manhattan neighborhood.

Wyatt glanced over. "Nervous?"

Beth took a breath, then shook her head. "Not really, just anxious to get this over with."

When there was no answer, Wyatt rang the bell again. After a short delay, Kyle opened the door. His longish hair was messy, and he wore sweats. "Beth...Wyatt...I wasn't expecting anyone."

Beth stepped forward. "Can we come in?"

"Sure, come on in," Kyle said, and brushed his hair from his face. "I was out jogging. Just got back. I'd have showered and dressed if I'd known to expect company."

"We're not company," Beth said, walking ahead. "I need to talk to you about something."

Taking his role of good guy, Wyatt shrugged. "It's important."

The living room walls were brick; the floors were hardwood. Out the windows was a view of the Manhattan Bridge. To the left was a sliding door leading out to the patio. Beth took a seat by the fireplace and Wyatt sat on the sofa, adjacent to her.

Kyle kicked off his running shoes and plopped on the other end of the sofa. "So, what's up?"

Wyatt sized him up. Beth's brother was a good-looking guy, late twenties. He had an honest face, and a trustworthy demeanor. Yet looks could be deceiving.

Beth put the envelope beside her, then clasped her hands in her lap. She looked directly at Kyle. "Why do you want me dead?"

Her brother turned ashen. "What in the world are you talking about? Who wants you dead?" He dug his hand in his hair. "Are you crazy?"

Beth glared at him. "I don't think so, Kyle. Somebody is trying to kill me, and I think you know who."

Her brother didn't say a word, but he slumped into the chair. "Will you please tell me what's going on?"

Wyatt leaned closer. "Beth is hoping you can tell us."

When Kyle didn't offer any immediate answers, Beth tossed the envelope at him. It slid across the coffee table and he picked it up. "Take a look at that. It's evidence. I copied it straight from accounting records."

While her brother studied the documents, Beth remained silent.

When Kyle looked up, he said, "I can see that stock was liquidated. Is that a crime?"

"It is if it's unauthorized, and if the funds show up in a personal account." Beth let that sink in for a second. "Uncle Martin accused me of embezzlement."

"He told me funds were missing."

"And you didn't think to question him?" Beth stared at her brother.

Kyle shrugged. "Why would I?"

"Clearly, our uncle manipulated those funds."

"I knew nothing about it," Kyle said, holding his hands up. "Uncle Martin asked me to sell the stock. He said the liquidation was part of a big deal that was in progress. It was vital to the company, and couldn't be revealed just yet."

"And you believed him?"

Kyle sat up straighter. "Of course I did. I had no reason not to."

"You need to understand the position your sister is in," Wyatt said.

"I was accused of wrongdoing," Beth said.

Kyle furrowed his brow. "I didn't know anything about it. I don't track funds through accounting, unless there's cause. I didn't realize the profit went into Martin's account." He paused. "You have to believe me."

"Beth was framed," Wyatt said.

"I can see that the accusation was false. I'm just acting CEO, you know. Without Dad there, Uncle Martin runs things—he gives me directions, and I had no basis to refuse. If I do a good job, I might run the company for real one day."

Silence followed. Kyle looked at Beth. Wyatt

looked at Kyle.

Then Beth let out a long sigh. "Jesus, Kyle, you're my brother. You need to wise up." She stood up and paced the floor. "I can see that our uncle pulls the strings. I get that, okay?"

Kyle looked relieved.

"You aren't the conniving type," Beth said. "You wouldn't have thought of perpetrating lies. That's why I was so confused."

A shadow crossed Kyle's face. "Somebody is trying to kill you?"

"There have been a few attempts," Wyatt said. "I'm staying close to make sure the killer doesn't succeed."

Kyle stood and raked both hands in his hair. "That changes everything." He turned toward his sister. "Do you think our uncle is after you...wants you dead?" He shook his head. "It's inconceivable."

"I don't want you to say anything to him, not just yet," Beth said. "Martin is using you; he thinks you are oblivious to his tricks. Let's keep it that way."

Kyle looked incredulous. "I can't just keep quiet if he's trying to have you murdered."

"Yes, you can...for now." Beth sat on the edge of the chair. "Don't let him know that you've caught on. You might be able to help me."

"How?" Kyle said. "What can I do?"

"Our uncle is up to something...very bad. I just don't know enough yet."

"You need to go the police," Kyle said. "Maybe they can find out who is trying to kill you...at least offer protection."

Beth shook her head. "I don't think so." She looked at her brother. "If I go to the police, Uncle Martin will have some explaining to do. But he's a slimy one. It's too early to reveal my hand. I have to get the goods on him before I go to law enforcement."

Kyle didn't say anything.

"Try to understand," Beth said. "It's my life we're talking about."

When Kyle went over to her, Beth stood up and gave him a hug. There were tears in her eyes. "It's just good to know that you aren't in on it."

Kyle held her at arm's length. "You should know me better than that. I admit that I was duped by a man who is family. But I wouldn't intentionally harm you."

"It's frightening," Beth said. "I wasn't sure where to turn, and if I could trust *anyone*."

Kyle hugged her again, then released her. "He won't get away with it. Uncle Martin has had his issues, and I haven't been particularly fond of him. But this is beyond the pale."

"I have to go," Beth said. "For now, just pretend we didn't talk. You don't know anything."

"I'll do my best, even though I still think you should inform the police."

Beth kissed him on the cheek. "Thanks, Kyle."

Wyatt followed her out, leaving her brother to recover from the visit. Once in the fresh air, Beth said, "Let's walk a bit. I need some space to process all of this."

"We need to talk, figure out what's next. Kyle wasn't much help; he didn't know any more than we do."

"No, he didn't." Beth took his arm and walked down the sidewalk. "But I'm telling you, this deception goes much deeper than I'd thought."

Wyatt liked having Beth on his arm. He drew her closer, wishing he could wrap her in a protective embrace. She'd bravely faced her brother without knowing what she'd find out. It could have gone much differently.

"I'd foolishly hoped that my brother would confess, that he'd trumped up the charges against me, along with my uncle. That he'd explain it all, make sense of the situation," Beth said. "Uncle Martin could have come to him with a plea for pity, asking for money."

"You thought you'd find reassurance that your family wasn't behind attempted murder?"

Beth stopped and looked up at him. "Stupid, right? I mean, what does it take? But I hadn't been able to fully accept the situation. It was easier to hold out believing there was an explanation, that some stranger was after me, not my own uncle."

"And what do you think now?"

Beth narrowed her eyes. "My uncle has set the rules, so he can suffer the consequences. It's time to beat him at his own game."

"And just how do you propose we do that?"

"I might have clung to a shred of hope," Beth said, "but that doesn't mean I haven't prepared for the worst."

Wyatt saw the look in her eyes. She was mad now—heaven help Martin Foster. Whatever situation he'd gotten himself into paled in comparison with what he'd soon experience. Beth was a force to reckon with; she had been since he'd known her. When pushed, she'd push back. And she'd had enough.

"Call a cab, and take me to an internet café." Beth smiled. "My computer is out of commission. And I need to look something up."

Wyatt didn't ask. He'd find out soon enough.

*****

The place wasn't too busy, and Beth took a seat with empty booths on both sides. "Good, I won't have some idiot looking over my shoulder."

Wyatt took a seat to wait, and let her search without interruptions.

When Beth had copied her brother's hard drive, she'd also set up remote access, since it would come in handy later. First she installed a private network, so nobody could tap into her searches. Technically, she wasn't allowed to do that on a public computer, but she'd uninstall it before she left.

There was no need to broadcast the information she was about to access, so she clicked into incognito browsing. The password she'd set up worked, and remote access to Kyle's computer was authorized. Good so far. Now she just had to find what she was looking for.

Only Beth wasn't certain what that was. If Martin operated under the radar, there had to be evidence. Sure, he would have covered his tracks if he could have. Yet there were usually mistakes. More than once, Beth had discovered the undiscoverable in her research. One clue had lead to another, until the picture had become clear.

She needed information that she could use, and it had to be there. Computers left records; that was what they could be counted on for. And Martin had to have made a mistake in his haste to save his own ass. "I'm going to get you...you traitor."

She spoke to the computer, cajoling it to help her. "Tell me what I need to know...come on. I know you have it."

Clicking away, Beth searched for what wasn't obvious, anything that was a red flag or didn't make sense. Hours flew by. Her stomach rumbled and she was parched, yet she wouldn't stop. This was her chance, a way to gain the upper hand. It was all about information, knowing Martin's secrets. And she was positive that he had them.

Then there it was, disguised as a legitimate purchase. Martin had paid an exorbitant fee for a speedboat. He'd been smart enough not to write a company check, yet he'd kept a record of the transaction—an oversight that would cost him, big time. He'd taken pains to hide it, so it must have been important.

There were more details, facts that might prove useful. Beth encrypted the information and emailed it to Cooper. He'd understand it, maybe better than she did. Further searching didn't net anything more, so she logged out.

Beth was hopeful, her morale high. One mistake meant there were more. And she'd find them, every one. Martin's days were numbered. He'd crossed the wrong woman and would live to regret it. She got up and waved to Wyatt that it was time to leave, anxious to fill him in on what she'd discovered. Maybe he'd know the significance of it.

Wyatt pushed the door open, and Beth stepped outside. It was nearly dark; she'd been in there longer than she'd thought. "I'm starving," she said. "You need to feed me."

"Only if you tell me what you found out in there," Wyatt said. "I see that look on your face."

"What look is that?"

"Uh huh...I think you know. Is barbecue okay? I know a decent place a few blocks over."

The mere mention of food made her stomach growl. "Lead the way," Beth said. "If I don't eat soon, you'll have to carry me."

As Wyatt had promised, the restaurant wasn't far. He secured a booth with some privacy, and they ordered ribs. Beth had a beer to go with it, and Wyatt stuck to Coke. Before she could tell him what she'd found, Beth devoured a chunk of bread slathered with butter, and washed it down with a few gulps of beer. "Those ribs better hurry up."

"So...let's hear it. I know you learned something. It's time to share."

First, Beth told him how she'd set up remote access to Kyle's computer, and that it had worked without a hitch at the café.

"You're very resourceful."

Beth took another gulp of beer. "I'm trying to stay alive."

Wyatt waited, sipping his Coke.

"So, get this..." Beth leaned across the table and told him what she'd learned. As she spoke, things became clearer.

Wyatt was impressed. "You got into some interesting records. A speedboat, huh? I don't think your uncle is into sport."

The waiter slid the plates of food in front of them. "Can I get you anything else?" Wyatt shook his head.

Beth stared at the food, then leaned back and put her hands over her eyes. When she uncovered them, Wyatt was looking at her.

"Oh. My. God."

Wyatt didn't move.

"I just realized what was so bloody interesting about my journals, what had my uncle so freaked out." Beth rubbed her face. "It's ridiculous that my journals were taken. I recall every word I've written. I can just recreate it. And by stealing them, it *pointed out* that there *was* something significant in there."

"I'm waiting."

"In the world of shipping, drug smuggling is rampant. Of course, my father hadn't fallen prey to the temptation. I'm sure of it," Beth said. "But illegal goods come into the country via container ships all the time."

Wyatt's eyes lit up, as if he was catching on.

"I sketched about it, drew cartoons of modern-day pirates, transporting contraband. It's drugs mostly; that's big money. A shipping company looking for more profits could get into smuggling. It's done all the time."

"If you say so."

"I researched it, don't you see?" Beth was excited. "I found it intriguing that polite society hasn't a clue. Respected citizens serve as distribution points. It could be anyone, someone you wouldn't suspect."

"I see where you're going with this."

"I've got him; this is it. My uncle must have freaked out when he knew what I'd dug up. I didn't hide it. I'd had no reason to. It was a purely intellectual exercise, cartooning fodder."

Wyatt smiled. "But you hit too close to home. Martin is desperate for money to save his own hide, and he'd have no moral compunction about drug running. It would provide the answer to his woes."

"That's got to be how he plans to get the money," Beth said. "No wonder." She shook her head. "It adds up. It makes sense that he wants me out of the way, but..."

Wyatt finished the sentence for her. "But...that doesn't explain why he wants you *dead*."

CHAPTER THIRTEEN

Beth refused to dwell on the negative. If any moment could be her last, then she might as well enjoy the ribs. This place had some of the best barbecue around. The smoked meat was slow-cooked, slathered in sauce, and served crispy. The pork was succulent on its own, but the tangy sauce made it out of this world.

"I suppose this tastes especially good, because I was so hungry," Beth said, wiping her greasy hands on a napkin. She looked over at Wyatt, tearing the last bits of meat off the bone with his teeth. He had sauce all over his hands and some on his face.

Beth liked to see a man eat, and Wyatt could keep up with the best of them. He'd cleaned his plate, including all the coleslaw, corn on the cob, and the jalapeño cornbread. All that remained was bones, smears of sauce, and drips of butter. A mountain of wadded-up napkins was piled beside his plate, and he tossed them into the middle of it, then shoved it aside. "That was damn good."

Beth grinned. "You want the rest of my slaw?"

Wyatt eyed it, then lifted a hand. "I'm stuffed."

Beth was relieved that she'd had a breakthrough. To celebrate, she'd ordered another beer. Now sated from the food, and relaxed by the alcohol, she leaned back. There wasn't much she could do for the rest of the night. Cooper had the data she'd sent, and Jessica was digging on her end.

Although the plot against her hadn't been unveiled as yet, she'd made significant headway. It was only a matter of time until the rest of the evil unraveled. Then Beth would have her life back. What she needed was a break.

The aura of the wedding lingered. Visions of the bride surrounded by bridesmaids in blue satin were unforgettable. The blue sky overhead, the romantic music, and the warmth of friendship and love had swept Beth into a dream world that hadn't quite vanished.

Beth wasn't ready for the wispy memories to fade. Not just yet. Eventually, life would rise up and pull her back to reality. But there was no harm in delaying that fate. "Do you know what I want to do?"

Wyatt's expression was soft, his dark eyes warm; he might have agreed to anything just then.

"I want to go dancing," Beth said, "with *you*."

"I faked you out, and you think I can actually dance?"

Beth laughed. "You move awfully well. I'll settle for that."

"Do you have a place in mind?"

"Only the club that has the best dancing in New York." For years Beth had frequented the Bell House. It had recently moved to its current location, which was an improvement, since the new building had an added bonus: a working ventilation system.

DJs played eclectic blends of music, with hip-hop, blues, rock, and even reggae. The regulars had bemoaned the relocation, complaining that the club had lost its grittiness. But Beth liked it as much as ever; the music hadn't suffered from the change in venue.

The cab ride was entertaining, as Wyatt talked

more than he had since she'd sought him out in LA. She tried to remember whether they used to talk much, but her youth seemed like the distant past, and she honestly couldn't recall.

Mostly, she'd argued with him on any topic that had been handy. Now she couldn't remember the basis for even one of the disagreements she'd had with him. Whatever she'd found to bicker about couldn't have been as important as it had seemed at the time.

While Wyatt told her about the Navy—what he was allowed to share, anyway—Beth surreptitiously lusted for his fine body. The denim of his jeans stretched over his lean but muscular thighs. His strong arms strained against the sleeves of his jacket. And his longish hair was silky, and gleamed under the city lights as the buildings rolled past.

The air was tense with sexual desire, mostly hers. Beth listened to the sound of Wyatt's deep voice, watched the sparkle of his dark eyes, and when his jacket fell open, tried not to stare at his flat abdomen. He was quite a specimen of masculinity, virile and delectable.

Wyatt was tough, his looks rugged. Yet he had a softer side, one that Beth wished to cuddle up to. She wanted to fall into his warm embrace and listen to the beat of his heart. But for now, she'd settle for a slow dance.

The cab slowed and pulled to the curb. A smile lifted the corners of Wyatt's mouth. "Have you heard anything I've said?"

"Huh? Of course I heard you." Beth rolled her eyes.

"I thought it was men who were lousy listeners," Wyatt said, then took her hand to help her out.

The place was in a former warehouse in Brooklyn. The main hall had an upscale feel, with striking chandeliers and arched wooden ceilings. There was a dimly lit lounge in the front offering a respite from the crowds and music. Beth ordered a shaken cocktail, but Wyatt was on duty, so stuck to club soda.

Although Wyatt was ever vigilant, Beth figured she was briefly out of harm's way. Even while talking, Wyatt had kept an eye out, and had mentioned he was sure the cab hadn't been followed. That put her mind at ease, since there was little likelihood of the bad guys showing up.

Beth grabbed Wyatt's wrist and pulled him over to a table. The music was Green Day's "Oh Love." She nursed her cocktail through the song, but when "Let Yourself Go" came on, she had to dance. Wyatt was athletic and danced fast as well as he did slow.

It was a joy to watch Wyatt's hips move, plus have a chance to stare unabashedly at his solid chest and shoulders. In the dim lighting, he was sexier than hell, and had the moves to go with it. Beth caught glimpses of other guys around her, with black jeans, silver chains, and spiked hair.

On any other night, Beth would have looked to see if one was interesting—but not now. No man compared to Wyatt, with his powerful build and unshakeable confidence. His hero mentality, coupled with constant alertness for her safety, turned her on.

The role of protector fit Wyatt, and held an attraction that Beth couldn't easily put aside. She swirled around him, moving to the beat. His fluid motions and the swing of his silky hair aroused Beth, and heat flooded her belly. She was in deep, but she didn't care a whit.

Beth danced and danced, until her hair was damp

and Wyatt's forehead glistened with sweat. He was tireless, and his strength made her feel...safe. When the music at last shifted to a slow song, he pulled her into his arms and swayed to the tune.

The heat of his body merged with hers, and Beth's responded. Between her legs, she was warm and damp. Her nipples poked against her shirt, and her skin tingled. Wyatt put his hand in her hair and pressed her cheek to his chest.

Beth closed her eyes, letting him guide, while she breathed in his scent, sweaty and intoxicating. He tickled his fingers down her spine, then let his hand rest on her hip. The motion was possessive, controlling, and she wanted more.

It was time to leave, before Beth ripped off Wyatt's clothes and satisfied her desire. It had been bold to kiss at the wedding reception, but she had to go before she took it to the next level on this dance floor. She stood on tiptoes and spoke in Wyatt's ear, her lips grazing his skin. "Let's get out of here."

Out in front, Wyatt put his hand on her back. "I'll get a ride for us."

Beth put her hand on his forearm. "Wait...I have an idea." Likely she'd regret this, but the attraction was too overwhelming to deny. "I don't want to go home."

"Where to, then?"

"A hotel." It was good that it was dark outside, as Beth didn't want him to look too closely. There was still a chance that he'd refuse her. "Foster keeps rooms reserved at the Peninsula for visiting clients, just in case. I can get us in there."

To fend off Wyatt's piercing gaze, she said, "It's safer, don't you agree? We're out of sight; no one followed. Why not keep it that way?"

His dark eyes burned with emotion, and Beth glanced away. She ignored how bad an idea this was. If she carried this through—which she had every intention of doing—would it ruin everything? What if he didn't really want her after all?

But so far that evening, Beth had indulged her fantasy. Ever since she'd danced with Wyatt, she'd wanted more of him. The one kiss hadn't been enough, and having been in his arms, she craved his closeness. She glanced up, but he voiced no objection. He was leaving it up to her.

So be it, then—Beth wasn't going to back down. Not with the tantalizing prospect of being naked with Wyatt. No matter what came, she would have one night, and know the pleasure Wyatt offered. Dancing close, watching, touching—Beth craved intimacy in a way that only Wyatt could satisfy.

In the dark interior of the back seat, Wyatt put his hand on her thigh, and she laced her arm through his. The message she sent was clear, and he didn't ask any questions. The trip to the hotel was titillating, with Wyatt touching her, her anticipation high.

The hotel was in Midtown, not far from Central Park. In daylight, the rooms had good views. But Beth didn't care about that; all she wanted to see was the inside of a suite. She secured the room key, and stepped into the elevator with Wyatt beside her.

She leaned against him, pressed close, and Wyatt wrapped his arms around her shoulders. The gesture was gentle, loving, and her heart melted. When the door opened, Wyatt took her hand, intent on getting to the room.

Beth stepped inside and kicked off her shoes. The curtains were open and the city lights sparkled below. She walked over to look out, and Wyatt followed. He put his arms around her waist, so she rested the back of her head against his sturdy form. Her body was warm with need, and her skin tingled.

She turned in his arms and looked into his eyes, forgetting to breathe. If there was any question whether he wanted her, the carnal lust in his expression put that aside. Wyatt's desire for her was as sexy as everything else about him.

Wyatt looked into her eyes, hesitating a second as if to ask if she was sure. Beth leaned into him, and he lowered his mouth to hers. His lips were soft and warm; she pressed closer. Then he took control and dug his hands into her hair. He dragged the tip of his tongue across her lips, sending a delicious shudder through her.

She arched her back, relishing his hardness, but resisting the impulse to touch. Wyatt's kisses were confident yet tender. He was no stranger to pleasuring a woman, and Beth savored each second. He kissed her deeply, raking his tongue along hers and breathing into her.

Wyatt tasted so good, the embodiment of maleness. He groaned as he devoured her lips, then kissed her cheeks, her neck, and over the curve of her breasts. He was testing, teasing, and arousing her. That he took his time, appreciating every inch of her, moved her deeply.

"I want to see all of you," Wyatt whispered in her ear. Then he lifted her shirt and gazed at her lacy bra. He bent low and bit at her stiff nipples, making her cry in delicious agony. Reaching inside the lace, he cupped her breasts and licked all around, driving her crazy.

Then, impatient with the garment, he undid the clasps and tossed it aside. Bared before him, Beth was vulnerable, yet she trusted Wyatt and wanted him to take her. He kneeled on the carpet and cupped her breasts in his palms, then sucked her nipples with fervor, tasting her with abandon.

Beth raked her fingernails over his scalp and let a few silky strands sift through her hand. With a growl, Wyatt stood and scooped her into his arms. In a few strides, he was in the bedroom and he lowered her to the floor, but didn't let her go. The night lights glimmered against the window, and Beth stood barefoot and half-naked, permitting him to press his hot lips to her skin.

Still fully clothed, Wyatt removed Beth's jeans and panties, then held her close. Her skin against his clothes was immensely sexy, making her swoon against him. He yanked back the covers and laid her gently on the bed, then kissed her all over.

His lips touched under her jaw, along the column of her neck, and between her breasts. He slowed and pressed his hot mouth to her belly, sending spikes of heat to her core. He nipped and licked along her thighs, then pressed his lips over her mound.

Beth panted and moaned, grinding into the sheets. "Wyatt...please."

While she watched, every nerve ending alive, Wyatt stripped off his clothes. He slipped his thumbs into the waistband of his briefs and looking into her eyes, he lowered them. His cock was insanely gorgeous, and Beth reached toward him.

In the shadows of the room, Wyatt was chiseled, his muscles outlined in the low light. He leaned over and briefly pressed his soft lips to hers, then reached in his pants pocket and retrieved a condom. Beth grasped his hot shaft, his velvet skin searing against her palm.

She feathered her fingertips along the sides and rubbed her thumb over the sensitive spot under the rim. Wyatt grabbed her wrist and pulled her hand away; pre-cum dripped over the plum-shaped head of his cock. Deftly, he rolled on the condom then got on the bed with her.

When he straddled her, Beth wrapped her arms around him. Wyatt caressed her breasts and kissed her hard, then rubbed his thumb over her tender spot. She whimpered, writhing underneath him. Her voice came from the back of her throat. "I need you. God, how I need you."

Beth grasped his buttocks and drew him close. The tip of his cock touched her wet tissues, and she pushed up to encourage him. Wyatt's gaze locked with hers, then slowly, he entered her.

*****

Wyatt's cock dipped inside Beth's warmth. He gazed at her porcelain skin, her dark eyes, and her hair against the pillow. She was so lovely, and when he was barely inside her, he nearly came unglued. He didn't want to climax yet; he wanted to experience every second, make it last.

Her pert breasts were luscious, and he flicked his tongue across her stiff nipples. His reward was a feminine sound that she made in the back of her throat. His cock swelled to greater proportion. Shoving, Wyatt slid deeper, and Beth enclosed his heat like a velvet glove.

He held his breath, unmoving, for fear that he would lose control. Beth wrapped her legs around his thighs, holding him tight, and rocked up into him. Wyatt's lower body flooded with heat, his cock ached, and his blood simmered.

Beth dug her hands in his hair, whining softly. The sound of her voice was his undoing. Beth's pleasure excited him, and any resistance crumbled. He stroked into her, increasing his pace, and she gripped him as she matched his rhythm. Sweat beaded on his brow, and Beth's skin glowed. He pounded into her, taking her, not holding back.

She put her feet on the bed for leverage, and he stroked in a steady rhythm, angled just right. His panting drowned out her shallow breathing. Then her body tensed and Wyatt pumped hard into her. With a soft cry of pleasure, Beth shattered beneath him.

She clenched around his shaft, making a shrill sound, trembling in his arms. Wyatt's body went still, his jaw stiffened, then he poured his seed out, giving his all. He slowly stroked until he had no more left, then slumped over her.

Beth raked her fingertips along his spine and kissed his heated skin. Her sensuality stirred him deeply, and he kissed her neck, breathing her in. "Beth..." he whispered with his lips on her check. She turned her head, and he touched his lips to hers, feeling her warmth.

Wyatt kissed deeper, tasting and loving. Then he removed the condom, rolled onto the bed beside her, and pulled her close. She draped one leg over him, and he cupped her round ass, owning her, if only for that moment. He watched Beth as she fingered the thatch of dark hair at the base of his cock, and he already wanted her again.

Beth raked her palm over his abdomen and looked into his eyes. She had a bedded look that turned him on. Her dark hair was messy and her skin was flushed. He admired her narrow curves and stroked her creamy thigh. "You don't know how beautiful you are."

Her dreamy smile touched his heart. Beth put her hand on his jaw, then scooted up to kiss him. She tweaked his nipples and dipped her tongue into his mouth, making him hard. Wyatt flipped her onto her back and straddled her.

Holding her wrists above her head, he sucked at her rosy nipples. "So sweet." Then he released her hands and slowly kissed over her delectable skin. He pressed his lips to her ribs, before working down to her belly button. He held her hips and kissed over her sex, breathing in the perfume of her arousal.

"Bend your knees for me." Wyatt pressed his palms against the backs of her thighs, then buried his face between her legs. He dragged the tip of his tongue over her wet slit. Her whimper encouraged him to continue. He dipped his tongue into her honey-like juices.

Beth squirmed, and her hips rose off the bed. With his thumbs, Wyatt spread her open, unable to get enough of her beauty. He licked her tenderly, and she shuddered. Then he swirled his tongue around her tight clit, relishing her moan of pleasure.

Her thighs fell wider apart, making her open to him. Wyatt cupped her buttocks in his palms and ate of her sex like a special treat. He kissed and sucked and pleasured her, until she trembled under his ministrations. Then he flicked his tongue over her clit and she cried out.

Swirling the tip of his tongue, Wyatt drove her crazy, stopping before she came undone. He wanted her to beg, craved hearing the words. He looked up into her glassy eyes. "Please...Wyatt...please. I just..."

That was all he needed. Wyatt gently sucked, then massaged her clit with his tongue, nipping it intermittently. Beth's body shook, then went stiff as a board. She yelled out and came apart under his caress. He pressed his mouth against her wet sex to feel the waves rolling through her slender form.

When she collapsed on the bed, Wyatt crawled up to kiss her. Beth's lips were pliant, her body relaxed. She purred at his touch. He had taken her to the peak, and soared along with her. He was so turned on that control was impossible.

Wyatt kissed her ravenously, finding any patch of bare skin. Then he fished another condom from his pants and rolled it on. He was hard as steel, and his balls ached. He growled, "I have to have you, honey." Beth pulled him to her, so Wyatt's body covered her length.

"I want you inside me, so badly," she whispered, and his pulse raced.

Wyatt put her legs up over his shoulders and leaned down to suckle at her reddened nipples. Beth grasped his hair in her fists, and pulled him close. He rose higher and angled his shaft into her. She was sopping wet and hot as a furnace.

God, she felt good. Beth was tight, but her lubricated channel accepted the width of his cock. She made sexy noises as he plunged deep, until he was all the way in. Wyatt was afraid to move, for fear that he'd instantly come. Beth clutched his shoulders, and her strong inner muscles closed around his erection like a vise. He groaned, then stroked with ferocity.

Wyatt's arousal spiraled out of control. He gazed into Beth's eyes, falling into their depths, her sexuality swamping him. She pumped up toward him each time he burrowed into her, until he was dizzy with sensation. Then she screamed out his name and climaxed, shivering underneath him.

Before she fully released, Wyatt exploded inside

her. His panting and predatory moans drowned out her soft gasps. He stroked until he collapsed over Beth, and she put her arms around his waist. Breathing hard and with his heart pounding, Wyatt nuzzled against her hair.

He didn't want the intimacy to pass; instead, he preferred to hold on to the moment, with Beth so sweet beneath him. He kissed her temple, her eyelids, and then her soft lips. She responded to him in kind by kissing his chest, shoulders, then back to his lips.

If only he could say the right thing, but what he had with Beth defied description. Wyatt couldn't think or speak, only feel. He slid beside her and wrapped her in a strong embrace, with her head under his chin. It felt so right, so perfect, and he was in no rush to let her go.

It was somehow better that Wyatt had known her for so long, or maybe he'd cared more deeply for her than he'd admitted. He was beyond any delusion that he could resist her. He'd had a mere taste, yet it had whetted his appetite for more.

When Wyatt was able to move, he pulled Beth up for another kiss. She smiled and kissed him again.

"Bath time," he said, making her giggle. He led her to the sunken tub and filled it with warm water. Beth added some bubble bath then he dipped into the water, reaching back for her. Leaning against the porcelain, Wyatt held her to him, with her back to his chest. He rested his chin on the top of her head.

The warm water was soothing, and having Beth in his arms was sensual. For a few minutes, Wyatt languished, wondering if she'd fallen asleep. Then she lightly squeezed his thighs. "Remind me...why didn't we ever do anything before?"

If there had been a reason, it escaped Wyatt. There

must have been something that had kept them apart, but he couldn't bring it to mind. Whatever it had been no longer existed. "I don't know, honey. I can't think of a reason."

Beth gently rubbed his thighs, stirring his arousal. Underneath the water's surface, Wyatt massaged her breasts until her breathing became ragged. With one arm around her waist, he stimulated her, feathering his fingers over her sex, then playing with her clit.

When she spread her legs, Wyatt dipped two fingers inside her, and she gripped as he fondled. With his thumb, he teased her clit, hard as a tiny pebble. She pressed her head against his shoulder, gazing into his eyes as a gentle orgasm trembled through her.

During her climax, Beth was even more beautiful, her flawless skin flushed and her soft eyes glistened with need. She'd given him a gift, the gift of herself, and he cherished her openness. She turned to wrap her arms around his neck and kiss his cheek.

Wyatt was amazingly lucky to have lived as he had, yet still have the honor of sharing such intimate moments. The intensity of emotion that gripped his chest was nearly unbearable. Beth distracted him by pumping his cock and rolling her palm over the head, while massaging his balls in her other hand.

It didn't take much for Wyatt to balance at the edge of release. Her hands felt so damn good. When Beth increased the pressure, it was all over. He gave in to his orgasm with fierceness, all inhibition shattered. Beth's hand worked magic until he came hard.

When Wyatt helped Beth out of the tub, he dried her off and carried her to bed naked. He wasn't nearly finished. He had that night, and he didn't intend to waste it. Snuggled under the warm covers, he pulled her into a spoon position, and she nestled closer.

Beth didn't demand anything of him, didn't ask what it all meant. And that was good, because hell if he knew. Wyatt found her irresistible, and that seemed enough for now. What tomorrow would bring, he hadn't a clue.

Hidden away in a classy hotel, Wyatt could relax and give Beth his full attention, which was what he did. He refused to think of the next day, or the next. There was every reason why this wouldn't work out. Yet it was possible that any barrier to staying together would dissolve in the heat of passion.

Wyatt wasn't an idealist. Life had taught him otherwise. Yet he thrived on adversity, and if there was any way to make Beth his, he would fight to have her. But only if she wanted the same, and that was what he wasn't sure about. She hadn't verbalized her feelings, and Wyatt wasn't about to ask. For one night, it was enough that she'd opened her arms to him and let him love her.

CHAPTER FOURTEEN

Beth had fallen asleep nestled against Wyatt and woke up with his strong arm around her waist. It was still nighttime, and she had no idea how long she'd slept. Safe and warm, she had no inclination to get up. She turned her head and pressed her cheek to Wyatt's skin.

Delicious visions of the evening flooded Beth's mind, making her tingle. Her body hummed with satisfaction and her heart swelled with adoration. Wyatt had become an addiction within the span of a few hours.

She recalled how sexy he looked in the bedroom shadows, with his muscular build and sensual eyes. The attraction was powerful, and her will to forgo the pleasure had been nil. It wasn't her personality to deny such strong temptation.

Beth didn't regret it for a second. Quite the opposite: she wanted more. Being in Wyatt's arms, giving herself to him, had been an experience not soon forgotten. She'd treasure the intimacy, no matter what her future held.

In the dark room, Beth was safe, as she had Wyatt next to her. He was there to guard her, but also, he cared for her. He hadn't spoken of it, but she had been able to tell. No man could be as tender and giving, unless he felt more than attraction.

Yet Beth wasn't counting on anything permanent, as it was unfamiliar. She'd learned to rely on herself, and although it was a comfort to have Wyatt to protect her, that wouldn't last indefinitely. Thoughts of the next few days stirred butterflies in her stomach.

Trepidation about what was ahead made her want to bury her head in the pillow and stay in bed. For a few hours, she didn't have to fight her enemies, or struggle just to stay alive. The threats were distanced, ineffectual as long as she stayed hidden.

But that wasn't realistic. Beth had to face her attackers and win. For at least that long, Wyatt would be by her side. When that was over, even if she did survive, there was no guarantee her sexy bodyguard would be part of her life. Did she even want him to be?

Beth hadn't fallen in love before, and wasn't sure if she dared admit she had. Yet if there was any man who could steal her heart, it was Wyatt—and he had done so. Her eyes were misty over the thought of losing him. She loved him, whether he felt the same or not.

Having embraced heart-stealing intimacy with Wyatt, he was the only man for her. But he hadn't spoken of falling in love, and there was every chance that he wouldn't. He was his own man, a Navy SEAL and protector, beholden to no one. He'd made that clear, even with his own family. So why would he hook up with her, other than for a heated interlude?

Beth must have drifted off, because when she opened her eyes, Wyatt was looking at her. With his head propped on one arm, he smiled. His hair was a mess, dark stubble shadowed his jaw, and he hadn't looked more attractive. He touched her cheek. "Did you sleep well?"

"Better than I had a right to."

"Let's get cleaned up and have some breakfast."

Wyatt leaned over to kiss her, tempting her to skip both.

This time they showered together, and the hot water revived her. Wyatt took the liberty of washing her, leisurely running his hands over her figure, lingering at her breasts. She wrapped her hand over his thick cock, and he groaned in the back of his throat.

Washing was cast aside, and Wyatt made love to her instead. Wet and soapy, Beth was lured into the sensuality. He aroused her, taking charge, until she spiraled into a delectable orgasm. She dropped to her knees and stroked him until he exploded, feeding her pleasure as well as his.

Beth wondered that they were able to keep their hands off each other long enough to get dressed. They wore the same clothes they'd had on the day before, reminding her that she needed to go home sometime. But as long as they were locked away in the room, the romance continued to blossom.

Wyatt was hot, tender, and loving, through actions but not words. Surely, Beth couldn't expect him to make a vow of love after one night in bed. Yet she hoped for it, despite all the reasons it wasn't going to happen. Still, there was no good reason not to enjoy the closeness while it lasted.

The hotel bathroom was stocked with necessities, so Beth and Wyatt were able to get presentable. He kissed her before disappearing to the living room, giving her some privacy. She dried her hair and fussed a bit with it. Styling was hopeless, and she didn't have all her makeup with her.

Looking the best she could manage, Beth joined Wyatt by the windows to look out on the sunlit city. It was another day, another opportunity. She was more hopeful about her prospects; Wyatt had a way of inspiring her. Yet she dragged her feet about leaving the hotel, and was glad when Wyatt suggested room service.

"We're safe in here." Wyatt perused the menu. "What will it be?"

Beth made her selection then sipped coffee while she waited. She checked her phone, but there were no messages. All seemed a bit too quiet, but holed up at the hotel she was oblivious to whatever transpired outside its walls.

Wyatt answered the door for room service and the attendant delivered the trays. He'd ordered the works, including pancakes, sausage, eggs, toast, and fruit. "All I asked for was yogurt," Beth said.

"You need to eat more than that. You'll need your strength."

Unsure what he meant by that exactly, Beth didn't argue. Either he had a morning in bed planned—in which case she would need plenty of energy—or he anticipated new challenges from her uncle's quarter. She suspected the latter.

Beth messed about with her scrambled eggs, nibbled at the toast, and ate most of her yogurt. Her appetite wasn't what it should have been. She fought back anxiety, well aware that her life was as much in danger now as it had been the day before.

It was best not to dwell on it, so she focused on Wyatt instead. There was nothing wrong with his appetite, and he ate his own breakfast, then any food that she'd left. Once he was out of food, maybe even satisfied, he leaned back to finish the rest of his coffee.

Beth's view of Wyatt had shifted; she no longer saw him as only a friend. She was curious about what made him tick. Not every man opted to join the service, much less the SEALs. Yet he had, and now continued to lead a dangerous life. "Aren't you afraid?"

Wyatt raised his brows. "Of what?"

"Danger, the enemy...dying?"

"Fear is a natural reaction; it's what you do with it that matters. I don't let it slow me down or interfere with my decisions."

Beth supposed that said it all. Looking at Wyatt, she sensed his calm, composed demeanor. Even under attack, she'd witnessed his unflappable attitude. He approached any situation with confidence, and expected to win. She wished she was like that.

Only his family had seemed to unnerve him, but she guessed it had been his father mostly. "It's good that you and Jessica are in touch again."

In a rare unguarded moment, Wyatt confided in her. "What happened between my father and me wasn't her fault. She's my younger sister, and I shouldn't have shut her out." He crossed his arms. "I'm her brother, and she counted on me. I went off to join the service and didn't bother to see that she was okay."

Beth noticed the pain in his expression.

"I feel bad about that. Jessica has done well, and I couldn't be more pleased. But no thanks to me," Wyatt said. "My father had been running things when I left, and she could have fallen victim to his dishonest ways."

A narrow smile crossed Wyatt's lips. "Maybe that's why she chose to practice law."

"Her way of fighting for the right thing?"

"Something like that." Wyatt stood up and paced a

few steps. "I also doubted Jeremy. I can't say for sure, but if my sister is correct and he's supporting the right causes...then I have to hand it to him. It wouldn't have been easy to undo my father's debacle."

"Not everyone with money and power abuses it." Beth couldn't believe that she of all people would say that.

"That's true; but the abuses are rampant."

Beth looked up at him. "My father ran the company honestly. I looked hard...and I didn't find any reason to doubt that."

"Your father was the exception," Wyatt said. "He's quite a man, one I admire."

A bit choked up, Beth began clearing the table and discarding garbage. Mention of her father had stirred sadness that she usually held in check. She loved her father so much. The thought of Martin taking over, and of the dark depths he'd sunk to, was disheartening.

Since breakfast was finished, Beth went down to check out, with Wyatt by her side. Melancholy took hold, as she didn't want to leave. As long as she was alone with Wyatt, she could pretend. But such pretense would soon be exposed; he'd go back to being her bodyguard, and any other status would slip from her grasp.

Once in the back seat of a cab, Beth fully expected to be taken home.

"Coney Island," Wyatt said to the driver, his words a surprise but also a relief.

"We're not going home?"

"I'm inclined to stay under the radar a bit longer. I haven't heard anything from Coop yet. He has to be doing some digging, based on the new info you sent," Wyatt said. "I'm tired of being at the mercy of your uncle and his minions. Whatever we face next, I don't want to go in blind. While we're waiting on Stealth, I figured you'd be up for a rollercoaster ride." He grinned. "It will take your mind off your worries."

*****

Beth strolled the boardwalk, which stretched along miles of sand and sea. The beach was packed. The visitors and festivities quickly pulled her into life's frivolities. Wyatt took her on the Cyclone, and managed to get the last seat.

"I'll have whiplash if you put me at the end of this thing," Beth said, laughing.

"What a baby." Wyatt seated her on the right side, in order to buffer her during the ride.

"Maybe riding this rickety wooden rollercoaster will kill me before my enemies nab me," Beth said. The ride packed some serious punch with its drops and turns. Beth looked out over the coastline, just before she plummeted, screaming her lungs out on the way down. It was a bone-rattling thrill ride that clattered around bends, before plunging into heart-stopping swoops.

It got Beth's blood pumping, that was for sure. Wyatt purchased the ride photo showing her expression in the crucial moment before the car let loose into the first drop.

"That was a nice rush," Wyatt said, and Beth punched his arm.

"I got whipped around so much, I nearly cracked a rib."

Wyatt tickled her until she begged for mercy. "I thought you were made of tougher stuff."

"You wish." Despite Beth's whining, she agreed to ride a second time. It was a bit freaky, hearing the car squeak as it made the first hill.

Once it got to the top, she remembered why she'd wanted to ride again. On the descent her stomach did a freefall, and Beth yelled. The jarring ride was scary as hell—then it was over. Returning to the start, with the sound of the old cars clanking on the wooden tracks, was part of the whole experience. Although she wouldn't admit it to Wyatt, she'd loved the ride.

On wobbly legs, Beth took Wyatt's hand and strolled along the planked boardwalk. "I thought I was going to fly right out of the car."

"No chance," Wyatt said. "I was holding on to you."

"Oh, well, that's a relief. Are you going to buy me a Coke, or what?"

*****

Beth hadn't fooled him for a minute; Wyatt knew she'd enjoyed the thrill as much as he had. Flying along the rails had been fun. One drop after the other had his adrenaline pumping. The ancient, rickety look of the cars had added to the thrill.

While Beth had screamed in his arms, Wyatt just laughed. It had been a while since he'd really laughed like that. Holding hands with her now, it seemed like she belonged with him. He had more fun with her than he could recall. Whether some idiot was shooting at them or they were flying over the top of a carnival ride, Wyatt found special joy in being with Beth.

If only the relationship could work out. But the business of living wasn't a never-ending party, and he had to face how different her life was from his. Beth was an heiress, due to come into a fortune—barring her uncle cheating her out of it. Yet money came with strings attached; he knew that better than most.

Wyatt preferred a simple life, and couldn't envision being swallowed up by money and power. He'd vowed to defend and protect, and so he would for the rest of his life. It would be so much better to share his days with Beth; it would be an infinitely richer existence, filled with love.

When had he become a romantic?

Beth hadn't spoken of love. She'd responded to him with passion, and denied him nothing during one evening. That didn't mean she would make a commitment, even if he asked her to. And he shouldn't be considering such a harebrained move. He had no right to ruin her life. He'd handle the hell out of her current situation, then she'd be free. Beth would be the woman she was born to be, wealthy and pampered. Who was he to interfere?

Wyatt squeezed her hand and headed toward a drink stand. "Your uncle won't get away with it, you know. Legally, he's started a battle he can't win. There's no way he's going to ace you out of your inheritance. Once you're safe again, your fortune will be restored."

Beth glanced over, but didn't say a word. Didn't she believe him? "No response?"

"What do you want me to say?"

Wyatt bought the Cokes, and they sat at a wooden table to stare at the ocean for a while. Beth fingered her napkin, then pulled a tiny pencil from her pocket and began to sketch. Watching in silence, Wyatt admired her skill.

She deftly outlined a couple of figures and filled in some shapes. The cartoon came to life. It was Beth screaming her head off at the top of the rollercoaster, with Wyatt laughing at her. It was sweet, and he was touched.

Wyatt grinned. "That's us, I take it. Can I keep it?"

Beth handed the napkin over, with a sparkle in her eyes. "If you wish."

"You are very talented. I know you get ticked off when I say that, but it's true. You are the sharpest woman I've met, and your skill with computers is amazing. Plus, you are a cartoonist, a witty one."

Beth laughed.

"I do what I do best," Wyatt said. "I make the most of my physical ability. But I envy your talent. If I had it, I wouldn't waste it."

"I don't need a lecture."

"Well, you should make something of your life." Wyatt regretted blurting that out, but there was no way to take it back. "I don't mean it that way. I just think you should stop hiding in the shadows. Be proud, and make use of what you've got."

"I'll come out of the shadows when it's safe to do so."

Beth had a point there. As if on cue, Wyatt's phone vibrated. "It's Rip," he said, and took the call. "What's up, man? I'm doing my best to keep Beth out of sight, but I can't do that much longer. Tell me you've got something for me."

"I wish it was better news," Rip said. "I saw the stuff you sent to Coop yesterday, and I tapped into some police connections. Law enforcement out there has their hands full trying to curb the drug trade."

"No surprise there."

"Right, but Martin Foster commandeered several speedboats and put them into action. That doesn't leave much to the imagination. Put it together: the guy needs a ton of money, and drug smuggling pays well."

"You sound pretty sure about that."

"It's not like I got a memo detailing his involvement," Rip said. "But it gets worse."

Wyatt couldn't imagine it getting worse than a potential drug-running conviction.

"The top dog in drug smuggling in the harbor is the Triad."

"Shit."

"Exactly...if Martin has gone into selling drugs, he's tramping on their territory. My guess is that he's messing with some very bad dudes."

"Any suggestions?"

"Watch your ass."

Wyatt ended the call. He didn't like the situation one bit. It was time to quit fooling around and take down the enemy. He went into battle mode, but there was no clear enemy in his sights. Civilian life called for clever, subtler tactics, as he couldn't just gun Martin down.

Beth stared at him. "What did he say?"

"Let's go. I'll tell you on the way back."

*****

Wyatt was on high alert. He kept his eyes peeled, but didn't see anyone alarming. He got Beth home safely. While she showered, he reviewed his options. During the ride back, he'd come up with the rudiments of a strategy.

If Martin had embarked on drug smuggling, then Foster International had crossed the line. Yet he couldn't blow the whistle unless he knew for certain. Wyatt couldn't just saunter up to the enforcement agency and whisper that one of the largest shipping companies in the state had a scam going.

He needed more than that. But what if the feds

were already suspicious, and all Wyatt had to do was help them along? He'd hate to drag the company under. After all, it belonged to Beth's father and was her family heritage.

But if what he suspected was true, Martin had already dragged the company into the mud. The most important thing was to uncover the truth, and to save Beth from the danger that surrounded her.

There was one option, although Wyatt hesitated to try it. For too many years, he'd hardly spoken to Jeremy. His brother had appeared to be his father's boy, and followed his motto: anything for a buck. But maybe Wyatt had been wrong about him.

He wasn't sure he could trust him now, but he might have no choice. Jeremy controlled Mercer Industries, and in his position he had many connections. The oil and gas business was subject to inspection, just like all big companies. The feds had their hands in many pots.

Wyatt couldn't go to the feds, but possibly Jeremy would scout things out. It was worth a try. Wyatt didn't relish the idea of asking his brother for anything, but this had to do with Beth. If it saved her life, it would be worth eating crow. He only hoped his brother didn't hold a grudge.

Jeremy's voicemail was on, so Wyatt left a message. He got a callback within a few minutes. His brother was surprised to hear from him. "I guess you could say I've had a change of heart," Wyatt said. "We're family; you're my brother. And Jessica told me how you've whipping things into shape at Mercer."

"Yes, I know you wondered if I'd turn out like Dad. But you've been away too long. I'm not like him, and I didn't agree with how he managed the company."

"I'm glad to hear that," Wyatt said. "We should go

out for that beer, like you suggested. But I called you because...I need a favor. Beth is in a bind, and she's your friend as well as mine. And without getting into a long story, I can tell you that her uncle is likely operating on the wrong side of the law."

"That's unfortunate."

"Very much so. Here's the thing: I need to determine what I'm dealing with. I suspect that Martin is profiting in the drug market." Wyatt took a breath. "What I need to find out is if Foster is under the feds' microscope. Are the regulators looking his way? Do they suspect the company of any illegalities?"

"You're asking a lot," Jeremy said. "It's not like I'm privy to their internal memos. But...I do have an idea. I can't guarantee what I can find out, but I know a guy who works in the department. We've had lunch, played golf a few times."

Wyatt saw possibilities.

"I don't know if he'll tell me much, but I might be able to find out if the department is showing an interest in Foster. I can use some cover story about our families being close. Stephen Foster has been ill, and I'm curious if everything is being run properly."

"That might do it," Wyatt said. "And Jeremy...I need to know *soon*."

"Yeah, I figured as much."

If Wyatt could get the feds to take Martin down, then Beth wouldn't take the heat. It was a long shot, but that was the best he had. If the agency was already stalking their prey, then all he'd have to do is help them along. He'd figure out a way; Beth's life depended on it.

Beth came out showered and dressed, but pale as a ghost. She walked over and sat on the sofa.

Wyatt couldn't imagine what had happened.

"Jessica called. She leaned on her investigators and they got some scoop from their undercover guys."

"Undercover?"

"Yeah, she says that the only way to find out what goes on, like at Empire City, is to infiltrate."

Wyatt was impressed. "So what did she learn?"

"It fits with Rip's theory. Drug profits would offer Martin a way out, enable him to pay his debts," Beth said. "But his debts are *not* to the casino. My uncle borrowed from the mob."

"That was asinine."

"Jessica has seen it before. The mob holds the money owed over the gambler's head as leverage. It's clear that the debtor can't come up with the cash, and that's fine with them. It's even better, because they gain control of his life...and his business."

Wyatt was disgusted. "Like forcing Martin to use his shipping company to smuggle their drugs?"

"Yes, and Jessica learned from a reputable source that Uncle Martin has obligated himself to the mob. He's screwed up bad this time." Beth's eyes were wide. "If betrayed, the mob will kill without blinking an eye. And the method they use..." Her horrified look said it all.

There was no way to lessen the severity of the situation.

"It isn't just that Uncle Martin fears I'll interfere. I wish that's all it was," Beth said. "The mob is pulling the strings, and if he doesn't come through, there will be retribution."

"That's putting it lightly."

"So...my uncle has a motive for *murder*." Beth's skin was ashen. "He's afraid I'll reveal what I know and block his chance to cash in, get the mob off his back." She let out a long breath. "He will *kill me* to stop that from happening."

Wyatt went over and put his arms around her. He'd be damned if that was going to happen. The assholes had to get through him first, and they'd pay hell trying. He wouldn't let them get to Beth; not a chance.

CHAPTER FIFTEEN

More than once that night, Beth woke up worried about her father. She hadn't seen him since her life had hit the skids, and she felt the loss. Growing up, it had been her father who'd encouraged her, loved her, and had faith in her.

She wanted to give back, show him how much she cared. Regret seized her over the things she'd neglected to do sooner. Stephen Foster had been a gem of a father; he'd adored her and supported her decisions, no matter how far afield she went.

Her father hadn't complained about her radical wardrobe or ideas, and had hired her at the company, despite any protests, including hers. Alzheimer's had taken him so suddenly. She'd been told that happens, but it hadn't made it any easier.

At least he was well cared for, but he had to be lonely—at least during the times he was aware of his surroundings. And who knew what he thought? Just because he couldn't voice it, was unable to find the right words, didn't mean his emotions weren't as real as Beth's.

That morning at breakfast, Beth was overcome with the need to see him. "I'm going to the facility to visit my father."

Wyatt visibly kept his cool. "It's not a good idea. If there's one place your uncle is watching, that's it."

"He's my father," Beth said. "I want to make sure he's okay. I realize that he has quality care, but he needs his family."

"I couldn't agree more. I'm just asking you to wait."

Beth shook her head. "A killer is after me. If I delay, maybe I won't see him again. If something happens to me...this could be my last chance to see my father and tell him how much I love him."

"Just don't say goodbye," Wyatt said. "I'm not going to let anything happen to you, so don't think of this as a last visit."

"I'll get ready, so we can go before you talk me out of it." Beth ached inside. Not a day went by that she didn't think of her father, but the prospect of visiting was bittersweet. More than anything, she wanted to give him a hug and assure him that she was there. The hard part was going to be witnessing his decline. Each time she'd seen her father, he seemed slightly worse.

While she finished dressing, Wyatt commandeered a vehicle. "I'm not comfortable taking a cab," he said. "I texted Travis and he came through for us. One of his connections will have a car delivered within thirty minutes."

It seemed Stealth looked out for the team, and the fact that Wyatt was across the country wasn't a barrier. Beth had heard Travis offer backup, so she'd assumed he had resources. Apparently, they were even better than she'd guessed. The car was a sage-green Corvette with blacked-out windows.

Beth slid into the car, and Wyatt jogged around to the driver's side. He hopped in and scooped the keys from the floor mat. He dangled them in front of her eyes. "Travis has a buddy who's a car buff. The guy is fully retired, spends his time polishing up his vehicles."

"And he let you *borrow* it?"

"Yep, he was in a unit with Travis; they go way back." Wyatt turned the key and revved the engine. "And this ride is bulletproof." He tapped the dash lovingly.

"You mean the windows?"

"Nope, the body too...can't be too careful."

The drive to the outskirts of Jersey City was pleasurable. The car was fun to ride in, and the drive would have been like a date if Beth hadn't known where they were going. Wyatt left the music off. "This car is distraction enough. I need to be able to hear what's around us."

Considering her predicament, Beth wasn't about to complain about his penchant for situational awareness. She could listen to music after she made it through the crisis. The landscape rolled by, but Beth's thoughts were on her father. What would she find?

When the beige stucco building came into view, Beth mustered her courage. It broke her heart that her father was sick, but she wasn't about to abandon him in a time of need. The place had a large porch and was surrounded by a garden. She hoped her father had been able to sit outside sometimes.

Several of the top floors were designated for residents with memory challenges. The ground floor included a large living room with a fireplace, kitchen, and activity rooms. On her father's floor, there was a breakfast kitchen with a hearth and a smaller living room.

When he'd moved in, Beth had learned about the accommodations. Lots of activities were provided for the residents, including outings such as picnics, library visits, even concerts. But her father hadn't been capable of participating for a while.

The private nurse Irma greeted them in the hallway. Despite her motherly look, Beth was uncomfortable around her. There was no basis for it. The woman was highly qualified, and her conservative appearance gave the impression of dedication to her job.

"It's nice of you to take the time to visit," Irma said, then glanced at Wyatt.

"This is Wyatt Mercer. He's a family friend," Beth said. "My father will appreciate him coming by with me."

"Your uncle visited the other day," the nurse said, in a condescending tone.

Beth wasn't sure what the implication was. "I'd like to visit more often." Her uncle had visited ever since her father had moved into the facility. When she'd been on better terms with Martin, he'd often updated her after a visit.

Hearing that her uncle had visited so recently made her skin crawl. Beth didn't want the man near her father. Yet Uncle Martin had managed to obtain a signature from Stephen when he'd still been capable of signing. It gave Martin medical authority, so he could make crucial decisions. Beth hadn't liked that arrangement then, and liked it even less now.

The nurse hovered. "It's time for your father's medication. I'll go in with you."

Beth held her hand up, and Wyatt interceded. "That can wait." His tone stopped the nurse cold, even though she seemed to be fuming at being told what to do.

"I'll be right out here in the hall," Wyatt said, motioning toward a couple of chairs for visitors.

Beth was glad to have a few minutes alone with her father. She pushed the door open and stepped inside. The room was clean and organized. It appeared that the staff paid attention to every detail, with every aspect of living designed to minimize confusion.

Glass-enclosed memory boxes with family photos, jewelry, and a few special trinkets were lined up on the shelves. Beth had been told that seeing personal items helped a resident to find their room. Staff made a point to converse with each resident, in a way designed to trigger memories.

Most importantly, Beth had been assured the staff had been trained to respect a patient with Alzheimer's, which meant not pressing a resident who was unable to summon the right words. That had been one of the first signs of her father's decline: he'd begun using the wrong words for things, even though he was very clear about what he meant.

The bathroom door opened and her father came out. He was well groomed, but looked a bit weak, and his expression was blank. Beth went to him and helped him into a chair by the window, unsure if he recognized her. She pulled up a chair beside him and held his hand.

"How are you doing?" When she got no response, Beth kissed the top of his hand. "I came to visit. We can talk for a while."

Stephen Foster had been a robust, athletic man. He was still handsome, but had lost weight. He appeared more fragile, and his skin was pasty. "I miss you, Dad."

That seemed to get through. Her father looked into her eyes and mouthed, "Elizabeth."

Tears welled in her eyes. "Yes, it's me. I've come to see you. I love you so much."

Beth held her father's gaze. His eyes were expressive, and she sensed he had more to say. Maybe he couldn't find the words. "We can just sit, if you like. I'm just glad to be with you."

Turmoil swirled in her father's expression, and Beth squeezed his hand. "Whatever you want to say, I'm here. You know I'll understand."

A spark of hope was visible in the depth of his dark eyes. He lifted Beth's hand and pressed her palm to his cheek, so she leaned closer. "Drugged," he said, watching her reaction as if to be sure he'd used the correct word.

"Yes, you have medication to help you," Beth said. "The nurse has it; I can get her." Before she could move to get up, her father gripped her hand and shook his head.

Alarmed, Beth waited for him to speak.

"Bad...please...no." Her father's eyes drooped, as if he might pass out. His message hadn't been clear, but he'd been visibly upset.

Her father had memory issues, and difficulty putting the right words together—but he behaved as if he'd been sedated. She touched his shoulder and his eyes opened, but his distress was evident.

Beth remembered the photo albums he kept in the drawer. The doctor had mentioned that good memories could assist her father. She went to the side table, but the top drawer was empty, so she checked the next one down. There she found one of the albums, and lifted it out.

Unlike the rest of his belongings, the album was in disarray. A few pictures had slid out of the sleeves, and some papers stuck out behind the last pages. It looked like her father had frantically flipped through the book, with some intention other than viewing a cherished photo.

Beth sat on the bed and flipped to the back to see what the papers were. Her breath caught and her pulse raced. The papers were notes...in her father's handwriting. He'd written with effort, and the letters were ill formed, the lines wavy.

She lifted a couple of them out and stared. The messages were ones of desperation. *No, bad, drugs* were scribbled in haste, as legibility hadn't been of a concern. Then her heart stopped. The bottom note said only: *please Elizabeth*.

Beth's concern escalated. Her father had managed to hide the notes, with the hope that she'd find them. She yanked the drawer all the way out, looking for any other message. A few pills with a powder-blue coating rolled to the front. She scooped up the loose pills and held them in her hand.

Fragments of thought pieced together, like a collage blending into focus. Her father had been drugged, yet somehow he'd dumped a few pills in the drawer to avoid taking them. In his incapacitated state, he wasn't able to fight back. He certainly couldn't walk out.

So he'd done the best he'd been able to. In a lucid moment, he'd scribbled notes and stuffed them in the album, hoping that Elizabeth would find them. Surely she was the only one who cared enough to look through the album. But what if she hadn't?

And how long had this been going on? No wonder her father had seemed worse, too frequently sleeping or passed out. What exactly was the medication he was on?

Beth had to rescue him; she wasn't sure how bad off he was. But she could hardly just walk out with him. Wyatt might be able to carry him out, but that wouldn't be good. She had no right to make medical decisions for her father. The authorities would have every right to bring him right back to the facility.

There had to be a way.

Beth kneeled beside her father's chair and held the notes up. "I read your messages," she said in a low voice. A glimmer of understanding shone in his eyes. "I'm coming back for you, I swear." Tears rolled down her cheeks. "Hang on a little longer. I'll get you out of here."

Leaning down, Beth gave her father a big hug. She didn't want to leave him, but she had to take care of what was going on before the situation got any worse. She stuffed the pills in her pocket and dried her eyes with a tissue. Taking a deep breath, she yanked the door open.

The nurse was at her station with her back toward the hall. It looked like she was on the phone. Wyatt stood up, calm as ever. Beth grabbed his arm. "Get me out of here, *fast*."

Wyatt didn't make a scene or ask what was going on. He swept her down the hall and into the elevator, then stabbed the button for the lobby. His look conveyed that he was prepared for anything.

Beth dared not speak, as she had no idea if the place was bugged or not. Once outside, she dashed to the car with Wyatt beside her. He shoved her in and took the driver's seat, then locked the doors.

"My father's been drugged." Beth couldn't catch her breath. "I mean...it's not the right drug. He's sedated. He wrote these messages." She held up the scraps of paper.

"Jesus."

"I stole some of the pills. He stashed them in the drawer." Beth dug into her pocket and retrieved the blue pills. "I have to do something. I have to help him."

"Can you kidnap your own father from a medical

facility?" Wyatt said.

"I thought of that. It won't work. He'd be hauled back and drugged more. Plus I'd be detained." Beth banged the back of her head against the seat. "Then how would I help him?"

*****

Wyatt saw her distress, and struggled to come up with an immediate answer. But he was at a loss. His instinct was to go right back in and bring Stephen out. If need be, Wyatt could fight his way out. But that method was doomed, and offered no more than a temporary reprieve.

"There might be a way," Beth said. "I just had an idea."

"Let's hear it."

"My brother can help. It's the least he can do," Beth said. "The company pays the tab at this place. My uncle might think he calls the shots, but money talks. I don't have a right to make a change in my father's care, but since Foster is footing the bill, Kyle can make demands."

"That might work."

"It has to," Beth said. "I'm desperate here. I need to get Kyle over here immediately, to stop the nurse from giving my father the wrong medication."

"Hold that thought," Wyatt said. When they'd arrived, there had been several other cars in the parking lot, all family-type vehicles. He'd committed the locations to memory. Each was parked where it had been. Only there was a new arrival, and the vehicle didn't fit—nor did the guys sitting in it.

A smart mobster would have driven a car that didn't stand out. But so far the gangster recruits had botched job after job, and were set to do so again.

Wyatt had heard the cold-air intake when he'd stepped outside. The noise was coming from a souped-up Buick Regal.

It was a model that gangsters considered cool, and whoever was driving the silver one probably thought it made them invincible. But the car stuck out, all revved up and ready to race. Well, he'd see just how fast their ride really was.

"What now?" Beth glanced around.

"Hold tight, honey. There are a couple of idiots interested in us. I need to lose them." Wyatt put the car in gear and pulled forward toward the exit. He didn't look their way; he didn't need to.

As soon as he pulled out onto the street, the Regal followed. Wyatt wondered what their plan was, or if they even had one. Did they think that they could run him off the road and take Beth, or make it quick with a drive-by shooting?

For starters, if they intended to gain the advantage, they shouldn't have given him so much warning. This was going to be fun. There was only one thing Wyatt had to be careful of; he didn't want to ding the pristine Corvette he was driving. Travis wouldn't appreciate that.

On the main road, the bad guys hung back to keep Wyatt from spotting them. There were a few other cars on the road. Maybe his pursuers would see the odds weren't in their favor and give up the chase before it started. But no such luck.

Traffic ebbed and flowed, then the Regal edged behind, too close for comfort. It was a maneuver that put them in position to pull to the side of the Corvette. No way was Wyatt going to give them a clear shot at Beth. He was not in the mood to test the bulletproof windows.

He gave the Corvette some gas, and the finely tuned engine responded. The guy driving the Regal revved the engine and peeled out, trying to keep up. Somebody had gone to a lot of effort to make that car serviceable. Wyatt was anxious to see if it had the guts to back up its showy exterior.

Leaning into the accelerator, Wyatt let the Corvette fly. It was a giddy feeling, and if there hadn't been mobsters threatening, he would have thoroughly enjoyed it. He looked over at Beth. She had her seatbelt securely fastened and her eyes glued to the road.

Wyatt had to give the Regal some credit, as it passed several cars and quickly showed up in his rearview mirror. Too bad the driver was a moron, because the jacked-up vehicle was impressive. Since Wyatt had been born and raised in New York, he knew the roads well.

Likely the dudes behind him weren't locals—just a guess.

The Holland Tunnel was behind him; he'd lured the Regal away. He just had to turn around and get to the entrance before they did. Then they'd be toast. He cruised down the street, driving away from the route to the tunnel with the bad guys on his ass.

"Put your feet up on the dash and hold on to the headrest," Wyatt said to Beth. "Brace yourself."

With a glance in the rearview to see that the gangsters were still paying attention, Wyatt nudged the Corvette to thirty-five miles per hour. With one hand on the steering wheel, he did a maneuver with the emergency brake. The rear wheels locked, and the tires slid with a loud squeal. Yanking the steering wheel to the right, followed by a hard left, he rotated the Corvette in a semicircle.

Releasing the emergency brake, Wyatt dipped through an opening in the street divider, hit the accelerator, and passed the Regal, going the other direction. He increased his speed and headed for the Holland Tunnel.

"What was that?" Beth said, lowering her feet to the floor.

"A thing of beauty," Wyatt said, glancing at her. "It's good to know I'm not out of practice."

"Now I know why I take cabs."

By the time the mobsters figured out what happened and managed to turn the Regal to head in the right direction, it was too late. Wyatt rolled into the tunnel and looked behind him. His unworthy followers were many cars back, and traffic was stacked up in every lane, edging into the tunnel.

"We lost them," Wyatt said, turning toward Beth. "Are you okay?"

"I think so." Beth put her hand on his thigh. "Just get me out of this tunnel, so I can call my brother."

"And I need to text Travis to find out where to get those pills analyzed. We need to find out what your father has been doped up with." He looked over at Beth, but she was focused on the traffic. He had to get out of this damn tunnel, but short of making the Corvette fly, he was going to have to wait. Unfortunately, his patience had worn thin.

CHAPTER SIXTEEN

When Wyatt exited the tunnel, there was no sign of anyone following. The lanes were clogged with traffic, so there was no chance of the Regal edging ahead. As soon as they were through, Wyatt leaned on the Corvette's accelerator to speed through the streets, taking an alternate route to avoid traffic.

"Are they following us?" Beth said, glancing back.

"No, we're clear." Wyatt didn't like seeing her distressed. "So before our company showed up, you were telling me about getting Kyle involved."

"Yes, I'm just so shocked at my father's condition, but he's out of my grasp. I don't have any say about his health or safety."

"But Kyle does?"

"Legally, my uncle makes the decisions, but the facility has to listen to the financially responsible party. My father set up a medical program for the principals of the company. He did it long ago, because insurance was inadequate."

"That was smart."

"Yes, well, now his bills are covered. But as much as Martin might think he runs the show, he doesn't...not completely. My brother is acting CEO, and oversees the accounts payable department," Beth said. "He has the authority to see that my father's care is up to par."

"So he can intercede, temporarily."

Beth sighed. "That's my hope. I suppose if Foster didn't pay the bills at all, the care facility would kick my father out. But that's no good, because Martin would just have him moved to some state hospital. That would be much worse."

"You've thought of everything."

"Not even close—I'm desperate here, and grasping at straws," Beth said. "But I don't have any better ideas. Do you?"

Wyatt smiled. "All of my ideas involve way more drama." He could get Stephen out of there by force. In a situation like this, Beth's strategy was more likely to be effective—and had the best chance of improving her father's circumstances.

Surveillance of the care facility hadn't been surprising. It had been a given that Beth would visit her father, and had only been a matter of time. But the facility was rather out in the open, and a van with blacked-out windows would have stuck out more than the gangster mobile had.

That meant one thing to Wyatt: there was someone on the inside. Likely the nurse had been instructed to report in when Beth showed up. It hadn't taken long to get some guys on the scene.

Beth looked at him. "What are you thinking?"

"That we need to find out what those pills are." Wyatt pulled into an open parking space, to figure out where to go next.

"What do you have in mind?"

"I'll know in a second." Wyatt reached Travis, and filled him in on the latest events, while Beth watched him intently.

"I can hook you up with someone," Travis said. "The forensic lab we use has a location in the city. Fred Grimes is a sharp tech."

LETHAL PERIL

"We need it done fast, though."

"I'll let him know it's a priority," Travis said. "Here's the address."

Wyatt made note of where to go and ended the call. "I have a place that can analyze those meds," he said to Beth. "We'll go straight there."

The office was north of Kings County Hospital, and it was a bit of a drive, but not bad. There was an adjacent multistoried parking structure, so Wyatt took the first open spot. He took Beth's hand, then headed for the lab.

The reception area could have been any doctor's office, with its out-of-style furniture and linoleum flooring. One difference was the lack of magazines, but it wasn't likely that patrons waited around. It was more of a drop-off arrangement.

When the door opened, Wyatt got a quick view of the lab techs, wearing goggles and white coats. There were melamine tables evenly spaced down the long room. The vinyl flooring, acoustic ceiling tiles, plus various types of equipment, tubing, and wires completed the sterile look.

A middle-aged man with his goggles dangling around his neck approached. "You must be Wyatt...Travis's guy?" They shook hands. "I'm Fred."

"How soon can you have this done for us?" Travis motioned for Beth to hand over the pills. "We need these analyzed...like, yesterday."

"I got that it's urgent, but the best I can do is by tomorrow morning. Sorry, but you aren't the only emergency."

"What time do you open?"

"I'll be in by seven, and I should have an answer for you by then," Fred said.

Wyatt would have liked it sooner, but it looked like

217

that wasn't going to happen. "We'll be here."

When they stepped outside, Wyatt said, "I'm not taking you home...yet. Staying out of sight has been effective. Plus, we might as well stay in Brooklyn, since we have to be back here so early."

"I'm game." Beth looked up at him and wrinkled her nose. "I can't keep wearing these clothes, though. So if we're doing another overnighter, I have some shopping to do...for both of us."

Wyatt needed a change of clothes too. "Okay, we'll hit up the mall and see what we can find."

"Then for tonight, the Sheraton is close. Will that work?"

"Yep, it's not far," Wyatt said. "And I don't think anyone is going to be looking for us in Brooklyn."

The mall had plenty of stores, so purchasing new outfits didn't pose a problem. Beth got into shopping, and bought new shoes and a hat too. It distracted her, so Wyatt had no objection.

After she made her purchases, Wyatt took her to dinner. He didn't bring up any subjects that were a downer; Beth would have to face all that soon enough. He was content to eat in peace, something Beth had experienced too little of lately.

It was different, to just sit and enjoy a woman's companionship, without the need to talk. Wyatt liked Beth's company. He didn't like the prospect of flying back to LA when this was all over, and not seeing her again. And he would certainly miss her in his bed.

Beth excited him like no woman had, and he wanted much more of her than he was likely to have. She was everything he needed, and he wanted to spend his life with her. Yet he hadn't allowed his thoughts to go there. It would only make it more difficult when the time came to part.

The truth was that he loved Beth. Yet he hadn't told her. He had his reasons, and at the top of the list was that he didn't want her to feel obligated. He was her protector, her savior from the clutches of the enemy. But he did so out of duty, and from caring what happened to her. She didn't owe him a damned thing.

After the meal, Wyatt took her to the Sheraton for a good night's rest. The security of the suite put his mind at ease. He'd requested a room that was equidistant between the elevator and the fire exit, providing two escape routes. And he'd chosen one that wasn't near the stairwell, as it provided too much advantage to any potential abductor.

Wyatt flipped the safety latch on the door, then did a last check for messages. He removed his gun and holster, got undressed, then waited for Beth to come to bed. She emerged and walked over to him, wearing a hotel robe. In the low light, she looked like a goddess.

Her dark hair had grown out some, and it fell in short waves around her face. Wyatt looked into her eyes, pushing all thoughts of sleep aside. When she dropped the robe and got into bed naked, he stripped off the rest of his clothes and slid in next to her.

Beth smelled of roses and soap. Her skin was like satin, her hair silky. Wyatt drew her close, and the feel of her soft lips drove him to distraction. He may not be able to spend his life with her, but he sure as hell was going to enjoy every night they had together.

Wyatt made love to her, slowly and tenderly, telling her with his caresses how much he cared. Maybe she knew, because Beth responded with passion that left him weak in the knees. He took her more than once, unable to get enough. And she seemed to feel an equally deep need, reaching for him again.

When Beth finally nestled into his arms and drifted to sleep, Wyatt buried his face in her hair. God, how he loved her. He had no assurance of how much longer he'd be with her, but what he wanted most of all was for her to be happy—he'd make sure of that.

*****

The next morning, Wyatt was at the lab when Fred unlocked the door. He held Beth's hand and squeezed it for reassurance. Whatever the news was, he feared it wouldn't be good.

In a private room, the lab tech reviewed the results of the analysis, highlighting important details. "There are medications that can mimic dementia."

Beth scooted to the edge of her seat and clasped her hands in her lap.

"When patients have memory issues, they'll often ask their doctor if it's something they're taking," Fred said. "And sometimes it is."

The lab tech waited a moment, then went on, "The side effects of various drugs can interfere with attention, memory, language, and cognitive faculties." He took a breath. "An examining clinician might incorrectly suspect the presence of dementia."

Wyatt wished he'd skip the technical jargon and get to the point.

Fred looked at Beth. "The medication your father was given made it appear that he had Alzheimer's...when likely he didn't." He leaned on the desk. "It's not my place to accuse, but my professional opinion is that it was intentional."

Beth gasped.

The tech handed over the test results, including the name of the drug. Wyatt looked over Beth's shoulder, but didn't recognize the unpronounceable name of the medication.

"That is a potent drug. I'm quite familiar with it," Fred said. "With your father's condition as you describe it, a doctor would have no basis to prescribe this medication. It would be harmful, as I'm sure you witnessed."

Beth gripped the paper. "If the meds made him feel bad, couldn't my father have stopped taking them...or just refused?"

"Not really...because it's a heavy sedative. I doubt he was cognizant of what was going on, except in rare moments."

Wyatt understood what the tech said, but he wanted to hear it stated...just to be sure. "So, if I have this correctly, it appears that the drug was administered to Stephen Foster in order to give him the symptoms of Alzheimer's."

Fred hesitated before he spoke, his tone cautious. "I would say so." He looked at Wyatt. "I'm only sharing that insight due to your position here. If you are to protect Mr. Foster, as well as his daughter, you need to be aware of the severity of what you're dealing with."

"I appreciate your honesty," Beth said. "We'll decide what to do from here."

Once outside, Wyatt said, "It's malpractice, and considering the doctor prescribed with the intent to harm, it's a crime."

Beth wrapped her arms around her waist. "My father started taking medication for back pain. Uncle Martin was concerned about him, so sent him to his doctor for an examination."

"Let me guess: Martin's doctor prescribed the blue pills."

"I'm sure my uncle paid him well to continue refilling that prescription."

Wyatt could tell that Beth was shocked by the magnitude of the evil, the heartlessness of it all. He'd come in contact with cold-blooded killers before, so had taken the news better. Yet it disgusted him that Martin was such a soulless creature.

He took Beth to the closest café for an espresso, allowing her a few minutes to recover. The place was busy, so they sat on stools at the window seating.

"Martin paid off the doctor and orchestrated your father's medical care. He ensured that Stephen would be deemed incompetent, so it would be easy to take control of the company."

"And my brother didn't suspect a thing," Beth said. "I didn't either, for that matter." Her wide eyes revealed the sadness she felt. "I *believed* my father had that dreadful disease." She bit her lower lip. "My uncle harmed his own brother...for *money*."

"It does boil down to greed."

"Do you think that nurse Irma is in on it?"

Wyatt rolled his shoulder. "It doesn't matter too much now, but I suspect she's the one who tipped off the mob, and let them know that you'd come to visit your father."

"My father is a victim," Beth said. "He doesn't deserve any of this."

Wyatt reached over to squeeze her hand.

"It's appalling. My uncle has gone too far," Beth said. "He knew my father wouldn't back him up in his underhanded schemes, so...he made certain he was out of the way."

"And he's doing his damndest to get you out of the

picture too."

Beth stood up. "I have to get to my brother, so he can help. We have to rescue my father as soon as possible. I can't bear the thought of him all drugged up and semiconscious, hardly knowing where he is."

Wyatt pushed the door open for her, and they headed back to the car. Martin's intricate ploy was no longer hidden, his activities no longer executed in the shadows. No doubt he would soon be aware of that turn of events, and his fight for survival would escalate.

That would make him all the more deadly. Wyatt had to make sure the man was stopped before he did any more damage. But first, he had to help Beth save her father.

*****

It was late morning when Beth and Wyatt strode into Foster International. The office seemed unusually quiet. A few staff tapped on their computers. The conference room was empty, and the coffee room as well.

The atmosphere at the company was as dour as Beth felt. She wished she'd run into Martin and put an end to all of this. As furious as she was, likely she'd rip his eyes out before he knew what hit him. But such was not to be. The slime bag wasn't at his desk.

Kyle's office was empty, and his desk was orderly. It appeared that he hadn't been in yet. Hopefully, he hadn't been sent to negotiate with another out-of-town client. "He has to be around," Beth said, and Wyatt nodded.

Susan was at her desk, going through some paperwork. "Beth, it's been ages." She glanced at Wyatt and smiled.

"I know, and I'm sorry about that," Beth said. "We are overdue for lunch. But today...I'm on kind of an urgent mission. Is Kyle in? He's not in his office."

"I haven't seen him yet," Susan said. "Normally he's in early, unless he has a meeting. But there's nothing on the schedule. I tried to reach him, but just got his voicemail." She shrugged. "I'm sure he'll show up."

"Okay, thanks," Beth said, and headed for the door. "I'll call you...promise."

Wyatt followed her down the hall, while Beth called her brother. "Just voicemail," she said. "I'm worried. This isn't like Kyle."

"It doesn't make sense."

"Maybe he's still at home, although I don't know why he would be this late in the morning," Beth said, then frowned. "Unless he's sick, but I can't imagine he would be so ill that he couldn't call in."

"Let's go," Wyatt said.

*****

When Beth arrived and stepped onto the sidewalk, the neighborhood was quiet. Wyatt hopped out and followed her up the walkway. She was anxious to find her brother and be sure he was all right. It was weird for him to be out of touch.

Wyatt stepped up to the door, then gave Beth an odd look. The door was ajar. He rang the doorbell, but when there was no response, Wyatt motioned for her to stand against the wall. Crouching, he withdrew his gun and held it in front of his body.

Beth's heart pounded. She could hardly breathe, unsure what Wyatt would find inside. A twinge of fear went up her spine. What if there was an attacker hiding and waiting? She couldn't bear the thought of

Wyatt getting injured. And what the hell had happened to her brother?

After what seemed like an eternity, Wyatt returned. He opened the door and waved her in. "There's nobody in here."

The place was a mess. The upscale condo looked like a war zone. Beth put her hand over her mouth. "Oh, my God...where is Kyle?"

"I don't know," Wyatt said. "But he had visitors, and it seems they were after something."

Beth looked around, trying to figure out what anyone would want with her brother, or what he had that was of so much interest. But she came up dry. She had no clue what had happened here.

Wyatt methodically searched along with her. She marveled at how calm he seemed under duress. Books were in disarray on the carpet, tables overturned, and a vase was shattered on the floor.

"I can't tell if the crooks were actually looking for something or just creating chaos," Beth said. She feared the worst for her brother. Too many times, she'd narrowly escaped with her life. Would he be as lucky?

Wyatt called to her from down the hallway, and she found him in the library. It was as much of a disaster as the rest of the house.

Reaching high, Wyatt ran his finger over the top of an oak bookcase, then followed the seam along the side next to the wall. Beth watched as he gripped the sides of the case, and pulled. The right side moved, and the bookcase swung away from the wall.

Beth moved closer. Behind the bookcase was a steel door. "What the...?"

"It's a hidden room," Wyatt said. "We need to get inside." He pointed to the security keypad. "Any guesses?"

Beth shook her head. "I don't know what he'd use for a passcode, unless it's the same as he used on his computer. But I don't think he's that clueless."

Wyatt eyed the touchpad. "His laptop is on his desk, so whatever the intruders wanted probably wasn't on his hard drive. But you can check; maybe the password is stored."

Beth retrieved the computer and put it on her lap. She tried various files and records, but didn't find anything that looked promising. Then she remembered Kyle's filing system. She'd thought it was confusing, but he'd persisted in using it, claiming that he could find what he wanted.

Clicking around, Beth discovered a personal file labeled generically as *New File*. What better way to hide something than to disguise it as unimportant? She gave it a try and located a code. "Try this," she said to Wyatt, and read the sequence.

The keypad beeped each time the letter or number was correct. Wyatt tapped in the code, and there was a loud click, like a metal bolt opening. He held up his hand for Beth to stay back, then slowly opened the tall metal door.

Wyatt stood in the doorway, and Beth came up behind him. Inside, slumped against the wall, was her brother. She rushed over and dropped beside him. "Kyle...are you okay?"

Her brother looked dazed, and he rubbed his hands over his eyes. "You don't know how glad I am to see you. I didn't know if it was safe to come out."

Wyatt extended a hand. "Here, let me help you up."

Once Kyle was comfortable on the sofa, Beth got him a glass of water. She waited patiently for him to snap out of it. Her brother leaned his head on the cushion and stared up at the ceiling.

"What happened? Are you hurt?" Beth sat on the sofa next to her brother.

Kyle sat up and raked his hands through his hair. "I could have been killed." His eyes were glassy. "Thank God for that room."

"I didn't know it was there," Beth said. "When did you have that put in?"

"The previous owners installed it. I guess it's a panic room, and it's something I wouldn't have imagined I'd need." Kyle let out a long, slow breath.

"I was getting ready for work, and I heard noises. I was here in the library, getting a reference to take with me," he said. "I heard someone break in, and when I peeked into the hall, I saw two men wearing ski masks."

"Jesus," Beth said.

"I quickly ducked into the panic room and pushed the button to close the bookcase from the inside. And not a second too soon, I'm sure." Kyle shook his head. "That room is soundproof, and I had no way of knowing what was going on out here."

"I'm glad we found you," Wyatt said. "No telling how long you'd have been barricaded in there otherwise."

"I couldn't believe it was you," Kyle said. "I thought I was dead. I prayed they'd assume I'd fled, but for all I knew, those men were waiting. And the walls of the room are steel reinforced. My cell phone didn't work. I was trapped."

Beth hugged her brother. "What a terrible ordeal."

"I don't know who they were, or what they wanted from me," Kyle said.

Wyatt paced the carpet. "I have an idea, but your

sister needs to tell you something first."

Kyle furrowed his brow. "Does it have something to do with the threats against you, Beth?"

"It's more than just me. Father is in danger too. And now you." Beth proceeded to tell her brother about her recent discovery. "Uncle Martin will do anything to get what he wants. Our father is being held captive, drugged into incoherency, so he can't fight back."

"This is a disaster," Kyle said. "But does this mean that Father isn't ill at all?"

"It looks that way," Wyatt said. "We won't know for sure until he gets off the meds."

"And that's where you come in, Kyle. You can demand a change of physician for our father. No doctor in his right mind would prescribe those deadly drugs." Beth put her hand on her brother's arm. "You have to help. There's no other way."

Kyle slumped against the sofa. "I don't think we stand a chance against Uncle Martin. He's teamed up with hired killers. How are we supposed to combat that?"

"Listen, Kyle, we're all still alive, aren't we?" Wyatt said, and her brother nodded. "I'm here to make sure it stays that way. So you listen to your sister's plan, and do your part." He paused, but Kyle didn't offer any more objections. "You do *that*, and I'll make sure we all stay safe."

Beth wasn't sure if her brother trusted that Wyatt could make good on that promise, but he acquiesced and let her tell him what she needed. She carefully detailed how it would work, and acted as confident as she could. Her brother didn't need to know that she was concerned too. He just had to believe it would turn out well.

"Okay, I'm with you, then," Kyle said. "He's our father. You must know that I wouldn't turn away, no matter how afraid I am. I don't see that there's any other option than what you suggest."

*****

The disarray at Kyle's place was left as it was, and Wyatt drove to Thomas Stapleton's office. On the way, Beth called to let him know she was coming. As soon as they arrived, the secretary buzzed the attorney, and he came out to get them.

Beth had been to the office many times before, but not for such a dire reason. She was grateful that the family attorney was familiar with her affairs. It would make it simpler to explain the urgency.

Thomas gave them a polite greeting, then escorted them to his office. The mahogany bookshelves and desk shone brightly. The windows looked out to other high-rises, and the sun was bright that day. The attorney pulled up three leather chairs to his desk, and motioned for them to sit.

He took his seat and looked across at Beth. "Now, what's this all about?"

As clearly as she could, Beth told him the situation, taking care to cover each important detail. She didn't want to come across as overly emotional, as he might not trust the facts. But she did have the chemical analysis of the medication.

When Thomas read it, he raised his eyebrows. "Did you talk to the lab?"

Beth relayed what she'd learned. "As you can see, my uncle has put my father in danger."

Thomas steepled his fingertips and took a moment to digest this news. Kyle and Wyatt looked on.

"These are serious allegations," Thomas said. "And

since Martin is family, I have to consider whether there's a conflict of interest here."

Beth held her breath.

Then Thomas smiled. "But you needn't worry about that. Your uncle failed to pay his bills, and I haven't represented him for some time."

"So what do you think?" Beth asked.

"Your uncle has abused his authority, and that is grounds to request that the power of attorney be invalidated. That will restore any decisions, concerning his health or affairs, to your father. And if he cannot handle matters on his own, then, per his living will, Kyle will step in."

Kyle sat up straighter. "And what about his treatment? Am I on solid ground in demanding that his doctor be replaced?"

"I would say so. Once he's recovered, I'll file a malpractice suit against that quack who has been treating him, if your father agrees to pursue action against him."

"Isn't the nurse guilty also?" Beth said.

"It's routine for nurses to dole out medication as prescribed by the doctor," Thomas said. "But, as I said, the doctor is another matter. I'll deal with him once your father is safe."

"Don't I need some paperwork to take with me to the facility?" Kyle said.

"I'll do better than that," Thomas said. "I'll bring a copy of the living will, and I'll accompany you."

"How soon will this happen?" Beth said.

"Invalidating a legal document takes time, but I'm friends with a capable judge, and he owes me a favor. I'll contact him tonight and ask him to start the process."

Beth's heart sank. "So we have to wait?"

"I don't recommend it. While the legal procedure runs its course, I can get a temporary stay. It will keep your uncle at bay until we get all of this straightened out," Thomas said. "You're doing the right thing. Your father's going to be fine."

Kyle arranged to meet the attorney in the morning, and make a visit to the care facility. Before then, he'd contact his father's primary care physician and request that he meet them there to take over the care, including all prescriptions. Thomas would notify the current doctor that he was off the case, with other actions pending.

*****

Back at the car, Wyatt said, "As much as I enjoy this Corvette, I have to return it to the owner." He drove back to the hotel and left the keys where he'd found them. Then he sent a text for pick-up.

"Let's go inside and get something to eat," Beth said. "We can regroup."

Kyle seemed relieved not to be left on his own. The downstairs restaurant had an available table, and the greeter promptly seated them. While waiting for the food, they sipped their drinks and nibbled on bread.

"I want to see Father again, but I shouldn't go near the place. I seem to attract too much attention wherever I go," Beth said. "And I'm sure that nurse will be on the lookout for me."

"Did you have a theory about why those men were after me?" Kyle said, looking at Wyatt.

"Word travels fast, and I'm sure Beth's visit was hot news. Those dudes who followed us would have called in after they lost us, plus our trusty nurse would have been on the phone the instant we left."

Kyle raised his brows. "What does that have to do

with me?"

"I'll tell you...if *we* can figure out that you're able to intercede on your father's behalf, then Martin can too. I'm sure he knew all along, which is one reason that he stayed on good terms with you."

"Bamboozled me, you mean?" Kyle said. "I still can't believe I was so blind."

"Your uncle can't have you screwing things up this late in the game. If your father is taken off those drugs, he's likely to recover his memory. And your uncle certainly doesn't want that."

"Now I'm a target, too," Kyle said, throwing up his hands. "*Great.* I might not live through the night."

"Don't assume the worst," Wyatt said. "You're safe in this hotel, so I suggest you get a room and stay here for now."

"And what about in the morning?"

"Hang on a second, and I'll tell you." Wyatt typed on his phone, and Beth guessed he was texting Stealth.

When he was done, Wyatt looked over at Kyle. "It's all set. My boss is sending in backup. Hunter Davis is a capable man; you'll be in good hands."

"He's here in New York?" Beth said.

"Not yet, but Travis is putting him on the company jet, red-eye. He'll be here by morning," Wyatt said. "He'll be your bodyguard until this is over."

"I'll sure feel a lot safer with him along when I go out to the care facility tomorrow," Kyle said.

Beth patted her brother's arm. "Stick with us; we won't let anything happen to you."

"I'll have to take that on faith," Kyle said, looking at Beth. "So...what are you going to do now?"

"You'll see...just focus on staying safe and taking care of Dad. I'll deal with the rest of it."

CHAPTER SEVENTEEN

Martin stood in the shower, staring at the marble wall. His muscles ached and his sinuses were on fire. If he could keep up the pretense at Foster just a little longer, the money would start rolling in. A drug drop-off had been made, and another was scheduled.

He felt warm liquid on his upper lip and put his hand up to his nose. Blood ran over his fingers, then the water washed it away, but it kept coming. Red flowed to the tile floor and swirled at the drain. He could smell his own blood.

Tipping his head back and squeezing the bridge of his nose, Martin tried to stop the bleeding. The damn nosebleeds were annoying. When the blood dried up, he got out and dried off. The hot shower hadn't stilled his shaking, and he had the chills.

He had sleep issues, and had developed a habit of setting up lines of cocaine on his glass-topped nightstand, to numb the pain each time he woke up. Only it didn't really do that, or not for long. And during the day, after a sleepless night, he sought the solace of a drug-induced high.

On and on, he chased the high, but the effect was too brief. Years ago, maybe months—his memory wasn't what it had been—he'd snorted once a week. It had started at parties, just to feel good and join the fun. God knew his life had been a mess even then. And it had felt good, he was sure. So much that he had snorted every few days, then every day, and now...

Martin wrapped the towel around his waist and looked in the mirror. The dark circles under his eyes and sallow skin were a sign. He looked like he'd aged years in the past few weeks. Happiness eluded him, and he wondered if he'd find it again.

The highs where he felt invincible were harder and harder to get. He snorted more and more often, but that feeling was elusive. The drug could make him feel like a rock star, but it also smashed him back to reality just as easily.

Jockeying between exhilaration and depression, thoughts of suicide crept into his mind, urging him to end it all. That was crazy thinking. He had his whole future ahead of him, and a chance to be one of the wealthiest men in the city. That would change it all, give him another chance.

After dressing, Martin did a line, just to get him over the hump. He had to go to the office, and he couldn't very well arrive in the shape he was in. It seemed others were out to get him. If it wasn't Chen or his mob boss, it was Beth, or her ignorant brother Kyle. It was always someone, but he wouldn't let it get to him—he would beat them all.

*****

The nightmare continued—as soon as Martin arrived at Foster, the head of IT buzzed him. It couldn't be good news; it rarely was. Clive Thames had been director of the technical division for years. He was competent and not prone to errors. When he relayed information, his facts weren't often questioned.

When the director waved toward a chair, Martin sat. His mental state was marginally better, but he wasn't amped enough to endure bad news. "You need to tell me something?"

Clive leaned back and narrowed his eyes. "Since you requested that we keep a close eye on Kyle's computer, there's been activity." He frowned. "Care to share why you're so interested?"

That ticked him off. Who did this Clive think he was to question Martin's authority? He rose from the chair, and barely restrained his impulse to pummel the guy—one more asshole against him. Temper whipsawed through him, and he snapped, "It's not for you to know. Tell me what you have and quit wasting my time."

The air between them was taut enough to snap. Clive glared at him, as if he might refuse to do his job. Then he spoke, his tone strictly professional. "Someone has set up remote access to Kyle's computer and has recently used it."

It must have been Beth. "Can you trace it, and locate the person filtering out information?"

"Our system picks up the access connection, but the path to the other end linked to a public computer, in an internet cafe."

"That's very nondescript."

Clive glared at Martin as if he was stupid, but offered no further insight.

"Care to tell me what information the person obtained?"

"All of it, whatever was there," Clive said. "Access means *access*."

Fed up, Martin left without further comment. As if the situation couldn't get worse. Beth obtained any information she damned well pleased, and she had ill feelings toward her uncle. He wasn't delusional enough to think that she wouldn't use every shred of evidence she could get her hands on. The unsettling part was he didn't know what she had found out.

Kyle wasn't in yet, so Martin was spared having to speak to him. His own office, formerly his brother's, provided an inner sanctum where he could fortify his nerves. He felt anxious, and the encounter with IT had made him irritable.

He needed a bump to get him through the day, so he locked the door and retrieved his stash. At his desk, he moved the glass tube over the line of powder and snorted. The drug burned like hell as it went up his nose, and he swore. Maybe he needed to find a more respectable dealer, because it felt like the drug had been cut with some chemical, the way it set his nostrils on fire. *Imbecile*—couldn't his dealer produce pure stuff? He certainly compensated him well enough.

Martin leaned back in the chair and closed his eyes. Energy drove through his veins and a spike of euphoria shot up his spine. The morning looked more promising. He could conquer his enemies. Not one of them could thwart his shot at success.

His niece didn't know what kind of man he really was; she'd underestimated him. Plus, he had power behind him. His mobster friends backed him all the way, and would do business with him well into the future. Thoughts of the amount of money he'd soon amass chased away the blues. He couldn't be dragged down; he was too clever for all of them.

After locking up his precious cocaine, Martin emerged from his office and strolled down the hallway. He was taller, and there was a bounce to his step. Walking around the corner, he saw Susan at her desk. She was dressed well, every hair in place, as though she didn't have a care in the world.

As he passed the window, Susan called to him, "Are you leaving?"

Martin walked into her office. He loomed above the desk, asserting his authority, and her expression became suitably respectful. "I have to get out of this damned place before it swallows me up," he said. "Besides, I have business to take care of."

Susan frowned and pushed back her chair. "Do you want me to respond to the letter from the DEA, or set up an inspection time?"

"What I want you to do," Martin said, pointing a finger at her, "is *stall*."

"I could ask Kyle to reply. It looks like a standard letter, and might be a routine inspection," Susan said. "I don't expect any more than that. Do you?"

"Just put it aside. I'll take care of it." Martin had no idea how he was going to do that, but he couldn't deal with it right then.

"Yes, sir." Susan went back to work, so he left.

*****

The casino provided a welcome respite. Martin's evenings were an improvement over his days, and often he didn't wait for nightfall. Any time of day was a good time to rake in winnings. He could win big with the sun still high in the sky. He couldn't see it from the gaming tables anyway.

The alcohol combined with the drugs in his system, giving him that extra boost. Martin looked at the woman on his arm, unable to remember her name. He was confident about rolling the dice, and was about to win big.

He was sick of all the recent harassment. But at the club, the press couldn't get to him. He'd been hounded for a statement about that blasted subway accident. Hell, he hadn't ordered that idiot to try to kill anyone. It wasn't right that he had to answer for it.

He'd refused any statement. The last thing he needed was for the media to run with a story that connected him to the crime. If he steered clear of them, the fervor would die down. The entire incident had been a big mistake, that was all.

But now the feds were snooping around at Foster, nosing into Martin's territory. It was fine for Susan to quip about it being a routine inspection. There was no such thing. When the DEA came sniffing around, there was a reason.

Yet the agency couldn't know of his new arrangement. Martin had been careful, and planned to proceed in that vein. He couldn't afford any errors. But that wasn't going to happen. There was no cause to fret about a screw-up that wasn't going to occur.

The mob ran a tight ship, and Martin had followed their instructions. Chen had few redeeming qualities, but one of them was that he was very clear about procedure. No wonder the Asian gangsters had amassed so much wealth.

Martin scooped his winnings to his side of the board, and the blonde on his arm grinned. Then Chen appeared, ruining his run of luck. "Excuse yourself. It's an emergency."

Christ, what now?

The mobster led him to a table at the back of the cocktail lounge, where it was dark enough to be invisible. Bourbon was served, and Chen took a belt of it. Martin was wired from the few drinks he'd had earlier, so he twirled his glass on the table, dreading what was next.

"Your niece hasn't been home for days," Chen said.

"It's beginning to frustrate my men. Do you have any idea where she is?"

"How would I know?" Martin was livid about Beth hassling them so much. She was going to get him killed.

"You've been careless."

"What are you talking about?" Did Chen know that Beth had accessed company records? That seemed impossible, since Martin hadn't coughed up that tidbit yet.

"Beth went to visit your brother Stephen."

Martin's heart pounded. "Weren't you keeping an eye on the place? That was your perfect opportunity."

"Her bodyguard was with her. He did some tricky stunt in a sports car, and lost my team. It's too bad the fatal blow was derailed."

Martin wanted to reach across the table and squeeze the breath out of Chen. "How many times are your guys going to botch things?"

The veins on Chen's neck stood out. "Watch it...remember who you're talking to."

I know who I'm talking to...an incompetent fool. But he didn't dare say it.

"That chase isn't what concerns us now," Chen said. "Elizabeth has stumbled across your cover-up. The nurse informed us that a new doctor has been assigned to the case. It won't be long before your niece learns the truth, and you'll have to come up with some convincing answers."

"Like what?" Martin was mad enough to wring Beth's neck. She had to screw everything up just when it was going so well for him. She hated him; she always had.

Chen was silent, and Martin squirmed. The mobster downed the rest of his drink, then said, "Mr. Zhang is displeased by all these fuckups. He's made it clear that it's time for him to take matters into his hands." He leaned close. "You haven't been able to handle things on your own, and the entire operation is at risk."

Not to mention Martin's life. "What does he propose?"

"He has requested a private meeting with you."

Was this it, then? The boss was going to bump him off, put an end to all of this? Martin didn't think so, but his gut was riddled with anxiety. The mob had too much invested, and wasn't about to throw it away. The operation would go forward, and despite the petty annoyances, there was no real barrier to their ultimate success.

Except for one—Beth.

*****

The meeting with Mr. Zhang was scheduled without delay, and took place less than a day later. As usual, Martin did as he was told, and arrived on time. He stood in front of the hotel as instructed, and a black limo picked him up. The boss was already in the back seat. The meeting was held in the vehicle while the driver negotiated the city's traffic.

Zhang's appearance was menacing, even more than Martin recalled. His beady black eyes, sparse eyebrows, and balding head gave him a street thug look. He was pudgy, yet wore an expensive suit that strained at the seams. His hands were covered with gold rings, some studded with gems. He was the enforcer, a role that meant he ran the mob's New York operations. If he issued an order, it was followed, as the consequence for disobedience was death—no warnings, no second chances.

Thus, when the man spoke, Martin listened.

"I'm weary of the uninitiated botching the kill."

Martin recognized the label *uninitiated* as a term used for new members of the Asian mob who hadn't proven themselves yet.

"Elizabeth Foster has caused us enough headaches, and she has to die. Don't you agree?" Expecting no dissension, Zhang continued, "Sometimes you have to do things yourself."

Yet the mobster's idea of doing it himself was certain to mean having Martin perpetrate the dirty deed.

"I have a man in mind, an assassin who knows his business and will get the job done. There will be no more screw-ups—he won't miss," Zhang said, then relayed the details of how to hire the services of this professional. "It's over to you now. This man won't be cheap; the best costs money."

Martin balked. Once he hired an assassin, it would be the same as if he'd killed Beth himself. But if she wasn't stopped, his life wouldn't be worth a nickel. His only way out of the entire mess was to make sure the smuggling operation went off without a hitch.

It was Beth's life—or his.

*****

It took Martin a couple of days to get the money together. He'd drained his resources, so had to get creative. But this was crucial; he couldn't afford to blow it. He had no compunction about stealing the money—this was a matter of life and death.

It was just a loan, and soon enough, Martin would be able to repay it.

Even though he was way out of his depth, there was no turning back. But once Beth was out of the way, there would be no one to stop him. There was still the matter of his brother Stephen, but he wasn't likely to recover from the effect of those drugs anytime soon. And when and if that did happen, Martin would think of something. He'd successfully manipulated his brother before, and was sure he could do so again.

While he waited in a hotel suite for the call, Martin paced. He was keyed up and couldn't seem to relax. What he needed was a little tweak, just a taste of the stuff, but he'd not dared bring any with him. Zhang would have his head if he got caught with drugs in his possession while making this important connection.

The threat of immediate execution had gotten his attention, so Martin suffered the agony of withdrawal. It wouldn't be long, and the contract would be concluded. Then he could get back to his life, get the boost he needed, and hang out at the casino.

When the phone rang twice, Martin almost jumped out of his skin. He picked up the receiver and there was a dial tone. It was the prearranged signal. He picked up the brown envelope and went to the door of the suite adjacent to his. Trying to appear normal, Martin glanced around. There were no other guests in the hallway. After he slipped the envelope under the door, he returned to his room.

It freaked him out to think of the assassin right next door. The man was a killer, and would as soon snuff out Martin's life as anyone's. He closed the safety lock on his door, although it provided little comfort. This was a man who got the job done, so it was best to stay on his good side. Anyway, there was no way that Martin could bail now.

The envelope had contained photos of Elizabeth and other details that had been required. It should be everything the killer needed. This was it; the end of his niece's pursuit of him. Soon she'd be dead. It was a gloomy thought, yet somehow exhilarating.

Martin had power, and he was on top, the ultimate winner. Beth should have backed off while she still had the chance.

The phone rang again, and Martin picked up and heard a voice muffled by some electronic device. He demanded that full payment for his services be deposited in the overseas account before the job was done. Martin supposed that these days a professional didn't tolerate any doubt that he'd deliver. If the man took the assignment, the terms would be fulfilled. Martin wasn't inclined to debate with a man like that. Once the assassin was satisfied that the money would show up in the designated account by the following day, the line went dead.

Martin sagged into a chair, frozen to the spot, close to throwing up. The contract had been sealed; he was now responsible for Beth's murder—and the mob's hands were clean.

CHAPTER EIGHTEEN

After her brother checked in at the hotel, Beth went home with Wyatt. She ventured into the condo with trepidation, as the enemy had encroached too far into her life. Her personal space didn't exist anymore. It seemed no part of her life was sacred. Plus, Kyle and her father were at risk too.

Beth's house was as she'd left it, and she was grateful for the safe oasis. Wyatt checked each room thoroughly, looking in closets and scanning for bugs. It was a relief that he was vigilant, so she didn't have to be. At the moment, she wasn't sure that she would have been up to it.

Once Wyatt assured her that the place was secure, Beth said, "I'm exhausted; it's been quite a day...actually, quite a week. I'm going to take a hot shower and unwind."

She left Wyatt scrolling on his phone, likely following up on some details. But she couldn't muster the strength to care. Although she'd assured her brother that she had the situation under control, she'd overstated the case.

Beth went to the bathroom and shed her clothes. She waited for the shower to warm up, then stepped in. The spray drenched her, and she relaxed a little under the hot water. She was worried, and thought of her brother. He wasn't as adaptable to danger as she was.

And when had she developed that skill? Beth's life

had been sheltered. Until a short time ago, danger hadn't reared its head. It was a condition that she hadn't dreamed she'd face. Then circumstances had changed without warning.

Now what was she supposed to do? The nonstop threats had eroded her confidence. In Wyatt's capable hands, she'd defied several attempts on her life, escaped crooks in a car chase, and rescued her brother from a treacherous situation. She couldn't imagine what the next day held.

Her father would get the assistance he needed, and that meant a lot. She needed to stop thinking of her own trauma and focus on others. Without her detective work, and now Kyle's backup, her father's demise wouldn't have been far off. She shuddered to think of what might have become of him.

It seemed like a stroke of luck that she'd sensed something was amiss, then discovered her father's cryptic message. Grief stabbed at her heart over the prospective loss of her dear father. If only she'd been aware of his circumstances sooner.

By tomorrow, her father would be in good hands, free of her uncle's clutches. But it would take more than that. If anything happened to Beth, her father would be at his brother's mercy—a horrific thought indeed.

Beth finished her shower, then dried her hair and put on jeans with a light sweater. She needed a glass of wine to help her put aside her worries for a few hours. That shouldn't be too much to ask. There was a lot to deal with, and disaster loomed. Refreshed, she'd be in much better shape, so when all hell broke loose she'd stand a chance.

Beth found Wyatt in the living room sipping on a can of soda. "I need something stronger than that."

She went to the wine cooler, and retrieved a bottle of white wine. She opened the Pinot Gris and poured a glass, then went back to sit with Wyatt.

She looked over, noticing that Wyatt had showered too. His hair was still damp, a sexy look for him. His jaw was strong, and his lips were so kissable. She liked that he'd left a little scruff on his jaw; it was so masculine. He wore faded jeans and a tight cotton shirt that hugged his chest.

One look at him sent a tingle over her skin. Wyatt didn't have to do much to arouse her; just the sight of him stirred her desire. At the hotel, he'd made love to her with such passion it had left her breathless. Beth wanted him again, and doubted that he would turn her away.

If there was a silver lining to her life being topsy-turvy, it was Wyatt. Running from danger, Beth had gone to him, like she had so many times in the past. Once again, he'd willingly come to her rescue, and was intent on protecting her. He cared, and had stuck his neck out for her without fear for his own safety. That was one thing about him that hadn't changed.

But greedy as she was, Beth wanted more from him. She wanted his heart. Did she have a right to ask that of him? Wyatt was there to thwart attacks against her, and she'd grown to rely on him. Yet she looked to him for more than safety; he was the one man who satisfied her.

If Beth had made a list of qualities she looked for in a man, Wyatt would fit the bill. He was a hunk to start with, but he was fun, kind, loving...need she go on? She was hooked on him. If only it was meant to be.

But their lives were so different, and Wyatt was with her only temporarily. He had no inclination to return to the city permanently, or to offer his talents to his family's business.

Beth sipped her wine, studying the gorgeous man across from her.

Wyatt put his soda can on the table and looked into her eyes. His gaze locked with hers, and Beth forgot to breathe. He didn't have to say anything. When his eyes roamed over her, Beth's body responded. Heat surged deep in her core, making her weak in a delicious way.

When Wyatt reached out his hand, Beth took it. He drew her onto his lap and kissed her deeply. There was nowhere else in the world that she wanted to be. Just to be in his arms, with his soft lips pressed to hers, was enough. For a brief interlude, Beth was with him.

In that moment, Wyatt was hers. Beth couldn't bear to think of him leaving, so instead she kissed him harder, deeper. And he reciprocated, digging his hands into her hair, then tipped her head back. He devoured her, kissed her along the column of her neck, nibbled her earlobe, and delved his tongue into her mouth, lashing against hers.

Wyatt guided her to the bedroom and slowly undressed her. He admired her nakedness, stroking her bare skin with his fingertips. Then he impatiently removed his clothes and lifted her onto the bed. He made love to her again and again, insatiable, ceaseless in his desire for her.

Beth's titillation spiraled out of control, and she climaxed in his arms. As if she was dying of thirst in the desert, she craved him even more each time he attempted to satisfy her. Then he plunged deep, filling her and stretching her, until she cried out with pleasure.

Wyatt exploded inside her, groaning with release, and holding her tight. Beth was dizzy with joy, humming with warmth, and melting into Wyatt as though they were one. When he collapsed beside her and pulled her into his arms, she kissed his lips. Then, looking into his gleaming brown eyes, she whispered, "I love you."

And it was true. Whether she could be with him, even another day, she wanted him to know. So she'd opened her heart to him without regret.

A sensual smile crossed Wyatt's lips, but he didn't reply. He looked at her, emotion welling in his expression, yet he didn't voice what he thought of her vow of love. And that was fine with Beth; he didn't have to. She knew he cared, and understood that it was complicated.

Beth had told him, and that was enough—for now.

*****

The next morning, Wyatt was up early. Beth slipped out of the empty bed and quickly dressed. This was an important day. She went out to the kitchen and grabbed a cup of coffee, then sat across from Wyatt.

"I got a text from Travis. The jet left on schedule and Hunter will get transportation to the hotel. We can meet him there in about forty-five minutes."

Beth downed her coffee. "We need to go, then. It's best if you're there when he arrives."

"Hunter could handle it."

"Yes, but I'm thinking of Kyle. I want him in the right frame of mind, knowing that he's not alone," Beth said. "Besides, he's concerned for my welfare. It will be good for him to see that I'm fine."

The hotel wasn't too far, and they had plenty of time, but Beth wanted to arrive early. It would give her a chance to speak to Kyle before his bodyguard arrived.

Kyle opened the door, looking rested but slightly nervous. Beth gave him a hug. "I decided to be with you when Hunter gets here, and see if he meets with my approval."

Wyatt patted her brother on the back. "I wouldn't be concerned about today's events. I'm expecting all to go smoothly."

Before Kyle could share any concerns he had, there was a knock at the door. Wyatt opened it to let his teammate in. "Hey, Hunter." He patted his friend's shoulder, then looked at Kyle. "This is Hunter Davis, your bodyguard."

Hunter was taller than Wyatt, and just as buff. His jacket did little to hide his musculature. He had thick blondish hair and striking blue eyes. He shook Kyle's hand and nodded. "At your service, sir."

Wyatt motioned toward her. "And this is Beth Foster."

The former SEAL was polite. He smiled at her, then leaned over to kiss her on the cheek. "My pleasure, Beth."

Beth supposed he was a man of few words; she knew the type. And no credentials were needed. Travis screened thoroughly, and hired ex-SEALs exclusively. Wyatt had told her much about the team, giving her the utmost confidence.

"The attorney is going to meet us at the care facility to take charge of the situation," Kyle said. "I assume that Stealth brought you up to date on the circumstances. So if you're ready, we can get going. The sooner we get a new doctor on the case, the sooner our father will get off the damaging drugs."

Beth was glad to see her brother take charge. If

Hunter had jet lag, it didn't show. He appeared fit, alert, and prepared for duty.

"We should be on our way, then," Hunter said, and held up a hand as his way of saying goodbye.

Kyle gave his sister one more hug and smiled at Wyatt, then left with his new protector by his side.

"It will be fine," Wyatt said, as if sensing her anxiety.

"I'm sure it will, but you can't blame me for worrying. My uncle has proven to be unpredictable, and I don't want to be caught off guard."

Wyatt escorted her back to the lobby, then outside. Beth was under no delusion. Shortly, her uncle would know about the change of physician, and would be livid. Too damn bad; he shouldn't have done such a terrible thing to start with.

By now, Uncle Martin must know that she'd visited her father. Wyatt had kept her under the radar for a few days, but that reprieve had ended. It was time to fight back, and hiding was out of the question.

But food wasn't. If Beth expected Wyatt to measure up to his duty, she'd have to feed him. "How does breakfast sound?"

"I saw a café that wasn't too far to walk to. Shall we try it?"

Wyatt took her hand and strolled beside her. It was good to be outdoors, and the brisk air was invigorating. "I think my troubles have just begun," she said. "Up until now, my uncle only suspected that I might use information I have against him, yet that was enough to prompt his attacks."

Beth looked up at Wyatt, and he lifted her hand to kiss it. "He won't have to wonder now, will he?"

"No, he won't. Uncle Martin will be incensed when he learns about my interference."

"He should be bloody terrified," Wyatt said. "Unless he's more of an idiot than I thought, he'll realize the jig is up."

Beth rather liked the idea of her uncle being terrified. It would be satisfying to turn the tables on him, and let him know how it felt for once. Further discussion was cut off when Wyatt squeezed her hand. "Try not to react, but we're being followed."

*****

Getting rid of surveillance without escalating it into a heated chase could be achieved by making the pursuer believe that he'd lost his target, and not the other way around. As long as the guy thought he'd lost through negligence, rather than by design, he would give up the chase.

Beth followed Wyatt's lead, acting as natural as she could, even though she was probably unsettled by the new development. A bookstore was half a block up, so Wyatt ducked in there with her. The high shelves provided cover, but the guy followed them in.

Casually scanning books, flipping through pages, and pretending to chat, Wyatt moved around the store. Each time he disappeared with Beth was a chance to lose the guy. It was noteworthy that the man wore beige clothing, had short brown hair, sported a popular brand of jogging shoes, and was overall fairly average—all so he'd blend in.

The tail would have been difficult to spot, especially since he had been walking down the sidewalk in a group of other pedestrians. But Wyatt's perception was acute. He'd noticed the guy glancing their way when he assumed the look would go unnoticed.

And the fact that he'd followed them into the store

confirmed the surveillance activity. Wyatt caught sight of the man a few times, and, when he wasn't able to easily shake him, guided Beth outside again. A coffee shop was two blocks down, across the street.

"Where to?" Beth said, in a remarkably calm voice.

"I could use a jolt of caffeine," Wyatt said, and headed that direction.

The shop was busy, but the line moved fast. Wyatt ordered an espresso for each of them, and took a seat so he could see out the window. Across the street, the guy in beige waited at a bus stop. He appeared no different than the other passengers waiting for transportation.

Except that the man frequently glanced at the coffee shop. It was an amateur mistake. Any pro wouldn't need to keep looking, but would see his targets in his peripheral vision, and not miss when they emerged. After less than ten minutes, it was advantageous to move on.

When the guy was distracted, Wyatt led Beth out of the shop, and turned the corner toward a large mall. If the man noticed and followed, he might not be able to keep them in sight among the crowds. Most surveillance losses happened at starts and stops, so it was best to keep moving from place to place.

Inside the mall, Wyatt stood behind a kiosk with his arm around Beth, reading the headlines of a newspaper on the rack. He spotted the pursuer when he entered the mall and strolled down the center aisle. Maybe the guy hadn't seen them yet.

Wyatt led Beth into a hobby shop, and perused the goods. From the back of the store, he glanced toward the front but saw no sign of the man in beige. "Time to get going," he said, and took Beth's hand. Without looking back, Wyatt strode out of the mall, down the street, and around the corner.

A bus was just loading at the stop, so he hopped on with Beth in tow. Taking seats in the rear, Wyatt scrunched down, and Beth followed suit. The door closed and the tail wasn't on the bus. The driver went down the street, made two turns, then headed toward the next stop.

It seemed that public transportation had done the trick. Wyatt leaned over and whispered in Beth's ear, "We're clear."

Wyatt opted to stay on the bus for a ways, just to be sure. Then, holding tightly to Beth's hand, he caught a different line and rode it back to Central Park. He strode down the path between the trees, heading for a group of people on roller blades. There was a banner that read: *Dance Skaters' Association.*

"We lost the tail," Wyatt said, "so you can relax. But it's smart to stick to crowds for now." The skaters swarmed around, which suited him fine. He found a vacant bench and sat down with Beth to watch the activity.

Wyatt's phone vibrated, and he pulled it out of his pocket. "It's Cooper," he said. The nearby crowd laughed and twirled around on skates. No one was close enough to overhear, so he hit speaker, letting Beth listen to the conversation.

"Coop, I'm here with Beth."

"Well, I've been digging, and it's interesting that the boat rental wasn't a one-time thing. Martin hired another one," Cooper said. "And the boat company doesn't look clean either, but that's another story. It doesn't affect your situation."

"Yeah, sounds like Martin has a real operation going," Wyatt said.

"What I find alarming is the accounts. Without

giving too much detail over the phone, Martin is draining money from Foster. He's disguising it, but not that well. Anyone who looks closely could spot it. I'm documenting what I find for you, Beth. The evidence will strengthen your position."

"I need all of that I can get, and I'm glad you're monitoring his spending habits," Beth said. "I'll use whatever you find."

"Sure, just let me know when you need the stuff and I'll encrypt it then email. For now, I'll continue tallying his criminal activity for you," Coop said. "Are you keeping her safe, Mercer?"

Wyatt laughed. "That sounds easier than it is, but I'm staying on it."

When the call ended, Beth looked up at him. "My uncle's willful destruction has to stop. If he keeps up this pace, I'm afraid that Foster International will go under. The company has been in my family for generations. I can't let that happen."

"By stealing funds he's hanging himself. That's serious stuff." Wyatt took her hand. "Let's walk a bit."

The skaters glided by, and a few joggers passed. Wyatt's life wasn't like that—normal, even carefree. He preferred the challenge that danger provided. But for Beth, it was different; she wasn't used to it. He needed to put an end to her uncle's antics, and soon.

"It's good that Coop has evidence for us," Beth said. "But I have to make sure that it's sufficient, that the case is credible. It has to be airtight; I don't want my uncle to weasel out of it. Your sister has offered to help, though."

"She can provide a legal viewpoint and recommend how to proceed," Wyatt said, and pulled out his phone. "I'll let her know that we're on our way over."

*****

Wyatt hadn't been to his sister's law office before. The marble lobby had an enormous polished reception desk in front of frosted glass, etched with the name of the firm. It wasn't Jessica's name, so he didn't care too much. Maybe someday she'd have her own business.

When she did, Wyatt would suggest bulletproof glass over frosted decorative panes. There were too many unhappy clients, and stories about visits to the guilty lawyers. It didn't hurt to be cautious.

Jessica came out to greet them. She was dressed in an expensive skirt and jacket; Wyatt could tell by the cut and the quality of the material. His sister had definitely come up in the world.

Wyatt gave her a hug, then Beth did the same.

"Come on back," Jessica said. "We can use the conference room. We'll have more elbow room in there."

Formalities were put aside; this was a family matter. Beth had known his sister for so long that the two women might as well be family. "What's the latest?" Jessica said, then glanced at the frosted glass wall that blocked the view into the hallway. "It's soundproof; it just doesn't look like it."

"So much has happened that I hardly know where to start," Beth said, then proceeded to bring Jessica up to date. She recounted all that had transpired since the wedding, and got raised eyebrows when she revealed what had been done to her father. "And Cooper, the computer tech at Stealth, just called with new info."

After Beth finished telling her all the details, Jessica smiled. "I think I can help you out here. It sounds like your uncle is robbing the company blind." She rocked in the chair. "You probably want to know how to best go after Martin. The FBI's white-collar division handles embezzlement and other such crimes. With what you've told me, they'd be all over it, if they knew."

"I sure hope so," Beth said. "My uncle is a slippery one."

"I'll prepare the case for you," Jessica said. "I can put all the information into a package, with relevant code violations cited. Presented properly, the job will be that much easier, and I take it you want to nail your uncle soon."

"Today would be good," Wyatt said.

"I'll need a day or so, but it will be worth preparing," Jessica said. "I can deliver the case to the FBI office. Coming from a criminal defense attorney, it will have more impact, and I can follow up with the agency for you."

"You're a gem," Wyatt said.

Jessica grinned. "Maybe I should switch from defense to prosecution. It's invigorating to nail a crook."

"I couldn't agree more," Wyatt said. "I appreciate you handling this. Coop can email the evidence so you can get started." He scrolled on his phone. "I'll text to let him know what you're doing, and you can contact him directly if you have further questions."

"That will work." Jessica stood. "Then you better be on your way, so I can get started."

In the elevator, Wyatt said to Beth, "I have a feeling that things are coming together."

"Maybe, but I have a ways to go before I'm clear of danger. Poking around in Martin's affairs is like stirring up a hornets' nest." Beth leaned against him.

"This has to go down before he catches on, or the whole sting will crumble like a house of cards. Once provoked, who knows what he'll do."

Wyatt had worked up an appetite. Breakfast hadn't happened, and his stomach reminded him. "I'm hungry. How does steak sound?"

Beth spotted a grill not far from the law office. It was past the noon hour, so the lunch crowd had filtered out. There was a red leather booth open, so Wyatt nabbed it.

"What will it be?" Wyatt said, looking at the menu. "Steak, steak, or steak?"

Beth laughed. "I'll have the skewer; at least it has vegetables with it."

The waiter took the orders and was back with the iced teas in a flash. Wyatt watched Beth add sweetener to hers, admiring her wavy hair and dark eyes. His gaze lingered, then his mind wandered to sexier thoughts. He needed to focus.

"I'm glad that you and your sister are on good terms again," Beth said.

With so much hanging in the balance, Wyatt couldn't believe that was what she cared about. Women just had a different way of viewing life; that's all there was to it. "I wasn't on bad terms with her, just out of touch. But don't worry your pretty head about it. I adore my sister, and I won't make that mistake again."

Beth smiled, and Wyatt wasn't sure if it was because he'd called her pretty, or because he'd said that he adored his sister. It was best not to question her good spirits, so he let it be.

The steak arrived sizzling on his plate, just how he liked it. The meat was juicy and tender. With the baked potato slathered with sour cream, it really hit the spot.

Beth played around with her meal, carving the chunks of steak into smaller bites, and stirring the vegetables around the plate. She ate some of it, then pushed her plate aside. When she looked over at him, her brown eyes sparkled.

"What?" Wyatt swiped at his mouth with a napkin. "Did I do something?"

"I do enjoy watching you eat."

Wyatt laughed. Then his phone vibrated; it was Rip. Since he couldn't take the call in a public place, he texted: *Call you right back.* "We better take this outside." He tossed some money on the table, and Beth followed him out.

There was a concrete bench in a grassy area along the sidewalk. Wyatt took a seat there with Beth beside him. Rip answered on the first ring.

"I'm here, buddy," Wyatt said. "And Beth too."

Rip said, "The game has changed. Your enemy just upped the ante."

"What do you mean?"

"I have some connections to the NYPD through my family," Rip said, "and the force keeps their ears to the ground."

Wyatt frowned. "And their undercover team found out something?"

"Rumor in the underworld is that a professional assassin has been retained, and the killer has an impeccable track record. He's got Beth in his sights. I just don't know when or where the hit is supposed to go down. That's the sort of detail we aren't likely to find out in advance."

Wyatt glanced over at Beth. She hadn't said a word, but her expression said it all.

"You need to be prepared...keep your eyes on Beth.

The police are on alert, and will do what they can. But this guy has to surface first."

"That's what I'm afraid of," Wyatt said.

"It's time to earn your fee, Mercer. I heard Hunter is out there, and you know Travis will provide additional backup if you need it."

"I appreciate the heads-up." Wyatt stared at his phone. The thing about a solo assassin was that all it took was one bullet to make the kill. An army of bodyguards would be useless if he got a clear shot at his target.

CHAPTER NINETEEN

A professional assassin was after Beth, and she had no idea how to stop him. The killer could appear from nowhere, and it could be over before she ever saw him coming.

Wyatt appeared calm, considering the circumstances. "We have to be prepared. That's the most important thing. I've dealt with killers before."

He must mean overseas on deployment—but this was civilian life. The situation was different. Beth didn't know if she should stay or run. Yet there was nowhere to run; the assassin would seek her out wherever she went.

"It's hopeless."

"No, don't talk like that." Wyatt took her hand. "Take a breath; slow it down. We have the edge because of the advance warning."

"I can't just hide. I can't stay out of sight...forever. Sooner or later, I'd have to show my face," Beth said. "There is no escape."

"Let the guy come. He might think of this as an easy job, but he's wrong—he didn't count on me." Wyatt's expression revealed determination, igniting a spark of encouragement. "Right now, you're okay."

Beth took a deep breath.

"The restaurant was one you haven't been to before, and this bench is a safe spot for the moment. It's out in public, not where a killer will look for you. Being visible can be a good way to hide, as a pursuer misses the obvious."

"You sound so confident," Beth said. "I'm just...not ready to die."

"No one is talking about dying." Wyatt's eyes were hard. "I'm here to protect you, and that's what I will do. You aren't alone...remember that."

Beth nodded. "But how do you prepare?"

"I'll guide you, and make sure we do all that we can to defend you," Wyatt said. "I hate that you're at risk, but stay strong. You're going to make it through this."

Beth's stomach was in knots, but she was unwilling to show weakness. "I have to make it; too much depends on it."

"Okay, then." Wyatt scrolled on his phone.

"Who are you contacting?"

"Travis...we need some gear, starting with bulletproof vests. He can set us up."

That was some consolation, but there was still a yawning chasm between Beth and safety. Wyatt seemed to know the right things to do, so she trusted him to protect her. Meanwhile, she could figure out how to dismantle her uncle's operation. She'd leave him to his area of expertise, and she'd focus on hers.

On the way to the tactical gear shop, Wyatt enlightened her on his close protection strategy. "Guarding isn't about brute force, or showing off. It's being smart, making yourself a difficult target."

Beth glanced at the cab driver, but the radio was on and he didn't seem to be paying any attention to them. "I'm all for being a difficult target."

"You have to know who you're dealing with, so you don't underestimate his skill," Wyatt said.

Beth doubted that she would do that; if anything, it was the opposite.

"A man who kills for profit views you as a target,

nothing more. And he is deadly because he can melt into the background."

"I can't conceive of a man who murders for profit," Beth said.

"He has a detached view, and is able to compartmentalize his feelings."

"You know a lot about it."

Wyatt didn't flinch. "I've learned from experience; I've dealt with such men before. It's important not to think a killer will show mercy, or care about morality. That's a mistake that can get you killed."

No doubt the assassin would need to keep a cool head under stress. Beth had witnessed Wyatt in emergencies, and he'd been in control—relaxed, even. It must be a skill he'd perfected, and she doubted a paid killer could rival him on that score.

"Personal protection, self-defense, or any effective security depends on the ability to think like the opposition," Wyatt said.

"I have to be a mind reader?"

Wyatt laughed. "That's what you have me for...my tactical ability."

The cab waited while Beth was in the store with Wyatt getting fitted with gear. The white Kevlar vest she tried on could be worn underneath clothing. It fit snugly, but didn't constrict her movement. Wearing it didn't make her invincible, but it helped.

Wyatt's vest was thicker, and he wore it over his clothing. "Seeing the vest can be a deterrent. It offers some advantage. And I plan on being between you and any bullet, so I'll opt for this thicker version." He picked some add-ons to protect other body parts, but explained that his gear was heavier. "I need you in something you can walk around in."

"As long as it protects me, that's all I care about."

"The layers of fabric catch a bullet in flight and disperse the force of its impact. It can stop bullets from most handguns and shotguns."

Beth understood Wyatt had told her that to make her feel safe. Yet having to wear a bulletproof vest was a reminder of the severity of her situation.

Wyatt ushered her back into the cab, then directed the driver to go to Mercer Resources in Lower Manhattan. "While we were in the store, I got a text from my brother," Wyatt said to Beth. "I asked for a favor, and it looks like he came through."

Beth hadn't been to Mercer in a while, but it looked about the same. It was several buildings attached by overhead walkways. Employees were visible through the windows as they crossed from one building to the other. Beneath the front walkway the company name was prominent in raised lettering on the concrete support.

The complex was formidable, as was the company and the wealth it represented. Oil and natural resources had supported the Mercer family for generations, much like shipping had for the Fosters.

When they entered the spacious lobby, the receptionist asked them to sign in. Shortly, Jeremy appeared, wearing a dress shirt and slacks. The shirt was a bit wrinkled, and he had the sleeves rolled up, giving the impression that he'd been working hard that morning.

Jeremy's office was a mess, with stacks of papers covering the desk, and chairs askew.

"Did we interrupt a meeting?" Wyatt said.

"No, that was earlier. Please, sit down." Jeremy waved a hand toward the chairs.

Beth tried to imagine Wyatt working in such an office, dealing with the daily flood of memos, meetings, and negotiations. The picture was all wrong. There was no way she could envision him in that environment. He'd been wise to stick to other pursuits.

Jeremy sat in his executive chair and leaned on the desk. "Rumor has it that the DEA has eyes on Foster International."

"That's certainly going to put pressure on Martin, and tighten the screws on an already explosive situation," Wyatt said.

"Plus—and you didn't hear this from me—the agency has a person undercover at Foster, who is feeding them information." Jeremy rocked back in his chair. "The employee discovered a few of Martin's suspicious actions, after his brother vacated the management of the company."

"*Vacated* is misstating the fact," Wyatt said. "But that's a long story. I'll fill you in later."

"And dealings with Beth, how she was treated, and why, has piqued interest—although I don't see how that relates to the DEA's interest in illegal drug activity," Jeremy said. "But it's not for me to figure out. I'm just relaying what I gleaned from picking my friend's brain. He wouldn't have offered any of this information, but when I probed, he seemed willing to share. I suppose when the agency is hot on the trail, they aren't immune to pride of accomplishment."

"The agency hasn't accomplished that much yet," Beth said. "But we might be able to help them along."

Jeremy continued, "Once I had my friend talking, I just let him talk. His person on the inside mentioned that Martin keeps close tabs on Kyle, even has IT monitoring his activities. Can't say I understand that one either. Your brother isn't in on this, is he?"

"No, he's not," Beth said. "But my uncle can't

afford to take any chances."

"Is it usual for the agency to recruit an undercover asset from within a company of interest?" Wyatt said.

"I can't say what's usual. In this case, the employee contacted the agency and agreed to feed information, on an ongoing basis." Jeremy paused. "That's what I have for you so far."

Jeremy looked at Beth. "You mentioned helping the agency? Do you know more about the smuggling operation?"

"I think I can put together more evidence."

"The DEA is already looking," Jeremy said. "Given more to go on, they'd put more resources into the investigation, I'm sure."

"If we put a package together," Wyatt said, "will you deliver it to the agency?"

"I'll be glad to coordinate that for you."

Once outside, Beth grabbed Wyatt's arm. "It has to be Susan...the employee working undercover. She's loyal to Foster, and has been with us for years. She wouldn't tolerate a traitor in our midst."

"Plus, she backed you up, even after Martin booted you."

"She knows which side she's on," Beth said with a smile. "And she's going to help us win."

Wyatt took her hand and headed for the cab.

"It's good of your brother to help." Beth glanced at Wyatt. She had learned to read his expressions. He had softened toward his brother, and it was clear that Jeremy wasn't like their father. It was satisfying that the brothers were on good terms, despite what the impetus for that had been.

Before Wyatt opened the car door for her, he said, "You can't go home."

"How did I know you were going to say that?"

"You catch on quickly."

"Yep, vary my routine, don't go to the usual places," Beth said. "You pick the hotel. I don't really care, as long as I can take this vest off for a while. Wearing it is going to take some getting used to."

Wyatt chose the Inn At Irving Place, which offered Victorian-inspired rooms in twin brownstone buildings. It housed a restaurant with a list of specialty cocktails, and a luxury tea service in the late afternoon. He signed in using a fake name and paid with cash.

"This isn't the type of place I would have guessed you'd select."

"It's not the sort of establishment that anyone looking for you will think of either."

The hotel was furnished with antiques, making its décor appear authentic. Before going upstairs, Beth couldn't resist Lady Mendel's Tea Salon. The tea was brewed in flowered pots, then served with a tray of biscuits.

Wyatt sat across from her, holding his porcelain cup in both hands. "This is quite a place."

Beth slid a finger through the handle of the delicate cup to take a sip of the Earl Grey. "I appreciate you being a good sport. This isn't exactly your style." She smiled. "I'll make it up to you."

"Promise?"

Beth drank her tea and nibbled a biscuit. "I'm tired of being on the run. I just want all of this to be over, so I can go home."

"It will be over soon."

Whether that was true or not, Beth preferred to think so. She finished her tea and went up to the suite. The historical theme transported her to England, and created a romantic mood.

Beth kicked off her shoes and took off her shirt. Then she removed the vest. Wyatt's gaze locked with hers, and he proceeded to strip away the rest of her clothing, then his own. His skin was taut over rounded muscles, and his body was hot. She had no will to resist him.

He made love to her on the Victorian-styled bed that creaked under his weight. Beth was swept up into the thrill of the encounter, and a slow, delectable climax washed through her. Undeterred by the décor or time of day, Wyatt stroked into her with a ferocity that left her weak.

There was a forbidden nature to making love in the afternoon that added to the allure. Sighing with pleasure, Beth relaxed against him, and he held her close. She listened to the beat of his heart and nestled into his warmth.

"Impending danger hasn't dampened your appetite," Beth said, and looked into his eyes.

"Not so far," Wyatt whispered, then brushed his lips against hers. "We'll see how the rest of the afternoon goes."

*****

The next morning over tea and scones, Beth faced reality. She couldn't just sit around, waiting for an unknown assassin to make a move. That was foolhardy. While she had the opportunity, she had to take action.

She'd realized the depth of her uncle's betrayal. He must have agreed to the attacks on her, even if he hadn't personally wielded the weapons.

That was enough. And Martin had to be operating in cooperation with the mob. The gangsters wouldn't have allowed him to tread on their turf otherwise. She wasn't familiar with the Triad, but suspected the group was similar to any mob. They were territorial, and didn't condone anyone skimming their profits.

But there was one thing her enemies hadn't counted on, and that was that she'd still be alive. That was such an unwelcome fact that the powers that be had seen fit to sic a deadly assassin on her.

With a price on her life, she didn't have much to lose. If she didn't give her all to taking out her enemies, then they would surely take her. With the mob's backup, her uncle had her outmanned.

Beth thought about the resources she had at her disposal. She had Wyatt to protect her, and she was grateful for him. Yet that was a defense, and came into play only once the action had started. That might be too late. What Beth had in her favor was what she'd had for a long time, but hadn't utilized to her full ability.

She was handy with computers, and had no compunction against hacking for the right reasons. She possessed wit and intelligence, and if she wished to tip the odds in her favor, she'd need to use both. Her uncle might assume that she was defenseless against such insurmountable strength. Yet she was not without her own weapons.

Wyatt had commented on her brilliance before, and admonished her for not using it. If ever there was a reason to do so, she had one now. Commitment to purpose stirred fire in her heart. She wasn't about to let her uncle and some thugs push her around anymore.

Beth let Wyatt know what she intended. The hotel had a business office with a useable computer. She clicked away on the keys and re-created the research on drug smuggling in the harbor. She didn't need her journal, as she remembered it clearly. And the few facts that needed verification were simple enough to check.

Hour after hour, she compiled the information—only this time she didn't write a general research document. She focused on Foster International, explaining how the shipping company, with Martin Foster at the helm, raked in illegally gotten gains.

What she didn't know she left blank, certain that when investigations were ramped up the rest would be uncovered. But she had a damn good story, well documented. When it was complete, she copied it onto two portable drives. One she put in her pocket, and the other she had the hotel lock in their safe.

When Beth completed her task, she briefed Wyatt. "Uncle Martin is content to conduct his clandestine activities, counting on no one getting wise to his tricks, but evil shrivels in the bright light of day. His worst nightmare has been that I would reveal his crimes.

"My best chance is to make this information public, as quickly as possible," Beth said. "I'm sure my uncle's unsavory associates won't welcome seeing their activities broadcast in the media."

"That's not their style."

"I've decided to take the story to a small press, and let them break the news." It was one thing Beth could do for her friend. "I know a reporter at the newspaper where Amanda Moreau worked. I'm going to give him my research and let him run with it. I'll think of it as a tribute to my friend, for her loss. The creeps aren't going to get away with it."

"You've got your uncle right where it hurts."

Beth smiled. "Trials can drag on, and so can investigations. But the press is so *immediate*."

*****

The next day, Beth went to the *Bay Ridge Gazette* in Brooklyn. She was fond of the small news office, and used to visit sometimes. Amanda and a couple of other reporters had liked her cartoons, and she'd enjoyed chatting about her research. It had been good to find compatriots of a similar mind.

Bay Ridge was on the harbor in the shadow of the Verrazano Bridge, its lofty silhouette a constant presence. The *Gazette* was downtown in a multistoried office building. The sidewalks were busy with shoppers, and cars were parked in a line along the curb.

Armed with information, Beth strode into the newspaper office with Wyatt by her side. Her friend Camden Johnston was at his desk. He wore slacks paired with a polo shirt, and his hair needed a trim. He removed his glasses then grinned. "I got your message, and I'm anxious to see what you have. Knowing you, Beth, it's got to be good."

Beth and Wyatt were in the news office all morning, until well after lunch. Cam sent out for food and then passed around sandwiches. He'd read the information several times, made comments, and asked Beth lots of questions. While she waited, her friend did some background work of his own and made some calls.

Wyatt paced the office like a caged tiger, and frequently peered out the front window.

After lunch, Cam met with his editor. The meeting ran long, and Beth began to wonder what it was going to take for the paper to run the story. She'd provided enough for a week's worth of articles, and even written one herself, in the hopes that the paper would just run it as written.

Beth had included a couple of her drawings that highlighted drug-smuggling operations right under the nose of the DEA. She'd depicted respectable citizens oblivious to the criminals in their own backyard. It was a nice touch, whether the paper printed the cartoons or not.

Wyatt came over and sat beside her. "So, what do you think?"

"I thought the media thrived on controversy," Beth said. "I handed over a scandal about one of the largest shipping companies in the city. You'd think the editor would snap it up."

When Beth was about to give up, Cam emerged from the meeting. He sat at his desk, stone-faced.

"Well...what did he say?" Beth said.

Then a wide grin spread over Cam's face. "He's going to run it in the evening paper."

Beth breathed a sigh of relief. "I was nervous; you took so darn long."

"My editor is thorough," Cam said. "Once it hits the newsstands, you can bet the larger papers will pick up the story—but we had it first."

"You must know the right people," Beth said with a smile.

It was only a matter of hours before the newspaper would hit the stands. There was no reason to hang out and wait; Beth would see it soon enough. She thanked Cam, then Wyatt shook the reporter's hand. "I guess we can go," she said.

*****

Wyatt exited first to check out the situation. The newspaper office was a location that Beth had been known to frequent, one that her enemies would be likely to watch. He'd kept an eye out, but hadn't observed any suspicious activity. The office faced the street; it was the last storefront before the corner. Beth followed him out to the sidewalk, staying a couple of steps behind.

When Wyatt rounded the corner, he spotted a homeless guy in a wheelchair. The man had long, stringy hair, and his clothes were dirty and tattered. He sat with his feet flat on the ground, but his shoes didn't match the rest of his attire.

Wyatt put his palm out behind him to let Beth know to slow down. She hadn't rounded the corner yet, so wasn't visible to the homeless guy. Pedestrians flowed past, taking no notice. Wyatt gripped his laser pen and held it at his side.

The homeless man wore new jogging shoes, a tipoff that he wasn't what he appeared to be. Wyatt saw the man glance toward Beth's position, and in the blink of an eye, assessed the situation. This guy was a potential threat, but Wyatt could hardly gun him down without knowing for sure.

The moment Beth emerged from around the corner, the homeless guy made a sudden move, lurching up. Wyatt flashed the laser beam at the man's eyes, causing him to throw up his arm to block the beam. The ray slowed the man down, but Wyatt wasn't close enough to cause blindness.

Beth looked at the man, then at Wyatt, who took a step toward her. He was out on the sidewalk; she had barely rounded the corner, standing slightly behind the homeless guy between them. The laser had been a deterrent, and a way to test whether the guy had ill intent. The man lowered his eyes, feigning a defenseless pose, but he threw off his rags and whipped out a gun. In one fluid motion, he crouched and raised the gun toward Wyatt.

A bullet from the .22 wouldn't penetrate Wyatt's body armor, so a shot to the heart wouldn't kill him. But a head shot would. It was a risky situation with Beth so close. The assassin could swing the gun slightly left and hit her first, then deal with Wyatt afterwards.

When the assassin crouched low and pointed the gun at Wyatt's head, Beth yelled, "No!" In the same instant, she leapt onto the assassin's back, threw her arms around his neck, and tried to tackle him to the ground. The gun went off, missing Wyatt, and screams came from the crowd. The man outweighed and outmuscled Beth, but she was fierce in her attack.

Wyatt had his Glock out, but couldn't take the chance that he'd accidentally hit Beth. The assassin growled and violently shook, trying to throw Beth off, like a bear trying to shake free of a swarm of bees. With one hand, she reached for his eyes, but when her grip loosened, the assassin propelled her off his back, throwing her into a parked car.

Beth hit her head and crumpled to the sidewalk, unmoving.

The momentary distraction was Wyatt's undoing. He lunged toward Beth, but the assassin got off a shot, hitting him in the leg, and he buckled. Crippled, Wyatt put his weight on one knee and flashed the Glock at his attacker. Pain seared though his injured leg, but he blocked it out.

There was no time to aim, and the gun was too high. The shot missed, and the assassin flew at him with a head butt to the stomach.

The impact knocked Wyatt off balance, but he recovered and kicked with his good leg. The gun flew out of the attacker's hand. Screams filtered into

Wyatt's consciousness as background noise, and vague masses of people huddled at a distance. The assassin grappled for the Glock, but an elbow to the neck backed him off.

Wyatt's left hand was wet and his pants were soaked—he was bleeding profusely. Weakness seeped into him, and he was dizzy. Instinct and adrenaline kept him going; he had to get to Beth. He pointed the gun at the assassin, but the guy was a moving target—the bullet grazed his skull, but didn't stop him.

The attacker lunged at Wyatt and kicked the gun from his hand—then, lightning fast, scooped up the Glock and raised it toward Beth. With a roar, Wyatt tackled the man's legs, and the shot hit a parked car. The assassin kicked him in the face, but still Wyatt fought. They struggled in a pool of Wyatt's blood.

The assassin swiveled the weapon at Wyatt, but he grabbed the guy's wrist and twisted, until the gun clattered to the sidewalk. Wyatt was in his element now; he was trained in street fighting. With blows to the head and ribs, he pummeled the assassin, but the guy was strong and fought with deadly determination.

The sound of sirens pierced the air, and the assassin kneed Wyatt then rolled away. Through hazy vision, Wyatt jumped at the man, but his left leg wouldn't hold him. Doubled over, clutching his belly, the assassin limped down the sidewalk, and disappeared into the crowd of people.

Wyatt crawled to Beth and felt for her pulse. She was breathing; thank God she was safe. "Beth..." The roar of sirens was louder, and people hovered, pressing close. Then Beth's eyes fluttered, just as darkness engulfed him.

CHAPTER TWENTY

Beth opened her eyes to see Wyatt unconscious on the sidewalk. There was blood everywhere, too much blood. His chest moved with shallow breathing; he was still alive. She took off her jacket and pressed it to the leg wound to slow the bleeding.

Uniformed police swarmed around her, but she held on to Wyatt. "Call an ambulance. We have to get him to a hospital." An officer kneeled beside her and bent over the victim. He put his own jacket on top of hers to help stop the blood.

Crowds gawked, noisily chattering, but Beth saw no sign of the assassin. The last thing she remembered was the gun pointed at Wyatt. She prayed that he'd survive. It looked like he'd lost a lot of blood; his pants were soaked, and his skin was pale. She put her fingers to his neck, but his pulse was weak.

Hurry...please hurry. Then a siren blared, such a welcome sound, and the paramedics were on scene with a stretcher. The police wanted to detain her for questions, but she pleaded for them to let her go with Wyatt.

The paramedics elevated Wyatt's lower body, and applied a pressure bandage to stop the bleeding. Beth rode in the ambulance, holding his hand with tears rolling down her cheeks. "Don't die...please don't die."

*****

Wyatt was taken to Veterans Hospital and wheeled into emergency. Beth wasn't allowed to go with him. She paced the waiting room, scared and alone. The paramedics had told her that he'd lost a lot of blood, but she'd known that. He was soaked in it.

She looked at her shirt, stained with red. Wyatt had to live; he just had to. That was all she cared about.

Beth went to the ladies' room to wash up. The back of her head hurt and a bump had formed. She might have a concussion, but she wasn't about to seek treatment. Until Wyatt came through, she would wait, and avoid being detained for some stupid examination.

Her injury was minor compared to what he'd suffered. The vision of Wyatt unconscious in the ambulance sent a new wave of agony through her. He was such a good man, and she loved him so much. Life couldn't be so unfair as to let him die.

Wyatt had protected her. He had been willing to die for her. Beth's heart was breaking. She couldn't think about the future, and was unable to see beyond Wyatt's recovery. He had to recover.

He was strong, a valiant fighter, and was meant to live. He'd fought in the service, but had made it home in one piece. He was a survivor, and he would surely conquer this.

Yet Wyatt had lost so much blood. A bullet in the leg could be deadly. A man could bleed out. But even severely injured, he'd fought off the assassin and saved her life. Beth couldn't face losing him. She couldn't deal with that possibility, but she might have to.

While she waited, a police officer came to talk with her. He asked her some questions, then scheduled an interview for a better time. She was grateful for that, plus she was relieved that the press wasn't hounding her. It would be a while before the media learned where Wyatt had been taken.

A doctor came to talk with her. Wyatt had been taken to surgery. He'd suffered massive blood loss from the gunshots. His body temperature had dropped and his blood pressure was dangerously low. "Rapid blood loss can prevent oxygen from reaching the brain and vital organs. In some cases, the injury is so severe that the body doesn't have the ability to overcome it."

Beth's eyes welled with tears.

"Wyatt is lucky the shot wasn't close range, and there was no direct hit to the bone. The muscle took most of the damage, likely one reason he didn't bleed to death before the paramedics arrived," the doctor said. "But he's young and strong. The surgeon will do all he can, and then we'll have to see."

"How long will he be?" Beth said.

"He'll be on the operating table for five hours, and then he'll be in recovery for a while. If I were you, I'd go home and rest. We'll call you when he's out."

There was no way Beth was going home until Wyatt's condition was stable. When he opened his eyes, she would be there. She didn't care about sleep or food, only whether he would be okay. She wouldn't leave the hospital until she knew he'd make it.

Beth bought a new shirt in the gift shop, and tossed the stained one in the garbage. Then she went to the cafeteria for coffee. She sipped the hot brew, recovering some from the shock of the day's events. Her numbness faded and the effects of the emotional trauma settled a bit. By her second cup, her sorrow and worry became superseded by anger.

She was more furious with her uncle than she'd ever been. He was responsible for all of this, and she would see that he answered for his crimes. The evening paper wasn't out yet, which was fine with her. She had an important call to make.

Beth stepped outside and found a quiet place in a courtyard intended for visitors. It was unoccupied, giving her the privacy she sought. She pulled her phone from her pants pocket and made a video call to her uncle. She waited for Martin to answer, adrenaline pumping through her veins.

There was no way she'd go see him in person, even if she had been willing to leave the hospital. Her uncle had been volatile and unpredictable, so she intended to stay beyond his reach. His tendency toward violence had permanently severed their relationship.

Her uncle's face appeared on the screen. He hadn't shaved in days; his eyes were red and puffy. His hair hadn't been cut in a while, and he didn't look that dissimilar to the homeless guy she'd encountered earlier. It seemed his lifestyle didn't agree with him.

Fear showed in Martin's expression. His stunned look gave her immense satisfaction.

"You're *dead*," her uncle said.

"Not quite." Beth stared at the screen.

Martin looked at her as if she might be an apparition.

"You were expecting a call from your assassin, I assume?" Beth sighed. "I daresay you won't hear much from him, unless he likes to brag about his failures."

"What would you know about it? You're just a spoiled brat."

278

"I wouldn't be rude, uncle. You've gotten yourself into a tight spot."

To her uncle's amazement, Beth detailed all that she knew about his recent operations. Her voice was calm, but her message was lethal. She recited from memory the details of his business transactions, accounts, and illegitimate profits. When she ticked off his crimes, beginning with conspiracy to commit murder, it had a potent effect. The list continued, including embezzlement and drug smuggling.

"Need I go on?"

It seemed her uncle had little to say.

"You harmed your own brother...*my father*," Beth said. "And a man who is very dear to me is in critical condition. If he doesn't make it, I will hunt you to the end of the earth and kill you myself."

Martin's face was pale, his eyes dark and brooding.

"You've attracted the attention of government agencies, and I've seen fit to help them along in their investigations. Whatever happens to you won't nearly make up for the damage you've caused."

Martin blanched. "I won't survive prison."

"I guess you didn't think ahead," Beth said, then, not wishing to look at his ugly face any longer, she ended the call.

Beth's hand shook as she set the phone on the bench beside her. That call would squelch her uncle's enthusiasm about coming after her. And once the evening news hit the stands, it would mark the end of his despicable methods.

*****

Martin stared at the blank screen long after Beth was gone. It couldn't be true. That little twit couldn't have outmaneuvered him. She should have died weeks ago.

If those bumbling idiots had been able to get the job done, he wouldn't be in this position.

Only minutes before the call, his drug of choice had lifted his mood. He'd expected confirmation of the job. The assignment had been paid for; Zhang had assured him the hired killer wouldn't miss—just like he'd assured him of so much else.

Yet it was all a lie. Martin had been betrayed. In good faith, he'd done all that had been asked of him. He should be living the good life, but instead he was doomed. His niece had been a thorn in his side since her youth, but he hadn't dreamed she was capable of such deceit. That she would do this to her own uncle was beyond the pale.

There was no possible hope in life if one couldn't trust family. That truism came down hard, a final crushing blow to his spirits.

He'd had no choice, really. What Beth had cited as his misdeeds had been committed without premeditation. Once indebted to the mob, there had been no option left for him.

Yet his niece didn't understand, and the Triad juggernaut wouldn't back him up. He knew that was so, especially now that their darling assassin had proven to be useless. Martin was on his own, but that had been his lot in life. He should have known from the start how things would pan out.

He shouldn't have believed what they told him. And now it was too late.

Martin went to the bar and rummaged for a bottle of bourbon, his last. But he wouldn't replenish his supply. There would be no need for that.

He sat in a chair by the window, looking out. The city was heartless; it moved in an unending progression, unfeeling towards its inhabitants.

There was no one who cared, not one person who would miss him. Martin chugged the bourbon, relishing the burn. He could feel; he was alive.

Slowly, he rose from the chair and walked with leaden feet to the bathroom. The bright white paint, the sheen of the marble countertops, and the polished tile floor were surreal. The room was intimidating, the walls closing in.

Martin could barely breathe. He opened a drawer and retrieved his stash. There wasn't enough left to line up on his nightstand for later, but it would be enough.

He gulped the rest of the bourbon, and swayed, unable to stay upright. He wore only his silk bathrobe with nothing underneath. The tile was cold under his bare feet. He emptied out the remainder of his stash, an amount that should have lasted a few more days.

It was a relief to know that he wouldn't need it.

Martin snorted several times. A burst of energy flooded his system, and momentary euphoria lifted him out of his melancholy. He would have made it all right, if he could have. But he hadn't been capable of that.

Prison loomed ahead, a destiny he was unable to face. The bourbon took hold, and Martin's world spun uncontrollably. Then the cocaine's magic faded, the high vanished, and depression swallowed him up.

Martin sank to the floor like a rag doll, and his head rested on the cool tile. He might have risen once more, if he could have—but he was unable to move.

CHAPTER TWENTY-ONE

After the surgery, Beth had been by his side. Wyatt had been drugged up, but aware of her presence. "I love you," he'd said. He'd spoken the words, or maybe he'd only dreamed that he had. He should have told her how he felt the night she'd confessed her love. He hoped that he hadn't missed his chance.

The first couple of days had been an ordeal, and Wyatt was still a bit hazy. His bad shoulder was stiff and his leg hurt like hell. He'd been easing off the pain meds. They made him groggy, and he disliked not being alert.

During his hospital stay, Wyatt had learned the outcome of recent events, and found comfort in the fact that Beth was out of danger.

Hunter Davis pushed the door open and strolled in. "How do you feel, buddy?"

"Like I've been in a wrestling match with a grizzly bear."

"That sounds about right," Hunter said. "What's the prognosis?"

"It's lucky that the bullet lodged in muscle; no broken bones and no permanent nerve damage. The surgeon wasn't able to remove the metal, which I understand is not uncommon. It's better to leave it in—scar tissue will form around it, and there shouldn't be lasting symptoms."

"Guys often come home with shrapnel or pieces of

bullets in them. You'll be in good company."

"I've had plenty of visitors," Wyatt said. "My brother and sister have been here. And Beth has stayed with me most of every day. I sent her home to get some rest, but she'll be back."

"I've been watching the news," Hunter said.

"Yeah, we made the front page for a few days."

"And her uncle...looks like he overdosed?"

"Yeah, I hadn't expected that," Wyatt said. "There's been good resolution to all of this for Foster." He'd spoken to Hunter ahead of time, so he'd known to expect the news report. "Jessica's package was delivered to the FBI. When the story exploded in the media, the documents she'd sent them were valuable. She'd made it clear that Martin Foster had been the perpetrator of the illegalities, and conclusively documented that Stephen Foster played no role in the deception."

"What about the DEA?"

"Jeremy turned over all the evidence we had. I'm sure they'll keep a close eye on the boat rental company," Wyatt said. "It's a thankless task to keep a lid on drug smuggling, but we provided some leads anyway. With Martin gone, there won't be any further activity funneled through Foster."

"I assume the mob will back off, now that all of this has been broadcast to the public?"

"They've disappeared, as though they had no involvement in what transpired. I'm sure that's what they'd planned all along. When the scheme collapsed, the crooks were nowhere around."

Hunter pondered that for a minute, then said, "When do you get out of here?"

"Two more days, then I'll be on crutches for a couple of weeks."

"Travis will put you back to work as soon as you're able," Hunter said. "So enjoy your vacation."

Beth came in just as Hunter prepared to leave. She came over and gave his teammate a bear hug. "I'm so glad you showed up," she said. "You have no idea how much I appreciate you looking out for my father and brother."

"Glad I could do it," Hunter said. "Well, I should be on my way. I'll see you back home, Mercer." He smiled. "And you take care, Beth."

When the door closed, Beth stood at Wyatt's bedside. She looked him over, as if to be sure the medical staff were properly caring for him. "I thought you were invincible," she said.

"I am...but it doesn't mean that I don't get roughed up once in a while." Wyatt took her hand. "And you need to be more careful. You nearly got yourself killed." He still couldn't believe that she'd jumped the assassin. "That was quite a stunt you pulled."

Beth squeezed his arm. "You're the one in the hospital bed."

Being confined to bed, hooked up to wires, was damned inconvenient. Wyatt was still weak as a kitten, too. Otherwise, he would have pulled her into his arms and shown her how he felt about her.

Wyatt wanted to say the right thing, but he couldn't get the words out. He was just glad that Beth was safe. "It's finally over. You don't have to look over your shoulder anymore."

Beth gently kissed him. With her lips against his, she whispered, "Thank you...for saving me."

The intimate moment was interrupted when Stephen Foster came in. He looked sharp in his slacks and polo shirt. He was thinner than Wyatt remembered, but now he'd be able to regain his health. "It seems while I was in the care facility, I missed all the excitement," he said.

Beth flew into his arms and hugged him tight.

Stephen held her arms and looked her over. "It's so good to see you, Elizabeth."

"You're looking stronger every day," Beth said.

"I'm feeling pretty fit." Then his expression darkened. "I lost my brother...I'm so relieved that I didn't lose you too."

Stephen let out a long sigh. "My brother was lost to me a long time ago. I tried, many times, to help him. But only he could avert his path toward destruction. And...he failed to do so."

Then Stephen brightened. "I'm back at work already, a few hours a week. And Kyle is doing a great job as CEO. It's a trial by fire for him, but it will toughen him up. He'll come through it as a stronger man, and he'll make a good manager." He smiled. "Also, I gave Susan a raise when I learned of her bravery in fighting against Martin."

Stephen looked at his daughter. "I'm very proud of you, Elizabeth, for uncovering the deadly scheme. You rescued me from a treacherous situation," he said. "And thank goodness that you're safe too."

Her father sighed. "Foster might have folded under the financial stress, if the federal agencies hadn't closed us down first. But with good management, the company will turn around. It's a good business, built on a solid foundation. It will take a lot of effort, but the company will bounce back stronger than before."

Stephen walked over to Wyatt and squeezed his arm. "Thank you, Wyatt. If you ever need anything, don't hesitate to ask. I can't possibly repay you for what you've done."

"I appreciate that, sir," Wyatt said. "But consider us even. I did the job I was hired to do." That was true, but there was more to it. His feelings for Beth had made it more than just an assignment.

Stephen turned away from Wyatt and faced Beth. "I'm so proud of you, my dear. I was livid when I heard of your mistreatment. I want you as part of the company, where you belong. I'm offering you the position of president of Foster International. I recognize your underutilized capabilities. With your technical expertise on our side, we can turn things around, and restore the company to its rightful place in the industry."

Beth hugged her father. Her eyes met Wyatt's, and she smiled through tears. "I love you, Dad," she said, with her arms around her father's waist.

Wyatt's greatest desire was Beth's happiness. He'd known all along what her place in life had been. Her talent and brilliance were finally recognized. He wasn't about to interfere. He smiled back at her, though his heart was breaking.

*****

Wyatt had been back in LA for a couple of months. His recovery had been slow and painful. The physical therapy had challenged him—but whatever the therapist had instructed him to do, he'd done double.

He gave all he had to his recovery, determined to get back to work as soon as possible. The pain and recovery had been worth it, because Beth had her life back. He'd do it all over again without hesitation.

In the meantime, Wyatt had been assigned to desk work. He had unending admiration for Cooper and Rip, unsure how they dealt with being in the office so much. It was killing him, and he'd been itching to get back in the field. Travis agreed to give him the next assignment when he'd fully recovered. That couldn't come too soon.

Wyatt was on good terms with his brother now, who was doing much to offset his father's destructive precedent. He'd contributed to environmental programs and ran Mercer Resources honestly. Wyatt had offered his help, if Jeremy ever had need for protective services.

He also made an effort to keep in touch with Jessica. He'd been wrong to hold his father's behavior against her. In truth, he hadn't, but it had pushed him away. Jessica had been innocent of wrongdoing. He adored his sister, and vowed to be a good brother.

He had his family back. In the past, he hadn't dealt well with his father's abuse of power, and he'd nearly lost his relationship with his brother and sister as a result. He hadn't been able to see past his disgust for his father's methods. And it had nearly cost him important relationships.

Had he lost Beth too?

But that was different. She'd conquered her demons. Any part she'd played in her family's business would honor the tradition of generations. She could take her rightful place, and she deserved it.

Should Wyatt have told her how he felt? It wouldn't have made a difference. She was rich, immersed in a world that he wanted no part of. He'd accepted his family, but he wouldn't go back. He was a bodyguard, a protector, and that was what he chose to be. He saw no way that he and Beth could be together.

Wyatt had the napkin that Beth had drawn the cartoon on, and he admired it. His heart warmed, seeing her screaming on the rollercoaster ride with him laughing by her side. He missed her unbearably. There wouldn't be another woman like her; there was no other woman he wanted. He loved her with his heart and soul.

*****

It had been weeks, and so much had happened. Beth had finally gone out for coffee with Susan and thanked her for helping, even when things had gotten pretty scary. They'd become friends, and agreed to get together whenever they could.

Beth's father was healthy now, and was devoted to restoring the good name of Foster International. It was great to see him so robust. Kyle had taken on the full responsibility of his duties, rising to the challenge with enthusiasm, and she was proud of him.

Elizabeth Foster was in charge of her life now. Her father's faith in her hadn't wavered. He loved her dearly and supported her choices, whatever they may be.

She looked at the photo in her hand, then held it up. In the picture, she had been screaming her head off, riding the Cyclone with Wyatt laughing by her side. It had felt so good to lean against him, and she longed for his strength. She smiled—what a wimp she'd been.

She loved Wyatt with all her heart, and missed him desperately. The first hours after his surgery had been touch and go, but he'd come through it well. He'd finally opened his eyes and reached for her hand. She closed her eyes, reliving the moment. "I love you, Beth...so much," he'd whispered, then had fallen back asleep.

Beth had kept track of his progress, and heard that he'd be going on assignment again soon. In the precious weeks that Wyatt had been by her side, she'd gotten to know and understand him.

He wouldn't have wanted her around during his recovery—not that she would have minded. She'd take Wyatt on any terms. But she'd waited until he was strong enough to resume his duties.

Beth swung open the door to the building and took the elevator up to Stealth Security. Her heart pounded at the thrill of seeing him again, and she took a calming breath.

*****

Wyatt was hyped up about the new assignment. Travis had assured him that he wouldn't be disappointed. The client waited for him in the conference room, ready to tell him the details. Travis did enjoy his mysteries.

He opened the door and stepped inside. His stride was confident, his morale improved. He was back to work, part of the team again, and that was good. He stopped mid-step and stared.

Beth stood by the window, grinning. She wore a sky-blue dress, and her hair brushed her shoulders. Her brown eyes sparkled, and she took a step toward him in her silver high heels.

All the air went out of Wyatt's lungs. She looked amazing, and it was so damn good to see her. He grinned. "Don't tell me that you need my services again."

Beth stood close and took his hands. "This time...it's personal."

"I can't tell you how good it is to see you, but...what are you doing in LA?"

Beth looked into his eyes. "Seeing you would be reason enough."

Wyatt's heart pounded. He breathed in her floral perfume, felt her warmth, and would have swept her into his arms...but something made him hesitate. "Is there another reason?"

"A media agency in LA has hired me. The cartoons the *Gazette* printed went viral, and I guess they liked what they saw. The company has employed me in their department dedicated to political cartoons, and they even animate them to publish online. That's very popular these days."

Wyatt beamed. "You're willing to reveal your talent to the world?"

"It looks that way."

"What about Foster International?"

"It's in good hands," Beth said. "My father is at the helm again, with Kyle by his side."

"I suppose you'll still inherit?"

Beth shrugged. "I guess so, but my father is going to live a long, healthy life. So I won't be spending inheritance money in the near future, and I have my own career now."

Wyatt touched her cheek. He was just so damned glad to see her.

Beth put her hand over his. "Besides, can you picture me in an office for the rest of my life?"

"Nope...you're too much trouble." Wyatt put his arms around her narrow waist and pulled her close. "So your career brought you to California?"

Beth's expression revealed there was more to it than that. "Well...while I'm here, I'm sure there is some kind of mischief I can get into..."

After a beat, Wyatt said, "Marry me."

Beth pressed close and touched her lips to his. "You're a very brave man, Wyatt Mercer."

Wyatt deepened the kiss, tasting her sweetness.

His life had just taken a turn for the better...a lot better. She was a dream come true.

When he pulled back from the kiss, Beth's eyes sparkled. She ran her fingertip over his lips and looked into his eyes. "Yes, my love...I'll marry you."

ABOUT THE AUTHOR

Emily Jane Trent writes romantic suspense and steamy romances about characters you'll get to know and love. If you are a fan of stories with a heroine that's got spunk and a hunk of a hero that you'd like to take home with you, these stories are what you're looking for. Emily's romantic tales will let you escape into a fantasy – and you won't want it to end - ever.

Made in the USA
Lexington, KY
14 August 2018